tyrannosaurus
wrecks

Also by Stuart Gibbs

The FunJungle series
Belly Up
Poached
Big Game
Panda-monium
Lion Down

The Spy School series
Spy School
Spy Camp
Evil Spy School
Spy Ski School
Spy School Secret Service
Spy School Goes South
Spy School British Invasion
Spy School Revolution

The Moon Base Alpha series
Space Case
Spaced Out
Waste of Space

The Charlie Thorne series
Charlie Thorne and the Last Equation
Charlie Thorne and the Lost City

The Last Musketeer

STUART GIBBS

tyrannosaurus wrecks

A funjungle NOVEL

Simon & Schuster Books for Young Readers

New York London Toronto Sydney New Delhi

SIMON & SCHUSTER BOOKS FOR YOUNG READERS

An imprint of Simon & Schuster Children's Publishing Division

1230 Avenue of the Americas, New York, New York 10020

Text © 2020 by Stuart Gibbs

Cover art and principal illustration by Lucy Ruth Cummins

© 2020 by Simon & Schuster, Inc.

SIMON & SCHUSTER BOOKS FOR YOUNG READERS

is a trademark of Simon & Schuster, Inc.

For information about special discounts for bulk purchases, please contact Simon & Schuster Special Sales at 1-866-506-1949 or business@simonandschuster.com.

The Simon & Schuster Speakers Bureau can bring authors to your live event. For more information or to book an event, contact the Simon & Schuster Speakers Bureau at 1-866-248-3049 or visit our website at www.simonspeakers.com.

Book design by Lucy Ruth Cummins

The text for this book was set in Adobe Garamond Pro.

Manufactured in the United States of America

0121 OFF

First Simon & Schuster Books for Young Readers paperback edition March 2021

10 9 8 7 6 5 4 3 2 1

The Library of Congress has cataloged the hardcover edition as follows:

Names: Gibbs, Stuart, 1969– author.

Title: Tyrannosaurus wrecks / by Stuart Gibbs.

Description: First edition. | New York : Simon and Schuster Books for Young Readers, [2020] | Series: FunJungle series ; 6 | Summary: The local police prove unhelpful when a 500-pound dinosaur skull vanishes from a secret excavation on Sage's family's ranch, so Teddy and his friends conduct their own investigation.

Identifiers: LCCN 2019013555| ISBN 9781534443754 (hardcover) | ISBN 9781534443761 (pbk) | ISBN 9781534443778 (eBook)

Subjects: | CYAC: Dinosaurs—Fiction. | Fossils—Fiction. | Impersonation—Fiction. | Reptiles—Fiction. | Mystery and detective stories.

Classification: LCC PZ7.G339236 Ty 2020 | DDC [Fic]—dc23

LC record available at https://lccn.loc.gov/2019013555

To the amazing Jennifer Joel,
who made all of this happen

Contents

THE SMOOTHIE OF JUSTICE

All the trouble with the tyrannosaur started the same day Xavier Gonzalez and I helped apprehend the Zebra Spanker.

Although we caught him at FunJungle Wild Animal Park in central Texas, the guy had already spanked zebras in thirteen other zoos around the country. He would slip into the exhibits while an accomplice filmed him, and then smack the poor unsuspecting zebras on their rear ends. The zebras would be understandably startled, and the Spanker would flee. The videos were then uploaded to YouTube, where they had become a sensation, each gaining more views than the last. Over thirty million people had watched the newest one.

The Zebra Spanker always wore a *lucha libre*–style Mexican wrestling mask, so no one knew what he looked like—or anything about him, really. It was rumored that he had done the first spanking as a lark, just to amuse his friends, but when it had gone viral, he had decided to keep it up. No one was even sure *why* he had chosen zebras—although I suspected it was because zebras are often among the easiest animals to get close to at zoos.

Zebras can actually be quite dangerous; a kick from their hind legs can shatter your ribs or crack your skull—and their bite can do some serious damage as well. But they are quite tolerant of humans and thus, their exhibits are usually built without the thick glass walls or wide moats that lots of other animals require. At many zoos, the zebras are only a few feet from the tourists, and so the Zebra Spanker rarely had to do more than reach over a wall or fence to strike his targets.

The Association of Zoos & Aquariums wanted the Spanker caught as fast as possible—although, sadly, this was a tall order for most zoos, which had shoestring budgets and small security teams. However, FunJungle wasn't like most zoos. It was really a hybrid of a zoo and a theme park, and had become one of the biggest tourist attractions in America since its grand opening a little over a year earlier. FunJungle had a large security force, although it wasn't exactly a *good* security force; it was mostly composed of people who had failed to get jobs in any other form of law enforcement. The man in charge, Chief Hoenekker, was competent, though, and he had been posting guards full-time at the zebra exhibit, figuring that even his least capable employee could still be a deterrent.

This turned out to be wrong.

The Zebra Spanker struck shortly after FunJungle had opened one Tuesday morning in the middle of June. Normally, the park would have been packed by that time, as school was out through most of the country, but there had been a massive storm the night before, dousing some parts of the Texas Hill Country with four inches of rain, and more was predicted. Since much of FunJungle was outdoors, many tourists had opted to do something else that day.

Even so, the FunJungle guard on duty, a young man named Chet Spivey, should have been better prepared. The Zebra Spanker's modus operandi was to strike early in the day, when crowds were small. But on that fateful morning, Chet hadn't reported to his post on time because he was busy chatting up a cute new barista at Clara Capybara's Coffee Café. The Zebra Spanker and his videographer arrived at the zebra exhibit to find no one else around at all; the few tourists who had braved the weather had headed for the more popular FunJungle exhibits first.

At the time, Xavier and I were on Adventure Road, the main route around the park, heading toward SafariLand with Sage Bonotto, another friend from sixth grade. Xavier and I had become friends quickly upon my arrival at Lyndon Baines Johnson Middle School, as he was a FunJungle fanatic and aspiring field biologist; he had sought me out, knowing my mother was a renowned primatologist who worked at the park. I had gotten to know Sage because he was my lab partner in science. He liked animals too, particularly the lizards and snakes that were abundant on his family's ranch. Sage was also the class clown, the kind of kid who would rig cans of Silly String to discharge in your locker, or leave whoopee cushions on the teacher's chair.

My friends had slept over at my place the night before. I lived in FunJungle employee housing, which was a trailer park located behind the employee parking lot. The original plan had been to camp out, as there was a nature reserve right out my back door. However, the storm had chased us inside, forcing us to sleep in my small bedroom and make microwave popcorn instead of s'mores.

I had unlimited access to FunJungle since both my parents worked there. (Dad was the staff photographer.) I had gotten Sage in through the employee entrance at the rear of the park. Everyone who worked there knew me, and they often let me bring a friend in for free.

Xavier didn't need my help to get in; he was a junior volunteer at the panda exhibit and thus had his own employee pass.

"We should try for another campout, later this week," Xavier said. "Since this one got rained out."

"We could do it at my ranch!" Sage offered. "There's this great place on the riverbank I want to show you. . . ."

"On the riverbank?" Xavier repeated skeptically. "Won't it be two feet underwater after last night?"

"Yes, but I bought a submarine we can all sleep in," Sage replied sarcastically, then added, "We're obviously not going to sleep there if it's flooded, dingus. But if it's dry, I promise you, it'll be one of the most awesome nights of your lives."

"I've done a lot of camping," I reminded him. In fact, I had spent the first ten years of my life camping, living in a tent in the Congo while my mother studied gorillas. "Unless you have a herd of elephants on your ranch, I doubt this will be as awesome as what I'm used to."

Sage gave me a smug smile. "Trust me. It'll be better."

"What's better than a herd of elephants?" Xavier asked incredulously.

"You'll see," Sage replied.

Xavier narrowed his eyes suspiciously. "You've been acting really weird lately. What's going on with you?"

"Nothing's going on," Sage said, in a tone that indicated something *was*.

Xavier turned to me. "See? Weird." Then he gasped with excitement as he noticed we were passing Savanna

Sally's Smoothie Shack. "Ooh! Who wants a smoothie?"

"And you're calling *me* weird?" Sage asked. "We just ate breakfast. Teddy's dad made us each, like, fifteen pancakes."

"I'm still hungry," Xavier explained. "Plus, I get twenty percent off with my employee discount!" He hurried over to the shack and announced, "One extra-large Safari Sogoodie Smoothie, please."

As the name indicated, Savanna Sally's was located near the fake savanna of FunJungle, which was in the enormous African Plains exhibit. Hundreds of Central African animals lived together there, including giraffes, impala, eland, cape buffalo, rhinos—and zebras.

"Extra-large?" I looked at Xavier's ample waistline, concerned for his health. "Maybe you should go with a smaller size."

"Smoothies are good for you," Xavier said. "They have fruit in them."

"And ice cream," Sage said, pointing to Savanna Sally's, where one employee was dropping a scoop of vanilla the size of a marmoset into the smoothie maker.

"There's a lot more fruit than ice cream," Xavier stated. "So that makes it healthy."

"That's not how nutrition works," Sage argued.

Xavier started to argue back, but he was cut off by the whir of the smoothie blender, which was as loud as a helicopter.

In Xavier's defense, the Safari Sogoodie was marketed as one of the healthier food options at FunJungle, but this was true only because most of the FunJungle food options weren't healthy at all. At one shop, you could even get deep-fried fudge, which my father referred to as an "instant heart attack." There *was* fruit in the Safari Sogoodie, but it was mostly high-sugar stuff like apples and grapes; and while the menu claimed it had blueberries in it, there were really only about five; purple food coloring was added to make it look like there were more.

The server handed the smoothie to Xavier and charged him $8.99. Like many of the beverages for sale in the park, it was oversize, to make people think they were getting some value for their money. Xavier needed two hands to hold it.

"Yikes," Sage said, eyeing it warily. "Once you're done with that, we can fill the cup with water and use it as a hot tub."

"You're hilarious." Xavier took a sip of his Safari Sogoodie. The smoothies had originally been designed to be consumed with straws, but straws had been banned at FunJungle—and almost every other zoo in America—because people tended to drop them in the exhibits, and then the animals would eat them and get sick. Without the straw, Xavier's lips were immediately dyed purple by the food coloring. Sage and I couldn't help but laugh at him.

"What's so funny now?" Xavier demanded.

"You look like a clown suffering from hypothermia," I told him, which made Sage laugh even harder.

Xavier wasn't pleased by this, but before he could say anything, we heard the braying of a startled zebra. It was a very distinctive sound, sort of a cross between a pig's snort and a squeaky gate. I knew it well from my childhood in Africa.

"That's a zebra," I said. "And it sounds upset."

"The Zebra Spanker must be here!" Xavier exclaimed.

"Oh, come on," Sage told him. "There's no way—"

At which point, a man in a neon orange *lucha libre* mask came running toward us with Chet Spivey in pursuit. "Stop that man!" Chet yelled. "He just spanked the zebra!"

It turned out that Chet had arrived just in time to spot the Zebra Spanker in the act. The Spanker had climbed over a railing at a scenic viewpoint and dangled into the African Plains to spank a large male zebra named Hochuli. (Given their stripes, all the male zebras at FunJungle were named after NFL referees.) The braying had alerted Chet to the crime, but the Spanker had already clambered out of the exhibit and was on the run. As they approached us, the Spanker had a huge lead on Chet, and it was getting bigger, as Chet, like most of FunJungle's security, wasn't in very good shape. He was already wheezing for breath, like he had run a marathon rather than only a hundred yards.

There weren't any other people around to stop the Zebra Spanker except us. We were standing right in his path.

The Spanker was a big guy— much bigger than he looked in his videos. Over six feet tall and as muscular as a silverback gorilla. He didn't appear very concerned by our presence. If anything, he seemed to think we would be *excited* to see him, like he was a celebrity. He actually grinned at us as he approached and exclaimed, "Hey, kids! It's me!"

I wasn't excited to see the Zebra Spanker at all; in fact, I *loathed* him. One of my biggest peeves was how many people ignored the warning signs at FunJungle—or any zoo—and bothered the animals, be it by tapping on the glass of their exhibits, yelling to get their attention, or throwing food to them. So I had no patience for anyone who climbed into exhibits and smacked animals that had been minding their own business.

But Xavier hated people who bothered the animals even more than me. If he caught people banging on the glass of the panda exhibit while he was on duty, he would point their bad behavior out to the crowd at the top of his voice to shame them, and then call FunJungle security to have them ejected from the park. (The security guards almost never showed up, but the threat of them usually sent the perpetrators scurrying off in fear.)

As the Zebra Spanker bore down on us, Xavier scowled

at him with disgust and then, without even thinking about it, he threw his entire smoothie into the culprit's face.

The thick, viscous mass of smoothie temporarily blinded the Zebra Spanker—and since it contained so much ice cream, it might have given him an external brain freeze as well. He yelped in surprise and careened toward us.

I stuck out my leg and tripped him.

The Zebra Spanker didn't fall right away. He only stumbled and then tried to keep running, which is a very bad idea when you're visually impaired and surrounded by open-air exhibits. The Spanker veered off Adventure Road, slammed into a low railing, and tumbled over it into the otter habitat. He landed on his rear in the fake stream and was instantly beset by hungry otters, who were lured by the smell of fruit on him.

This scared the pants off the Zebra Spanker. He still couldn't see, and now little furry things that smelled like fish were crawling all over him and licking his face. "Help!" he wailed. "Someone get me out of here!"

Xavier, Sage, and I raced to the railing and looked down into the exhibit. Sage took his phone and started recording everything.

"Ha!" Xavier yelled at the Zebra Spanker. "Getting into the exhibits isn't so much fun now, is it?"

"Please!" the Spanker moaned. "This isn't funny!"

"I think all your fans might disagree." Sage zoomed in on

him and told us, "We definitely need to post this."

Chet arrived at the railing, still gasping for breath and clutching his side in pain. He was so winded, it was difficult for him to speak into his radio. "Dispatch, this is Officer Spivey. The Zebra Spanker has been contained. Although I'm going to need some help getting him out of the otter pit."

"The otter pit?" the dispatcher responded in disbelief.

"Yes," Chet answered. "He fell in after being hit in the face with a . . ." He turned to Xavier. "What was that, anyhow?"

"A smoothie," Xavier said proudly. "The Smoothie of Justice."

Sage's phone rang, interrupting his video. On the screen, I could see it was his mother calling. He stopped filming the Zebra Spanker and answered excitedly. "Hey, Mom! You'll never guess what Teddy, Xavier, and I just did!"

I couldn't hear his mother's response, but it was obviously bad news. The expression on Sage's face shifted from jubilation to shock. "What?" he asked. "How?!"

Sage listened to his mother a bit more, the frown on his face growing bigger and bigger. "Okay," he said finally. "I'm coming home."

"What's wrong?" I asked him.

Sage turned to me, his eyes red with tears, and said, "Someone stole my tyrannosaur."

OTTER PROBLEMS

"Uh, Sage," Xavier said cautiously. **"I hate to** break this to you, but . . . tyrannosaurs have been extinct for sixty million years."

We were sitting in the shade of a jacaranda tree near the otter exhibit. Sage had wrapped up his phone call with his parents. They had originally planned to pick him up later that afternoon, after he had spent the day at FunJungle, but with their current crisis, my father had agreed to drive Sage back to his ranch. Which meant we should have been walking back to my trailer to get Sage's things. Only Sage was still in shock.

Now he looked to Xavier angrily. "It's not a *live* tyrannosaur. It's a skeleton."

I couldn't control my surprise. "You have a *T. rex* skeleton?"

"Sort of. It's still being excavated on our property."

"That's what your big surprise was?" I asked.

Sage nodded sadly. "I hadn't told anyone about it yet. I wasn't allowed to."

Xavier asked, "How did someone steal a skeleton that's still in the ground?"

"I don't know," Sage answered. "My parents just said Minerva was gone."

"Minerva?" Xavier and I asked at once.

"That's what we call her," Sage said. "We had to name her *something*."

More FunJungle employees had arrived to get the Zebra Spanker out of the otter exhibit. One of the small-mammal keepers, a woman named Lauren Bohn, was there too, making sure the otters were okay. She yelled over to us, "You guys know why my otters are purple?"

"It's a smoothie," I replied. "From Savanna Sally's."

"Aw, nuts," Lauren said. "That can't be good for them. With all the food coloring they put in those things, these guys are gonna have purple poop for a week."

One of the park employees who had come to deal with the Zebra Spanker was Marge O'Malley. Only a few months before, Marge had been chief of FunJungle security, but after several major mistakes—such as accidentally destroying the FunJungle Friends Parade—she had been booted off the force and demoted to crowd management. She was still acting like she was in charge, however, bossing the security guards around—and the guards were dutifully following her orders. Under Marge's guidance, they lowered a ladder into the otter habitat.

"I should go in and apprehend the perpetrator," Marge announced. "I've had combat training." She turned to Chet. "I'll need your taser in case he attempts to fight me."

I had a feeling this was going to go poorly. Marge was in even worse shape than Chet and not particularly coordinated. She had only had a single class in combat training, and that had ended abruptly when she had knocked herself unconscious while attempting a roundhouse kick.

If any of this concerned Chet, he didn't show it. In fact, he seemed pleased to not have to descend into the otter pit himself. He quickly surrendered his taser to Marge, who clambered over the railing and onto the ladder.

Several families of tourists gathered to watch.

"Who was excavating Minerva?" I asked Sage. "Your family?"

"No, we only found her," Sage replied. "Then we called the University of Texas and they sent out a whole team to dig her up."

"That's who realized she'd been stolen?" I asked.

"Right. The team showed up to work this morning and

discovered she was gone. Then they called my folks and my folks called me." Sage spoke in a dull monotone, which was the complete opposite of how he usually talked. It was like he had found out his dog had run away.

"Maybe Teddy can figure out who took her!" Xavier exclaimed. "He's solved lots of mysteries."

This was true. Several crimes had occurred around Fun-Jungle over the past year, and I had gotten involved in figuring out who was behind them, often against my will. But I had also ended up in a great deal of danger, which is why I wasn't in a big hurry to get involved in another case.

In the otter pit, I heard the distinct sound of Marge O'Malley tumbling off the ladder and landing painfully on the ground. This was followed by a long stream of bad words from Marge. Some tourists quickly led their children away, but many more came running over, excited to see what had sparked so many expletives.

Lauren Bohn looked into the exhibit, concerned. "Oh boy," she said to Chet. "Please tell me she didn't land on one of my otters."

Sage turned to me expectantly, his dour mood having faded a bit. "Do you think you could help with this case?"

"I don't know . . . ," I said cautiously.

"You've found stolen animals before," Sage pressed. "Like that panda. And the koala. So maybe you could help find Minerva, too! Your dad has to take me back to the ranch anyhow, right? Why not take a look around and see if you can find any clues?"

"Aren't the police investigating this?" I asked.

"I guess," Sage said, though he didn't seem pleased about it.

"You're way better than the police," Xavier told me supportively. "Remember when Henry the Hippo got killed? The police didn't even try to investigate that case! They laughed at you when you called it in."

"They thought it was a prank," I pointed out. "Not that many people murder hippos. In America, at least."

"But someone *did* murder Henry," Xavier said. "And if it hadn't been for you, no one would have ever figured that out. . . ." He trailed off as he noticed two tourists hurrying toward the otter pit.

It was a young couple, and both of them were wearing T-shirts for Snakes Alive, which was a small zoo that had recently been built on the interstate near the exit for FunJungle. Xavier hated the place even more than he hated people who banged on the glass of animal exhibits. While most of the animals at Snakes Alive were reptiles, they also had a few mammals, like a troop of colobus monkeys, a lion, and a small pack of hyenas. The owners made no secret of the fact that they were trying to siphon off business from our park. Their billboards all proclaimed: *More Fun than FunJungle— and a Whole Lot Cheaper!*

But that wasn't Xavier's issue with Snakes Alive. He was upset about their animal care, which was rumored to be dismal. Neither of us had visited the place yet—we didn't want to support it—but several other kids from school had gone. My friend Dashiell had described it as "the place where fun goes to die." Despite this, Snakes Alive still seemed to be attracting enough tourists to survive.

"You shouldn't support Snakes Alive," Xavier informed the tourists. "It's not accredited by the Association of Zoos and Aquariums."

"So?" the guy asked. "It was still cool."

"Zoos in the AZA are required to maintain high levels of animal care," Xavier explained. "Snakes Alive doesn't."

"The animals looked fine to me," the tourist woman said. "They had a giant cobra—and a place where you could feed hot dogs to baby alligators."

"That was so cool!" the guy exclaimed. "Is there any place you can feed alligators here?"

"No!" Xavier gasped, horrified by the thought. "And alligators shouldn't be eating hot dogs anyhow. Hot dogs aren't found in nature."

"Neither are Doritos," the woman said, "but we've got a raccoon in the park by our house who eats them all the time."

"That doesn't mean they're healthy for it," Xavier said, exasperated. "Snakes Alive isn't a good place for animals!"

"Maybe not," the guy said, getting annoyed now, "but you know what they don't have there? Little dorks who give you crap for visiting the place."

"Besides," the woman added, "it's not like FunJungle is much better. You've got people climbing in with the otters."

We turned back to the otter habitat. There were now half a dozen FunJungle security guards heading down into the otter pit to deal with Marge and apprehend the Zebra Spanker. We could still hear Marge cursing, while the Zebra Spanker was angrily claiming that he had been assaulted by otters and demanding to see a lawyer.

The tourists in the T-shirts continued on, figuring they had made their point. Xavier could only sigh in exasperation.

Sage returned his attention to me. "Will you at least come see the dinosaur dig?" he asked.

I had to admit that sounded cool. I had never been to a fossil site before. Even a desecrated one would have been interesting. "I'm not promising to get involved in solving this crime," I said. "The police should handle it. Not me."

"Of course," Sage agreed. "And you can invite Summer, too, if you want."

Summer was my girlfriend, who also happened to be the daughter of J.J. McCracken, the owner of FunJungle. I wondered if Sage was inviting her along because he thought she was cool—or because she had helped me solve crimes before.

I still found myself hesitating, though, wary of getting dragged into something dangerous again. "I'm not sure . . ."

Sage said, "We all get to ride ATVs to get out to the site."

"Deal," I said. A ride across Sage's ranch on all-terrain vehicles *and* a dinosaur fossil site was too much fun to turn down. And I figured that I could control my own destiny. If I didn't want to get mixed up in the mystery, I didn't have to. Taking a look at the crime scene didn't mean I would end up in trouble again.

As usual, things didn't work out the way I had planned. In a few days' time, I'd be in a bigger mess than I ever had been before.

THE DIG

Sage hadn't offered the ride on the ATVs merely to entice me to visit the crime scene. It turned out that we really couldn't get to the dig site without them.

The Bonotto Ranch was massive, more than twelve thousand acres, which made it larger than a lot of entire counties in America. It had been in Sage's family for over a hundred and fifty years. Most of the other big ranches in the area from that time had been carved up and sold off piece by piece to build subdivisions and golf courses. What remained weren't necessarily working ranches so much as big spreads of land where rich people could graze a few cattle and pretend to be ranchers—like the McCrackens. But the Bonottos still made their living raising cattle, just as their ancestors had. The ranch had barely changed in the time that their family had owned it. It was mostly oak and cedar forest, interspersed with the occasional field of grass.

The driveway was nearly six miles long, and since it was unpaved, you couldn't go faster than fifteen miles an hour on it. Thus, it took at least twenty-four minutes to get from the front gate to the house—and that could be even longer if a herd of cattle was blocking the driveway, which happened quite often. Sage's parents couldn't take an hour every time they needed to drop him off at the gate for the school bus, or to collect him after a play date, so when Sage was in second grade, they had given him a car. The law in Texas said you could drive if you were on your own land, no matter how old you were. Sage's car was an old, beat-up Chevrolet, but it never went anywhere except to the front gate and back. Sometimes Sage even let me drive the car to his house.

The old Chevy was sitting at the gate when Dad brought Sage, Xavier, and me to the ranch. Sage had left it there when he had come to my house the day before. Summer was waiting nearby in her own car with her driver, a young guy named Tran. When I had texted Summer about possibly coming to visit a tyrannosaur fossil site—and a crime scene—she had been so excited that she had immediately canceled her horseback riding lessons and her jujitsu classes to clear out her day.

Even though Summer was incredibly rich, she didn't act like it. And she considered the fame that came as a result of her wealth to be a burden, rather than a blessing. (Summer always did her best to behave like a normal girl, but she was rich and pretty, so gossip sites and magazines were constantly doing stories about her, which were almost always wrong; they were often about her love life, romantically linking her to famous people she had never even met.) So Summer tried to call as little attention to herself as possible. Instead of having Tran drive her around in a limousine, she rode in a normal car that was several years old. She never held my hand in public, because she didn't want the press to realize I was her boyfriend and invade my life too. And while she could glam herself up for public events, she preferred to hide behind sunglasses and a baseball cap so people wouldn't recognize her. She was wearing those today, despite the clouds, as well as old jeans and a sweatshirt that she could get muddy.

My father also planned to join us that day. Although he had traveled all around the world taking pictures of wildlife for *National Geographic*, he had never been to a dinosaur dig either, so he had eagerly asked if he could join us, and Sage welcomed him. Dad insisted upon driving Summer, Xavier, and me up the driveway in his car while Sage took the old Chevy. Even though Sage drove that route almost every day, Dad still didn't feel comfortable letting a sixth grader chauffeur him around.

Sage's home was a small ranch house that had been built

by his great-great-grandparents. Beside it stood a barn, several cattle pens, and a long corrugated tin roof on poles that sheltered the many vehicles the Bonottos owned: In addition to Sage's car, they had three pickup trucks, two horse trailers, a tractor, a hay baler and eight ATVs—though three were gone when we arrived.

Two county police cars sat by the house. One was marked *Sheriff*.

Dad and Sage parked their cars. Dad had brought along one of his best professional cameras and a variety of lenses, which he carried in a specially designed backpack, where they were nestled in foam. He slung this onto his back while Sage led us to the ATVs.

There were other dirt roads on the ranch besides the driveway, but they were poorly maintained and thus required four-wheel drive. (Sage claimed there were some distant parts of the property that no one had visited in years.) Sage's parents and their ranch hands usually got around in trucks—or on horses—but there were ATVs for everyone else.

Sage handed out helmets and protective gear to us, and we suited up, hopped on ATVs, and headed for the fossil site. Since the ATV engines were too loud to shout over, there were radios built into the helmets so we could stay in touch on the way. I had ridden the ATVs on Sage's ranch before, but never on a muddy day. Riding through the mud turned out to be great fun—as long as you didn't mind getting spattered with it. Summer and Dad enjoyed it as much as I did, whooping with delight as we roared across the fields and slewed through the muck, but Xavier was more reserved. He drove much slower than the rest of us, taking every curve as cautiously as a deer in tiger territory. We had to stop repeatedly to wait for him to catch up to us.

Eventually, we made it to the dig.

It was located on a bend in a tributary of the Guadalupe River that wound across the ranch. I had been along this stretch before; normally, the river was about twenty feet across and only two feet deep, but given the previous night's storm, it had overflowed its banks and seemed to be at least a foot higher. The water was moving fast and so clouded with runoff that it looked like chocolate milk. The river snaked through a wide, grassy plain; its dusty banks framed by dirt bluffs that were about five feet high. The dig was on the riverside, out in the open, with no trees to shade it, where the river cut close to the bluff.

Five canopies had been erected around the site. They were the kind you got at the sporting goods store for parents to sit under at their kids' soccer games, although some of our neighbors in employee housing had put them up beside their trailers to give themselves some shade outdoors. Here, they stood over bare patches of dirt where all the grass had been scraped away.

A lot of people were standing outside the canopies; the sky was cloudy enough that no one was looking for shade. Everyone was watching us approach. They had probably heard our ATVs several minutes before we arrived.

I counted both Sage's parents, two uniformed police officers, and eight other people who I figured were paleontologists.

The mood around the dig was sullen and glum. The joy we had felt riding the ATVs instantly vanished.

We had to park on the high ground, atop the small bluffs. The other three ATVs the Bonottos owned were already there—along with Sage's mother's horse, Cleopatra. I figured the police and Sage's father had come out on the ATVs, which meant all the other people must have walked to the site, even though it was several miles to the nearest road. Cleopatra wasn't even tied up. She was roaming freely, happily grazing on grass and in no mood to wander off.

Sage led the way down a muddy path in one of the bluffs.

His parents came to meet us as we approached, looking as though our presence there was making them uncomfortable. Sage's father was a tall, burly man with skin so weathered by the sun that he looked much older than he really was. I had never seen him without a cowboy hat. Sage's mother was slim and fit; she was renowned as the best horseback rider in the county and had won plenty of equestrian awards when she was younger.

"Sage," his mother said, "we told you to come alone. This is supposed to be a secret."

"What's it matter now?" Sage asked. "Someone already stole Minerva. . . ."

"Not all of her," his father said tightly.

"I figured these guys could help us," Sage protested. "Teddy and Summer solved all those crimes at FunJungle. Maybe they could solve this, too."

Sage's parents both looked at Summer and me thoughtfully.

I wasn't quite sure what to do. So I just waved to them awkwardly.

Dad stepped up. "Joe and Lorena, we're sorry for intruding. We didn't realize this was a secret. We'd be happy to leave you to this. . . ."

Mrs. Bonotto asked Summer and me, "You found that stolen panda, right? When even the FBI couldn't?"

"That's right!" Summer said cheerfully.

Sage's father looked at her curiously. "You're J.J. McCracken's daughter?"

"Right again," Summer agreed.

Joe and Lorena shared a look. Somehow, without saying anything, they seemed to come to an agreement.

"All right," Joe said. "Come on down. But don't touch anything. This is a crime scene."

"We know how to handle a crime scene," Summer said confidently. "This isn't our first."

I didn't feel nearly as comfortable as Summer did. It now seemed that we were only being allowed to visit the dig site because we were amateur detectives—which I hadn't meant to happen. But there didn't seem to be any polite way to excuse ourselves, and Summer, Xavier, and even my father seemed too excited to leave.

I was also a little wary of why Mr. Bonotto had asked about Summer's father. J.J. McCracken was one of the wealthiest men in Texas, if not the country. I wondered if that had anything to do with our invitation to stay as well.

The Bonottos led us into the dig site. Now it was the police who grew annoyed by our presence.

I recognized the sheriff as we approached. Lyle Esquivel was a stocky man in his fifties with a thick mustache and bushy eyebrows. There wasn't much crime in our county—the incidents at FunJungle had been out of his jurisdiction—so Sheriff Esquivel and his force didn't really have much to do. They mostly busted people for speeding, and the sheriff came to school every year to give us a safety presentation, during which half the class always fell asleep.

The other officer was a young woman I didn't know. She was of medium height, with long hair and a name tag that said BREWSTER. She was taking pictures of the crime scene with her phone, though she paused to watch Sheriff Esquivel with us.

The other people on the dig were watching us too. I wondered if anyone might recognize Summer, but they didn't seem to. Summer's baseball cap, sunglasses, and newly mud-splattered clothes gave her a very different appearance than her clean-cut, fashionable public persona.

"These kids shouldn't be here," Esquivel told the Bonottos. "This ain't a tourist attraction."

"I'd like them to stay," Sage's father replied. The sheriff started to argue this, but Mr. Bonotto cut him off. "This is our property and they're our guests. They're staying. So let's get back to the investigation, shall we?"

Sheriff Esquivel gave him a long, hard stare, as though he was debating whether or not to pick a fight over this. Then the stare shifted to the rest of us. Finally, he turned around and led us toward the dig. "Before we were interrupted," he said sharply, "I was questioning how this crime could have possibly been carried out. Some of what you're telling me doesn't make any sense at all."

"We're being completely honest with you," Mrs. Bonotto said, sounding slightly offended.

"I don't doubt your honesty," Esquivel told her. "I just think you might have some of the facts messed up. You're telling me this skull weighed five hundred pounds?"

"At least," Sage's father said. "Probably more. We couldn't exactly weigh it."

"Wait," Xavier blurted out, unable to control himself. "Only the skull was stolen? Not the whole dinosaur?"

Esquivel turned and glared at Xavier, making it very clear he didn't appreciate the interruption.

"Yes," one of the women at the dig answered. "But as far as we're concerned, the skull pretty much *was* the dinosaur." She was thin and pretty, dressed in a button-down shirt with muddy jeans and work boots. Zinc oxide sunblock was smeared across her face like war paint, even though it was a cloudy day. Despite the woman's obvious distress at the crime, she did her best to be welcoming as she came over to greet us. "I'm Ellen Chen from the University of Texas. I'm the lead paleontologist on this project."

Dad, Xavier, Summer, and I all said hello.

"You need to understand," Ellen went on, "we've only found about thirty-five percent of a tyrannosaur skeleton here—"

"That's all?" Summer interrupted.

"Believe it or not, that's not too bad," Dr. Chen said. "And not that uncommon. No one has *ever* found a complete skeleton of any dinosaur. There have been millions of years for the pieces to get lost or destroyed. The most complete *T. rex* ever found was eighty-five percent, and some have been as little as ten. But the really important thing was that we found the skull. A mostly intact one, no less. Because a skull is by far the most important piece of a dinosaur fossil."

Now I couldn't help but speak up. "Why's that?"

"Because a skull tells you almost everything important you want to know about a dinosaur," Dr. Chen replied. "For starters, what species it was, but also what it ate, its approximate age, the size of its brain, whether it was sick or not, how important its various senses were, and hundreds of other things. You can't tell any of that from, say, a rib." She pointed dismissively at some nearby bones on the ground.

Up until that point, I hadn't even recognized that they were bones at all, even though a good deal of dirt had been excavated around them. They weren't intact ribs, but were broken into pieces; I had thought they were merely rocks that were being cleared out of the way. It made me wonder how anyone had ever realized they were fossils.

Dad must have been thinking the same thing, because he asked, "How did anyone even find this dinosaur in the first place?"

Mr. Bonotto looked proudly at Sage. "That's the work of this little man."

Sage grinned. "I'd been fishing in the river and was on my way back, climbing up the bluff, when I noticed what looked like a tooth, right over there." He pointed to a spot at the base of the bluff. A gouge two feet across and equally as tall had been removed from the dirt—the former location of the skull, I figured.

"So I started digging around it," Sage went on. "And then I realized it was connected to a bone, and then, well . . . I couldn't believe it."

"That must have been crazy," Summer said.

"Insane," Sage agreed. "So I rode home to tell my parents, and they didn't believe me . . ."

"Well, who would have?" Mrs. Bonotto interjected. "We'd been out here a million times and never noticed anything."

"So I brought them back out here, and I showed them," Sage continued. "And we called the university right away . . ."

"And that's where I come in," Dr. Chen finished. "I came out the moment I heard. And to be honest, I couldn't believe it either. Only fifteen tyrannosaur skulls have ever been found, and those were mostly in Montana. So to find one *here* . . . It's a landmark discovery. Or, it would have been . . ." She trailed off, suddenly overcome by emotion, blinking tears away. "I'm sorry," she sniffed. "I can't even begin to explain how big a loss this is."

"For the university museum?" Xavier asked.

"No," Dr. Chen said. "For *science*. There's still a great deal we don't know about the *T. rex*. So a new skull has the potential to teach us an enormous amount about the species.

It's also possible that this might have been a new subspecies. Or a new species of dinosaur altogether. But with the skull gone, we'll never know."

She hung her head in dismay, and the other members of the dig did as well. The overwhelming feeling of sadness descended over the site once again.

The whole time we had been talking, Sheriff Esquivel hadn't even tried to hide his annoyance that we had interrupted him. Now he took the chance to resume his previous line of thought. "On that note, as I was saying before, I have some serious questions about how an object of that size could possibly have been stolen at all."

"You think we just *misplaced* it?" Sage's father asked sarcastically. "It was the size of an ATV and weighed at least a quarter of a ton!"

"That's what concerns me too," the sheriff said. "You'd need a truck to get that thing out of here, and the closest road is five miles away."

"Three and a half," Dr. Chen corrected. "Trust me, I've walked it enough times."

"You guys park all the way out there?" Summer asked her, surprised.

"Yes," Dr. Chen answered. "Though we don't walk it every day. Most nights, we camp out."

"Here?" I asked, looking around. I didn't see any signs of a camp.

"About a quarter mile that way." Dr. Chen pointed downriver. "We don't want to compromise the dig. But last night, because of the rain, we all evacuated to a motel. So it took longer than usual to get out here this morning, because we had to drive back and walk in. Otherwise, we would have discovered the theft a lot earlier."

"*Alleged* theft," Sheriff Esquivel insisted. Ignoring everyone's angry stares, he continued. "How, exactly, is someone supposed to carry a five hundred-pound dinosaur skull three and a half miles without a truck?"

"The same way *we* would have," Dr. Chen said angrily. "We'd sling it in a tarp and carry it out."

Esquivel took a wad of chewing tobacco from a tin and tucked it into his lower lip. "How many people does it normally take to do something like that?"

"Eight to ten," Dr. Chen replied.

"And how long?"

"Hours."

"Could you be more specific?"

"*A lot* of hours. It probably takes about three hours to go a mile."

Esquivel shifted the chewing tobacco in his lip. "So you're

telling me that eight to ten people traipsed all the way out here to the exact site of a secret dinosaur fossil site, grabbed a five-hundred-pound tyrannosaur skull, and then spent nine or ten hours lugging it back to the road . . . in the middle of a rainstorm? How on earth is that even possible?"

Mrs. Bonotto glared at the sheriff. "You're the policeman. Isn't it your job to figure that out?"

Esquivel said, "I cased this site carefully before the peanut gallery got here. And I'll tell you what I *did* notice: There's an awful lot of mud around here. But there's not a single footprint leading away from this site. Only footprints coming here. If eight to ten people carried a giant skull out, you'd think there'd be at least *one* print leaving the scene of the crime, wouldn't you? Statistically, there should be dozens, if not hundreds. And drag marks as well."

Despite our annoyance at the sheriff, everyone seemed to realize that was a valid argument.

Sage mustered the best response anyone could come up with. "Maybe the rain washed all the footprints away."

Esquivel spat a stream of tobacco juice at Sage's feet, then walked over to the gouge in the bluff where the skull had been. It was only twelve feet from the river's edge and the mud was deep there. His boots sank two inches down into it. Then he lifted one foot out. It made a thick sucking noise and left a large, foot-shaped divot. "That's not just a footprint," Esquivel said. "That's a crater. And a person lugging something that weighed five hundred pounds would sink down even farther. I know last night's storm was big, but it wasn't a hurricane. If eight to ten people were here, there'd be some evidence of it."

I started to say something, but Esquivel cut me off. "Don't you even try to suggest that they somehow wiped away every footprint between here and the road. Because it would take hours to do that, if not days."

That was exactly what I had been about to suggest. So I kept silent.

"A helicopter!" Xavier announced triumphantly. "Someone could have stolen the skull with a helicopter!"

"Not a chance." Esquivel spat another stream of tobacco juice. "I served twelve years in the Marines. I know helicopters. Your average chopper can't lift a quarter ton. You'd need a big, military-grade one to do that, and those things are loud as all get-out." He looked to the Bonottos. "Did you hear a chopper last night?"

"No," Sage's father admitted. "But maybe the storm covered the noise . . ."

"The storm's another problem," Esquivel said. "Flying a helicopter in rain and lightning like we had last night would have been borderline insanity. There are people who could do it, but they're few and far between. Most of them are military. And even if one of those rare people *did* want to steal a tyrannosaur skull, they'd still have to get their hands on a helicopter that could lift it, which isn't easy. Plus, they'd have to know about this dinosaur, which you said was top secret."

"Why *was* it top secret?" Summer asked.

"To prevent thefts like this," Dr. Chen answered. "A rare fossil like a tyrannosaur skull is worth millions of dollars. So whenever a discovery is made, its location—and ideally the discovery itself—is kept quiet. If word gets out about a dig like this, you'll get looters." She turned her attention to Sheriff Esquivel. "Which is probably what happened."

"So you claim," said Esquivel.

"How many people knew about this dinosaur?" I asked.

"You're looking at them," Dr. Chen replied.

I took in the small group of paleontologists and the Bonotto family.

Then I considered the location that the skull had disappeared from. There was no way anyone could have gotten close to it without going through the mud, and yet, as Sheriff Esquivel had pointed out, there were no tracks indicating that had happened. In addition, the shortest distance to the road involved crossing the swollen river, which seemed like it would be virtually impossible on a sunny day, let alone in the midst of a nighttime rainstorm.

Unlike Sheriff Esquivel, I didn't think that Sage, his parents, Dr. Chen, and the other eight members of the dig were all lying about the skull having been stolen. But at the same time, I couldn't imagine how anyone could have possibly made off with the skull.

Despite my fears of getting involved in trying to solve another crime, I found myself wanting to investigate, to ask more questions, to learn who the other people at the dig were, to walk around the scene and hunt for clues, to figure out what had happened.

But before I could even begin to grapple with all that, I got the strangest phone call of my life.

THE ANACONDA

Normally, I wouldn't have even answered the phone at a crime scene. There was too much else to focus on and I didn't want to be rude. But whoever was trying to reach me kept calling.

The first call came while I was standing there on the riverbank, taking in the dig site. I took my phone out, saw a number I didn't recognize, then flipped the phone to silent mode and put it right back in my pocket.

Sheriff Esquivel was saying, "Seeing as we are still on the hunt for footprints—or any other evidence that this crime even happened—all of you need to stay the heck out of my way. So why don't y'all move over there?" He pointed to some boulders along the riverbank, twenty yards from the dig.

"There?" Summer asked skeptically. "We won't be able to investigate anything from over there!"

"That's the point," Esquivel told her. "In case you've forgotten, I'm the sheriff around here. This is *my* job, not yours." He made a shooing gesture with his hands, the way someone would signal their dogs to get out of the house.

Summer looked ready to argue, but Dad shook his head, signaling her that this wasn't the time.

As we all headed to the rocks with the Bonottos, my phone started buzzing in my pocket again. I ignored it.

The mud along the riverbank sucked at our feet as we moved to the boulders. We were making fresh tracks in it; whoever had stolen the skull definitely hadn't come that way.

"The nerve of that man," Mrs. Bonotto muttered under her breath, glaring at the sheriff over her shoulder. "He's acting like we're the criminals. Why on earth would we lie to him about a skull being stolen?"

The boulders were still wet and slick from the rain. Some were as big as cars. Most were jumbled on the riverbank, though there were also a few in the swollen river, which surged around them, forming tiny rapids.

Sage scrambled up onto the boulders on the riverbank like they were a jungle gym. Xavier and Summer followed him. Summer moved with the agility and grace of a mountain goat. Xavier had more trouble. He had the climbing skills of a rhinoceros.

I would have followed, but my phone stopped ringing and then started vibrating in a different pattern. Text messages.

I removed it from my pocket again, this time to read what had been sent.

Call me back.

Its an emurgency.

Its searious.

Then my phone started ringing again.

"Who's calling you like that?" Dad asked. He had taken off his backpack and was assembling his camera to take photos of the dig.

"I don't know," I said.

"They seem awfully desperate to reach you," Dad said. "Think they might be in trouble?"

"Maybe," I admitted, and then answered the phone.

"Finally!" the caller said, sounding annoyed. I immediately recognized the voice—and the nasty attitude. It was one of the Barksdale twins calling me, though I wasn't sure which. Tim and Jim were equally mean and dumb. They were in the class ahead of me at school and they had caused plenty of trouble for me, as well as almost every other student.

"Tim?" I asked, taking a chance.

"No, it's Jim, idiot."

"Sorry, Jim, I'm in the middle of something right now . . ."

"Well, so am I. I've got a big problem here. Do you know how to get a cat out of a snake?"

I had been about to hang up until that sentence. I didn't really feel like helping anyone who had just called me an idiot—or repeatedly bullied me at school. But my interest was piqued. I had to ask, "What are you talking about?"

"Tim and I just got this new pet snake, and it sort of ate our cat."

"It *sort of* ate your cat?"

At this, my father looked at me curiously, but I signaled that I needed a bit more time on the phone before I could explain it all.

"Yeah," Jim said. I now noticed that he didn't sound quite as tough as he usually tried to. There was a hitch in his voice, like he might be trying not to cry. "Snakes swallow their food whole, right? So that means the cat could still be alive inside?"

This was wrong. Snakes *did* swallow their food whole, but they always killed it first. However, I didn't feel like breaking that news to Jim quite yet. I still had a lot of questions to ask. "How big a cat are we talking about here?"

"Pretty big for a cat. It's Griselda."

I knew Griselda. The Barksdales let her roam free around town. She was famous for being the biggest cat anyone had ever seen—and possibly the meanest. She often terrorized children at the playground, where she habitually left dead birds under the jungle gym and extremely large poops in the sand pit.

"Jim!" I exclaimed. "Griselda must be twenty pounds!"

"Twenty-five."

"What kind of snake did you get?"

"An anaconda."

"An *anaconda*?" I repeated, drawing a new round of stares from everyone. "How big is it?"

"Fifteen feet, I think. Maybe sixteen. So how do we get Griz back out of it? Can we do the hind lick maneuver or something?"

"You mean the Heimlich maneuver?"

"Yeah, whatever. I know that with humans, you're supposed to hit them in the stomach to make them throw up their food, but we don't know where the stomach is in this thing. It's like all neck."

"Not exactly," I said, amazed that one person could be wrong about so many things. That wasn't how the Heimlich maneuver was performed, and snakes were not all neck. "How long ago did this happen?"

"I don't know. Maybe an hour or so. We left Julius—"

"Julius?" I interrupted.

"The snake. That's his name. Julius Squeezer. We left him home with Griz so the two of them could play while we were gone. And then we came home and, well . . . we called to Griz and she didn't come. And then we found Julius with this lump the size of a cat in his throat. That's Griselda, right?"

"Probably so," I said.

To my surprise, Jim burst into tears.

Dad was still standing beside me, now taking photos of the dig site, but also trying to piece together what I was talking about by eavesdropping on my half of the conversation. Sage and Xavier were climbing around on the giant rocks along the riverbank while Summer hopped from one boulder to another in the river.

Over by the dig, Sheriff Esquivel was grilling Dr. Chen while the other eight people on her team sat sullenly nearby, waiting their turn.

The young policewoman, Brewster, was staring at me. But the moment I looked her way, she turned, pretending like she hadn't been looking at me at all.

On the phone, Jim was doing his best to control his sobbing. "What if we cut the snake open?" he asked. "Would Griselda still be alive in there? Like in 'Little Red Riding Hood,' where she cuts the big bad wolf open and her grandma is perfectly fine?"

"Um . . . that's a fairy tale," I said cautiously.

"What do you think would be the best to cut the snake open with? A machete or a chain saw? We have both."

"Don't cut the snake open!" I warned, more urgently than I had intended. I didn't want them to kill it—and I wondered if it might kill the Barksdales in self-defense.

"But Griselda's in there," Jim wailed.

"Griselda's gone," I told him. "Julius would have killed her before eating her."

"No!" Jim started blubbering into the phone again.

I almost felt sorry for him. But then I remembered he was a complete jerk who had consigned his evil cat to death by doing something incredibly moronic.

Dad was still eavesdropping. At the same time, he was using his telephoto lens to take photos of the crime scene from a distance.

"Jim," I said, "where did you get an anaconda that big?"

Jim stopped crying and shifted back into his usual, nasty persona. "Why do you care?"

In truth, I suspected he had obtained the snake illegally. There was a massive illegal pet trade in America that made billions of dollars a year. While there were plenty of legitimate reptile dealers, I doubted any of them were selling fifteen-foot-long anacondas. However, I didn't tell Jim that. Instead, I said, "It's important. So that more cats like Griselda don't die."

Jim's guard went up anyhow. "I don't have to tell you anything."

Over the phone I suddenly heard Jim's twin brother, Tim, call out, "What'd he say?"

Jim forgot about me and spoke to Tim. "That Griselda's dead. Because you had the stupid idea to buy that snake!"

"You wanted it too!" Tim challenged. "So maybe you're the stupid one."

"Don't call me stupid, idiot," Jim yelled back, and then the two of them started fighting. I heard punches being thrown, more insults being shouted, and glass breaking.

I figured I wasn't going to get any more information out of the Barksdales, so I hung up.

Dad was now taking pictures of Summer as she hopped from rock to rock in the river. He lowered the camera and looked to me curiously. "What was all that about?"

"The Barksdales bought an anaconda somehow," I reported. "One that's fifteen feet long."

Dad's eyes widened in surprise. "Fifteen feet?"

"And it ate their cat."

"They're lucky it didn't eat one of *them*."

"I think they might try to kill it," I said, worried.

Dad nodded, concerned, then slung his camera strap over his shoulder and fished out his phone. "I'll call the reptile guys at FunJungle. Maybe they can run out there and intervene before things get out of hand."

"Too late," I said.

I immediately called Tommy Lopez, who worked at the Department of Fish and Wildlife. Summer and I had helped Tommy with a case a few weeks before. Fish and Wildlife was responsible for policing the illegal reptile trade, so I figured they would want to know about the anaconda. I got a message saying that Tommy was out on assignment, so I left a message for him.

And then Dr. Chen started screaming.

THE STORM

"Are you crazy?" Dr. Chen shouted. **"Get off** there!"

At first I thought she was yelling at Sheriff Esquivel; maybe he had carelessly trod upon some fossils that hadn't been dug up yet. But then I noticed she was looking toward my friends on the boulders. Although I still couldn't tell who she was upset with. Neither could anyone else. Everyone looked her way, confused.

So she pointed directly at Summer, who had made it out to a boulder in the middle of the river. "You!" Dr. Chen yelled. "Don't you think we've had enough tragedy here today? We don't need a drowning, too!"

"I'm okay!" Summer yelled back confidently. "These rocks are totally safe!"

"No, they're not!" Dr. Chen came toward the boulders, looking genuinely concerned for Summer's safety. "They're wet and slippery, and that river is moving much faster than usual. If you fall in, you could drown! So please, do us all a favor and come back to land!"

Even from a distance, I could see Summer roll her eyes, but I found myself thinking that Dr. Chen had a point. The rock Summer was standing on was barely poking above the surface of the river—Summer had to place her feet right next to each other to stand on it—and the water was churning around her. I started to feel nervous myself.

Summer didn't show the slightest hint of concern, although she did follow Dr. Chen's request. She casually made her way back to shore, hopping from rock to rock.

As she did, I caught a glimpse of something out of the corner of my eye.

I turned back to the dig. Everyone there was distracted by Summer, looking toward the river.

Except one person.

One of the people working with Dr. Chen was a teenage girl, about fifteen or sixteen, I guessed. She was dressed for a long, hot day of dirty work, wearing overalls over a long-sleeved T-shirt and a wide-brimmed hat to block the sun.

The girl was scurrying away from a part of the dig and rejoining the rest of the team. It appeared that, while everyone else was watching Summer, she had taken the opportunity to slip away. She looked around furtively to see if anyone had noticed her, then did her best to act like she had been standing with the others the whole time.

It occurred to me that I hadn't taken a very good look at the seven other people working on the dig with Dr. Chen.

One was another teenage girl. She appeared to be friends with the first, as they were standing next to each other and dressed similarly, the way that girls who were good friends often did. They even had their hair done the same way, in ponytails that peeked out from under their floppy hats.

A middle-aged woman with short-cropped hair was close to them. I guessed she was one of their mothers, as she had a distinct mom vibe about her. She was dressed in the same sort of outfit my mother had worn when studying gorillas in Africa: jeans, a button-down shirt with the sleeves rolled up, and sturdy hiking shoes—only this woman's clothes looked a lot newer.

There were four people who looked old enough to be my grandparents: two men and two women. Despite their ages, they seemed to be in good physical shape, which would make sense, given that they had hiked at least three miles to the site that morning.

The final person was a man in his thirties. He was tall and gangly, and he wore a tie-dyed T-shirt, cargo shorts, a baseball cap, and a ponytail even longer than the teenage girls'.

"Those people can't all be paleontologists, can they?" I asked Sage's mom, who was standing close to me.

"Oh no," she told me. "They're all volunteer diggers. Dr. Chen is the only one here who works for the university. The rest are doing this for fun. Although I think the girls are getting some sort of high-school credit."

Summer leaped from the last rock in the river to the safety of shore. Upon impact, her shoes sank several inches into the mud.

Sheriff Esquivel now seemed to take notice of the eight volunteer diggers as well. He whistled to his one fellow officer, like she was a dog. "Brewster! You done taking photos of the crime scene yet?"

Brewster looked up, startled, and answered timidly, "Not quite yet, Sheriff. Maybe a few more minutes."

Esquivel frowned grumpily, like this had annoyed him somehow. "Well, get it done. And then get all these people's names and phone numbers and work out a schedule for them to come be questioned at my office."

"You're going to question *us*?" the mom asked. "Why? We didn't steal the skull."

"Do you want me to investigate this or not?" Esquivel asked sourly. "If no one knew the location of this dig but you folks, then you're all the suspects I've got."

"You're not going to question them here?" Dr. Chen asked.

"Nope." Esquivel nodded toward the north, where the sky had grown darker along the horizon. "Looks like we have more rain coming, it's a long way back to the car, and I'm not a big fan of being wet."

I hadn't noticed the potential storm until Esquivel pointed it out. It appeared that no one else had either.

"We ought to start heading out ourselves," Dr. Chen told the others on the dig. "Hopefully, we can make it to our cars before that gets here."

Esquivel turned to her, a thought having occurred to him. "The Bonottos said all y'all are parked out on Fletcher Road?"

"That's right." Dr. Chen was already gathering her things and preparing for the hike back out.

"That's on the other side of this river," Esquivel observed. "How do y'all normally get across it?"

"There's a big log spanning a narrow spot in the river down by our camp," Dr. Chen explained. "We rigged up a hand rope for safety. It was a little dicey this morning, but still passable."

"Too dicey to carry a skull across it in the middle of a rainstorm, I'll bet." The sheriff considered the fast-moving river. "And no one crossed this with a quarter ton of dinosaur skull either." He turned back to Officer Brewster. "Forget those crime scene photos and get me those names and numbers. ASAP. These people have three and a half miles to hoof it before the heavens open up again."

With that, he walked away from the site, his boots making great sucking sounds in the mud.

In the distance, lightning flickered in the clouds. It was still too far off to hear the thunder, but it was definitely coming our way.

"We better get going too," Sage's mom told us, then started back toward her horse and the ATVs.

Dad, Mr. Bonotto, Sage, Xavier, and Summer followed her. I took a last look around the dig site.

The dig crew was quickly gathering their gear to hike back out to their cars. They had already been upset about the disappearance of the skull, but now Esquivel's attitude and the coming storm had them all looking as morose as could be. As they pulled on their raincoats and gathered their umbrellas, Officer Brewster flitted about them, entering their contact information into her phone.

As Brewster moved from the mom to the grandparents, she suddenly looked my way. Our eyes locked and she held my gaze. I got the sense there was something she wanted to say to me.

"Teddy!" my father called.

I broke my gaze with Brewster.

Dad stood at the base of the small bluff, waiting for me. "Let's go," he said. "Before we get drenched."

I hurried after him, my shoes sliding in the mud. We clambered up the bluff and made our way to the ATVs.

Sheriff Esquivel was already sitting astride one. He took off without even a glance back, the motor shredding the prestorm silence.

Sage's mother hopped onto her horse as easily as I would have climbed onto a bicycle and galloped toward home.

The rest of us put on our helmets, climbed onto our ATVs, and drove back to Sage's house. The ride wasn't nearly as much fun as it had been on the way out. My mind was filled with thoughts about the missing skull; how it had been stolen was certainly a major mystery. And I was thinking about the Barksdales and their anaconda too, wondering where they had acquired it. Even though I hadn't liked their cat, I still felt bad for it; no animal deserved to die because its owners were careless. I even felt a little bit bad for the Barksdales as well.

We weren't far from the house when the storm arrived. By now the sky had turned so dark it felt like dusk, even though it was only around lunchtime. The rain began slowly, with the drops plonking down every few seconds. They were big enough that they had real weight to them; each one felt like someone flicking me with a finger as it smacked into my arm or shoulder. A few splattered on the visor of my helmet. We all gunned our engines and sped up, racing the rain.

We reached the covered shelter for storing the vehicles mere seconds before the rain really came down. Sheriff Esquivel had beat us back, so he had already parked his ATV and was halfway to his squad car when we arrived.

The moment I turned off my ATV, the deluge hit.

A serious Texas rainstorm can be quite a sight. Locals often joked that the Texas Hill Country got ten inches of rain a year—and it all fell within fifteen minutes.

This storm made me think that wasn't really a joke. It was as if someone had torn a hole in the sky. Water was suddenly pouring down so hard we could barely see the house thirty feet away. Luckily, we were protected by the tin roof of the shelter, but Sheriff Esquivel was in exactly the wrong place at the wrong time. The rain came down on him like an anvil, drenching him in an instant.

He was about twenty feet away from us and already had his keys out, intending to get into his squad car as fast as possible. But the rain caught him by surprise, knocking his cowboy hat down over his eyes. He promptly stumbled over his own feet, slipped on the slick ground, and face-planted in the mud. His keys flew from his hands and plopped into a puddle left over from the previous night's rain.

Under the shelter, we were still dry, but it had grown cool fast, and the wind kept blowing gusts of mist inside. Still, it made more sense to stay there than attempt a run for the house or the cars. If we did, we would certainly end up getting drenched like Sheriff Esquivel.

The rain was rattling so hard on the corrugated tin over our heads, it sounded like we were in a war movie. Thus, no one else could really hear when Sage came up beside me and asked, "So? Can you help us figure out who stole Minerva?"

"I don't know if that's such a good idea," I said. "The police are already investigating . . ."

"You call that investigating?" Sage pointed to Sheriff Esquivel, out in the rain. "He doesn't even think there was a crime!"

Outside, Esquivel pulled himself to his knees and crawled to the puddle his keys had fallen into, which was growing by the second in the downpour. The sheriff fumbled through the murky water, tossing aside clumps of grass he had grabbed by mistake. His hat fell off and landed upside down in the puddle. Esquivel snatched it out and slapped it back on his head. Even in the few moments it had been off, it had caught enough rain to pour down his shirt. Esquivel screamed in rage, splashed around in the puddle some more, and finally came up with his keys. He leaped to his feet to race to his car, but immediately lost his balance on the saturated ground and fell once again, this time on his back.

Everyone else in the shelter was so riveted to the sheriff's mishaps that they hadn't even noticed Sage and me talking.

"Esquivel's not going to be happy if I start snooping around," I said.

"He probably won't even notice," Sage replied.

"Plus, getting involved might be dangerous."

"No, it won't."

"Everyone always says that," I replied. "And then I end up in danger."

Out in the rain, Sheriff Esquivel was writhing about on his back like a turtle flipped onto its shell. He finally managed to flop over onto his stomach and then stagger to his feet again. He was now so coated with mud he looked like he'd been dipped in chocolate—although the rain quickly washed some of it away, leaving him dappled and soaked to the bone. He grabbed his hat once more, shook the water out of it, and clambered into his car. Then he drove off angrily, his car skidding and kicking up mud.

No one gathered in the shelter seemed the slightest bit sorry for him.

"*Please*," Sage begged me. "Sheriff Esquivel isn't going to do anything. And we need to know who stole that dinosaur."

The worried tone of his voice struck me. I turned to him

and was surprised by the desperation in his eyes. It made me think something much greater than a stolen dinosaur was at stake. "What's going on?" I asked.

Sage glanced furtively at his parents. They and everyone else were staring out at the rain, most likely trying to guess how much longer it would last, and thus, how much longer we would be stuck in the shelter.

Even though they were distracted, Sage pulled me farther away from them and whispered, "The cattle business has been really bad lately. My folks have taken out a lot of loans against the ranch, and they've just ended up deeper in the hole. A *lot* deeper."

I looked toward Sage's parents.

"They don't know I know," Sage said quickly. "But it's bad. Minerva's the only thing that can save us."

"What do you mean?"

"If that skull was really worth millions, it'd be enough to save our ranch. It was like stumbling across a treasure chest."

I now understood why Sage was so desperate. "Your parents were going to sell it?"

"According to the law, if it's on our property, we own it. But if we can't find who stole it and get it back . . . we're going to lose our home."

I frowned, feeling a growing sense of worry.

I was concerned for Sage and his family. I didn't want

them to lose the ranch that had been in their family for generations. And I didn't want my friend to have to move away from a place he obviously loved.

I was also worried because I shared Sage's belief that Sheriff Esquivel wasn't going to investigate this case properly.

And I was worried because I knew what all that meant: Despite my concerns, I was going to help find out what happened to the dinosaur.

6

MUD

Like many Texas thunderstorms, this one didn't last long. After fifteen minutes, the massive downpour stopped almost instantly, as though the clouds had run out of water. The lightning and thunder moved on into the distance, although the sky remained dark and ominous, threatening more rain.

We took advantage of the break in the weather to get to our car and head home. None of us wanted to be out on the ranch's poorly maintained driveway when another downpour started. As it was, poststorm, the long road was in bad shape. It was mostly mud slicks and puddles so big, they could have almost qualified as ponds. Lots of branches had been knocked loose by the winds, and at one point, an entire cedar tree had toppled into the road, its trunk snapped like a toothpick. Luckily, it had fallen in a clearing, which allowed us enough room to circumnavigate it; otherwise, we would have had to backtrack to the Bonottos' and hope they had a chain saw.

"I'm surprised Sheriff Esquivel got out of here all right in that rain," Xavier observed. "Especially since he took off like a madman."

"We're not off the property yet," Dad warned, in a tone that said he half expected to find the sheriff's car wrecked on the side of the driveway.

Summer pointed to the roadside ahead. "Looks like he did have some trouble." The bubble lights from the roof of the sheriff's car lay smashed in a puddle. It appeared that the sheriff had lost control and a low-hanging branch had torn them off his roof. Three sodden cattle stared at them, confused.

"He's not going to be happy about that," Xavier said.

"He wasn't happy to start with," I said. "He *really* won't want to investigate this case now."

"It's not like he would have been any help anyhow," Summer claimed. "Daddy says there are rocks that could do a better job fighting crime than the sheriff."

"He's not that bad—" Dad began.

Xavier interrupted him. "All those people from the dig were telling him the skull had been stolen and he was acting like they were just making up some crazy story!"

"I'm not saying he's right," Dad went on. "But the case *does* seem pretty impossible. For the life of me, I can't imagine how anyone could make off with something that big so far from a road. At night in the middle of a rainstorm to boot."

"Maybe they didn't take it all the way to the road," Summer suggested. "Maybe they only got it halfway and then hid it in the woods somewhere on the ranch for a while. And then they're going to come back later to get it. Maybe they're even coming back today!"

"It still would have been incredibly difficult to get the skull halfway," Dad told her. "And they still would have left footprints at the crime scene."

Summer started to dispute this, then realized she didn't have an argument. She closed her mouth again and frowned. "That's a good point," she admitted.

A few seconds of silence passed, all of us trying to come up with a way the crime could have been committed, and failing.

"What was that phone call you got about?" Summer asked me suddenly.

I realized she and Xavier had been out by the river when I had explained everything to Dad. "The Barksdales bought an anaconda."

"An anaconda?" Summer echoed. "Isn't that illegal?"

"If the Barksdales did it, it must be," Xavier said. Then he looked to me. "So why'd they call *you*?"

"It ate their cat," I said.

Summer burst into laughter. "No way! It ate Griselda?"

"Yes," I said. "They wanted to know how to do the Heimlich maneuver on it."

Summer laughed harder. Even Xavier chuckled a bit.

"*You* think that's funny?" I asked him, surprised he could find any humor in the death of an animal.

"Sure," Xavier said.

"You're not upset about the cat?" Summer asked, between fits of giggles.

"Normally, I would be," Xavier said. "But Griselda was a menace. Feral cats kill over a billion birds a year in the United States alone—and Griselda was worse than most. I'll bet she took out a couple hundred a year herself."

A big gust of wind kicked up. There was a crack like a gunshot and a big, thick branch snapped off an oak tree and dropped into the road in front of us. Dad slammed on the brakes, but even though we were going slowly, the car still skidded on the muddy ground. We slid a few yards forward before coming to a stop right next to the branch, our front bumper just kissing the bark.

Dad heaved a sigh of relief. "That was close. C'mon, kids.

We'll need to drag it off the road." He opened his door and climbed out.

The rest of us got out with him. The rain had turned the dirt road into a thick slurry. My feet sank so deeply into it that cold mud ran into my shoes, which was an unsettling feeling. Xavier and Summer didn't seem pleased about it either.

"This is my best pair of sneakers," Xavier groused. "My mom's gonna kill me."

More damp cattle stood by the side of the road, shin-deep in mud, watching us while they chewed their cud.

The branch that lay across the road was eight inches in diameter. If it had fallen a couple seconds later, it might have caved in the roof of our car.

"Have you heard anything from the reptile team at Fun-Jungle yet?" I asked Dad.

He fished his phone from the pocket of his jeans. "Oh yeah. Looks like I missed a message from them. They rounded up some folks to go to the Barksdales' and check things out." He tucked the phone away and then added, "They won't have any legal jurisdiction, though. If the Barksdales don't want to let them into their house, there won't be much they can do about it."

"Maybe the Barksdales will *want* them to come in," I suggested. "Maybe, after Griselda, they'll have realized that it's dangerous to have an anaconda in the house."

"That thought process sounds a little too intelligent for the Barksdales." Summer frowned at the worsening condition of her shoes as she slogged through the mud. "I mean, they were dumb enough to get an anaconda in the first place. Who does that?"

"More people than you'd think," Dad said. "In fact, there are people whose *children* have been killed by their pet snakes."

Xavier, Summer, and I shared a look of horror at that. "No way," Xavier said.

"Sadly, it's true." Dad knelt by the side of the branch and grabbed onto some twigs that protruded from it.

The rest of us followed his lead.

"On my three," Dad said, then counted, "One . . . two . . . three!"

We all heaved as hard as we could. The branch was surprisingly heavy, and it had fallen with enough force to stick fast in the mud. Our feet sank even deeper into the muck until they touched the rocks a few inches down, at which point we finally had enough leverage to move the branch. It held fast for a few moments, then came free so quickly that Xavier and I both stumbled backward and landed on our butts.

Now cold ooze ran over my waistline and into my

pants, which was a significantly worse feeling than having it in my shoes.

Xavier yelped in disgust, obviously having felt the same thing, and leaped to his feet. "Ugh! Gross!" he exclaimed. "I've got mud in my butt!"

Summer burst into laughter again.

"It's not funny," I told her, struggling to my feet.

"Yes, it is," she informed me.

Now that the branch was free, we could move it to the side of the road, but that still wasn't easy. It was heavy and unwieldy and difficult to drag through the muck. By the time we got it to the edge of the driveway, we were all smeared with mud.

My hands were coated with it. I knelt to wash them off in a puddle.

Summer joined me. "I hate to say this, but Esquivel might have a point about stealing that skull."

Xavier looked up from wiping his hands on his pants. "What are you saying? That everyone's lying about there having been a dinosaur?"

"No." Summer rubbed her hands feverishly in the murky water. "But it was hard enough moving that branch ten feet just now, and it didn't weigh anything close to what that skull would have. So how would someone have moved the skull without a team of people?"

"Maybe they *did* have a team," Dad said.

I stood up, drying my hands on my pants, which didn't work very well, as my pants were already quite wet. "You mean everyone from the site stole the skull?"

"No," Dad replied. "I mean, maybe a group of professionals took it."

"Professional dinosaur thieves?" Xavier asked, incredulous.

"They exist," Dad said. "A friend of mine wrote an article about it in *National Geographic* a while back. Not too long ago, everyone thought that dinosaur skeletons should only be in museums, but over the past few decades, a lot of private collectors have been buying fossils for themselves. That has made the prices skyrocket, which has led to a black market in stolen bones. So now, there are thieves that specialize in fossils. When millions of dollars are at stake, I'll bet you could easily assemble a whole team of those specialists."

"But how would they have found out about Minerva if she was a secret?" Summer asked.

"These professionals pay well for information," Dad answered. "Secrets don't stay secret for long when money's on the line." He picked his way back through the mud toward the car.

The rest of us followed him. Like Xavier, I had cold mud down my pants, which made me shiver as I walked.

Summer paused suddenly. "Even if there *was* a team

of thieves, how could they avoid *that*?" She pointed at the stretch of driveway in front of the car.

The activity of our moving the branch had churned up all the mud. There were hundreds of deep holes and gouges from our feet, plus two large divots where Xavier and I had landed on our butts. The mud looked like an entire army had trooped through it, rather than only four people.

Summer said, "If we did that just moving a branch, imagine what eight to ten people would do moving a five-hundred-pound skull more than three miles. It would take *days* to smooth out all the tracks they'd leave behind. Weeks, maybe."

"Maybe it was a *really* big team of people," Xavier suggested. "Like, ten of them stole the skull, while another ten smoothed out the tracks behind them." He looked to my father. "Do these gangs of thieves ever get that big?"

"I don't know," Dad said. "Maybe. Although it might take a hundred men to smooth out miles of footprints like those."

We all clambered back in the car, trying our best not to get mud everywhere, but that proved impossible. Both Xavier and I had it all over the seats of our pants, and it was thickly clotted on everyone's shoes. We were all wet and cold, and despite Dad turning the heat on, the rest of the slow, bumpy ride down the driveway was rather miserable. I was trying to figure out how someone could have moved the skull three and a half miles without leaving a trail of several thousand footprints, but all I could really think about was how nice a warm shower would be.

"Where'd the Barksdales get an anaconda in the first place?" Summer asked suddenly.

"I asked," I said. "But they wouldn't tell me. In fact, they got really defensive about it."

Summer said, "Well, if they got it illegally, then that must mean there's an unauthorized reptile dealer operating around here."

"I suppose that makes sense," my father said thoughtfully. "Although the Barksdales might have simply bought it from someone else who had purchased it illegally. Someone who didn't realize the snake was going to get so big and was looking for some suckers to pawn it off on."

"That'd be the Barksdales for sure," I said.

"Then why would they be so defensive when you asked about where they got the snake?" Summer asked. "There must be an illegal dealer. Who would investigate someone like that?"

"Not Sheriff Esquivel, I hope," Xavier said.

Dad said, "It ought to be the Department of Fish and Wildlife."

I checked my phone. "I haven't heard anything from Tommy Lopez yet. He must be really busy."

"Maybe *too* busy to investigate something like this," Summer said.

"Oh no," I said, recognizing the tone in her voice. "You're not thinking that *we* should do it?"

"I'm not thinking *we* at all," Summer said. "I'm thinking *me*. Nothing dangerous. Just asking the Barksdales some innocent questions about their snake."

"Anything involving the Barksdales is potentially dangerous," I said.

"They're never going to be honest with Fish and Wildlife," Summer declared. "And they've already refused to tell you where they got the anaconda. But I think they'd talk to me. Especially if I acted like *this*." Summer suddenly shifted her personality, going from her standard, low-key attitude to that of a slightly ditzy, fascinated girl. "You have an anaconda?" she asked breathlessly. "That's sooooo cool. Where'd you get it?" She batted her eyelashes and then pursed her lips, making herself appear coy and demure. Summer was very pretty, and when she laid it on like this, she could look like a magazine cover model.

"I think that would work," Xavier said quickly. He had become a bit flushed, watching Summer.

I had the sneaking suspicion that, if I hadn't already known Summer, and she had talked to me that way, I would have spilled my guts to her.

"The Barksdales won't trust you, either," I cautioned Summer. "They hate you. You pulled their pants down in front of the entire school, remember?"

"Doesn't matter," Summer said. "Teenage boys are idiots."

I noticed Dad laughing to himself.

"Please tell her this is a bad idea," I asked him.

"This is a bad idea," Dad repeated, but in a tone that indicated he didn't really mean it. I got the sense that Dad wanted to see how this all played out.

We came to a puddle so big it was practically a lake. The driveway disappeared into it and emerged on the far side, where three waterlogged cattle were up to their knees in it. There was no way around it, so Dad drove right through the middle. Water sloshed up against the sides of the car, giving the impression that we were in a boat rather than an automobile.

"Maybe I could take Violet with me too," Summer said thoughtfully. "The Barksdales definitely have the hots for her. They'd probably give her the PIN numbers for their bank accounts if she asked."

"Ooh!" Xavier exclaimed. "We could run some sort of sting operation! The two of you could question them while Teddy and I listened in somehow!"

"Right," I said sarcastically. "The girls could wear wires

and we could wait inside one of those nondescript vans like in the movies."

"Exactly!" Xavier said.

"I was *joking*," I told him.

He frowned at me. "Don't you care about bringing reptile smugglers to justice?"

"Of course," I said. "I just think that it should be handled by people whose job it is, and not us."

Xavier said, "If law enforcement were doing their jobs, the Barksdales wouldn't have an anaconda right now, would they?"

"Here we are," Dad said, keeping the conversation from going any further.

We had arrived at the front gate. Summer's car was still there, parked on the shoulder of the road. Tran got out to greet her, looking nice and dry, having waited out the storm in the comfort of the car. A paperback novel sat flapped open in the front seat; it appeared he had plowed through about half of it in the time we had been at the ranch.

Normally, Summer would have been game to head back to FunJungle with us, but she seemed desperate to get home and clean off. "I'll call you later to talk about our sting operation," she said, then gave me a quick peck on the cheek and climbed out of our car.

"There is no sting operation!" I yelled after her.

She gave me a devilish grin and got into her car.

Dad had barely pulled back onto the road again when my phone started buzzing. I took it from my pocket, hoping it was Tommy Lopez calling, but was surprised to see the caller ID listed as "Sheriff Dept."

I answered it cautiously. "Hello?"

"Is this Theodore Fitzroy?" a woman asked.

"Yes."

"This is Officer Karen Brewster. I just saw you at the dig site."

The volume on the phone was up loud enough that Dad and Xavier could hear this. Both looked at me, intrigued.

"Oh!" I said, surprised. "Hi. Did you get out before the storm?"

"No. It came up too fast. The digging crew and I had to wait it out in the woods, which didn't work so well. We all got pretty soaked."

"Sorry. Um. How did you get my number?"

"I called the department. We had it in our database. You're sort of a known quantity around here, given your involvement in various crimes."

"Oh," I said again, unsure whether to be flattered or concerned.

Dad signaled me to turn on the speaker function, which I did, so that he and Xavier could hear better.

"I hate to bother you," Officer Brewster went on, "but the girl you were out here with, that was Summer McCracken, correct?"

So someone had recognized Summer after all. I thought about denying it, but decided that it wouldn't be smart to lie to a police officer. "Yes."

"Is she with you right now?"

"No. She just got into her own car."

"Good. Because I'd like to talk to you about this case."

"Without Summer? Because she's been as much a part of solving crimes around here as I have."

"I'm not calling you to ask for your help. I'm calling to ask you some questions about Miss McCracken."

I felt a chill go up my spine that had nothing to do with the mud in my pants. "You don't think she had something to do with the theft of the dinosaur?"

"No, not her," Officer Brewster said. "But I'm quite sure her father did. In fact, he's my number one suspect."

RUBY'S

"What?" I gasped.

I wasn't the only one who was surprised. Xavier had
to clamp his hand over his mouth to keep from making a
sound and tipping off Officer Brewster that he was listening in, while Dad was so startled he briefly drifted onto the
other side of the road. Luckily, the roads out by the Bonotto
Ranch were rarely traveled, especially after a storm, so there
wasn't anyone else out there for us to run into.

"I'm telling you this in the strictest confidence," Officer Brewster said, "as you appear to be friends with Miss
McCracken. You can't say a word of this to her. Or anyone
else."

"Of course," I said, with a furtive glance at Xavier. "Why
do you suspect J.J.?"

"According to Dr. Chen, Mr. McCracken is the only person besides anyone on the dig team who knew about the tyrannosaur. She wasn't sure how he heard about it, but he has already offered to purchase the skeleton several times. Seems he wants it for his theme park. Maybe to go in the dinosaur exhibit."

That sounded plausible. There was an enormous dinosaur exhibit at the end of the World of Reptiles building featuring all sorts of animatronic prehistoric beasts. (It had always bugged me that it was in the reptile building, when dinosaurs had been proven to be more closely related to birds, but most tourists didn't seem to care; the exhibit was one of the most popular attractions at FunJungle.) I could imagine J.J. wanting an actual dinosaur skeleton for it. And yet . . .

"If J.J. had made multiple offers to buy the dinosaur, why would he steal it?" I asked.

At the same time, Xavier had apparently thought of something as well, because he quickly unzipped his book bag, dug out a journal, and started scribbling in it furiously.

"The Bonottos were hoping to auction off the skull to the highest bidder," Officer Brewster replied. "So they rejected the offers, which upset J.J. I'm guessing that he didn't want to get into competition with anyone else, so he stole the skull."

Xavier finished writing, tore out the page, and handed it

to me. It was a question for Brewster. I took it from him and read, "It doesn't make sense that he'd want it for FunJungle. If he puts it on display, then everyone will know that he's the one who had it frozen."

"Frozen?" Brewster repeated.

"Stolen!" I corrected. Xavier's handwriting was atrocious. "I meant stolen."

"I don't know," Brewster said, sounding annoyed that I was poking holes in her theory. "Maybe J.J. doesn't want Minerva for FunJungle at all. Maybe he wants a dinosaur skeleton in his living room. That's what most people paying top dollar for dinosaur bones are doing with them."

"I can't imagine J.J. having a skull stolen like that . . . ," I began.

"No one can ever imagine their friends committing a crime," Brewster told me. "And yet thousands of crimes are committed every year. Tell me, how did Summer McCracken end up coming along with you today?"

"I invited her," I said.

"Are you sure about that?" Brewster inquired. "Take some time to think about it. Is it possible she already knew where you were going and asked to come along?"

"Are you suggesting that Summer is also tied up in this?" I asked.

"I just think it seems a little suspicious," Brewster replied.

"J.J. McCracken wants to buy the dinosaur. He's told no. He gets upset. The dinosaur disappears. McCracken is the number one suspect. And who shows up at the top-secret crime scene the very next morning? His own daughter."

I felt myself growing angry at Brewster's accusations. I was about to dismiss her entire theory as idiocy, but Dad held up an open hand, signaling me to bite my tongue.

Take a breath, Dad mouthed.

So I did, calming myself down. He was right; there was no point in antagonizing Officer Brewster. Instead, I realized that I should try to divert her attention to someone else. Someone who made more sense.

"Summer definitely didn't know about the dinosaur before I told her," I said as pleasantly as I could. "I invited her. She didn't invite herself."

"Really?" Brewster asked, like she didn't believe me, which forced me to bite my tongue again.

"You said Dr. Chen was the one who told you about J.J. McCracken?" I asked.

"That's right."

"Well, what's to say that's the truth? Maybe Dr. Chen stole Minerva and is pointing the blame somewhere else."

"Dr. Chen didn't steal the skull," Brewster said confidently. "She has an alibi."

"What is it?" I asked.

Officer Brewster explained, "There's a bar by the motel where Dr. Chen and everyone else on the dig stayed last night. It's out by the interstate. The bar's called Ruby's Taphouse. Dr. Chen and the whole crew were there all night last night."

Xavier started scribbling furiously again.

"All night?" I repeated.

"Well, not until dawn. But until last call, which was somewhere around one thirty a.m. They gathered there for dinner and ended up staying late. I called the bar and confirmed it with Ruby herself."

Xavier ripped off another piece of paper and handed it to me. I made sure I could read his handwriting this time and then asked, "The teenage girls were there too?"

"Well, no," Brewster said. "Of course not. That'd be against the law. But according to everyone—even Ruby—they were allowed in for dinner and then, once everyone started drinking, they went to their motel room and watched a movie. They were asleep in the room when the mother came back."

"And every other one of the people from the dig was at Ruby's the whole time?" I asked.

"Except for the old man who disappeared for ten hours and came back soaking wet and carrying a dinosaur skull," Brewster said, sounding annoyed. "I'm not an idiot, Teddy.

I know how to confirm an alibi. These people all have one, and it's rock solid."

We arrived at a fork in the road. Dad braked to a stop and drummed his hands on the steering wheel, thinking. The left turn led back to FunJungle. But Dad seemed to be having second thoughts about going that way.

I couldn't ask him what he was doing without tipping off Officer Brewster that other people were eavesdropping on the call. So instead I said, "Sorry. I wasn't trying to question your abilities."

Dad came to a decision and took the right fork in the road, heading away from FunJungle.

Officer Brewster asked, "Did Summer McCracken say anything suspicious today? Did she indicate in any way that she had previous knowledge of this crime?"

Now it was my turn to get annoyed again. I didn't like the idea of anyone questioning the honor of my girlfriend. Although it occurred to me that Officer Brewster didn't seem to know Summer was my girlfriend. Otherwise, she never would have trusted me to rat on her. "Summer didn't know about this until I told her about it," I reiterated. "Plus, she is one of the most honest people I've ever met. If her father had anything to do with this, she didn't know about it."

Dad glanced at me as I said this, and I winced. In my

hurry to protect Summer's reputation, I had suggested that J.J. McCracken still might have been responsible.

Not that I could guarantee J.J. *wasn't* involved. I liked J.J., but I knew he could be somewhat slippery where ethics were concerned. There had always been rumors that he might have broken a law or two—or more—to amass his fortune, although nothing had ever been proven.

And yet, I still felt I needed to say something in his defense. "Not that I'm saying J.J. *did* do it. I don't think he would. Have you checked to see if *he* has an alibi yet?"

"Someone as rich as J.J. McCracken doesn't need an alibi," Brewster said dismissively. "He can pay other people to do his dirty work for him."

"But doesn't that mean that *any* rich person might have done it?" I suggested.

"They'd still have to know about the dinosaur first . . ."

"Maybe someone else did, but we just don't know about it yet."

"Do me a favor, kid. If Summer starts asking strange questions about the dinosaur—or does *anything* suspicious—let me know. I'll text you my private number right now."

"But—" I began.

Brewster didn't bother to listen. I got the impression she was done talking to me and wanted to get off the call. "And one more thing: If you *do* come across evidence that

J.J. McCracken is involved in this crime and you don't share it with me, then you could be considered an accessory to the crime. Do you know what that means?"

"Yes. It means I could be in trouble too."

"Exactly. So let me know if you hear anything." Brewster hung up.

"Boy oh boy," Xavier said. "She really has it in for J.J., doesn't she?"

"We should let Summer know," I said, starting to dial her number.

"I'm sure Brewster's counting on you doing that," Dad said.

I stopped dialing. "Why's that?"

"You're obviously friends with her. Brewster could tell that. She could have easily kept it a secret that she suspected J.J., but she didn't."

Xavier asked, "What point would there be to letting J.J. know she suspects him?"

"I'm not sure," Dad answered. "Maybe she wants to make him nervous. Maybe she thinks he'll make a mistake."

The woods ended abruptly as we came to civilization. The road we were on dead-ended at an access road, which paralleled Interstate 35, the main route from San Antonio to Austin. I had been told that, not many years before, there hadn't been much along this stretch of highway except for a few small towns. But as San Antonio had sprawled north and Austin had sprawled south, the highway had become one long stretch of suburbia. The access road was now lined with fast-food restaurants, cheap motels, convenience stores, and the occasional random business. Dad turned right onto the access road, passed a McDonald's, a Taco Bell, and a swimming pool supply store, and then pulled into the parking lot of a bar.

Ruby's Taphouse.

The bar looked like it had been built several decades earlier and never had a dime of improvement put into it since. The paint was peeling, the parking lot was more weeds than asphalt, and letters were missing from the neon sign so that it said *Rub 's Tap use*. Still, through the windows, the place seemed homey and far more inviting to spend time in than the fast-food restaurants.

Next to Ruby's was the motel that Officer Brewster had mentioned. It was called the Cozy Inn, and it appeared as though the same person who had built Ruby's had built it, too; it was also a bit rundown, but not awful. A two-story L of rooms hooked around a parking lot and a fenced-off swimming pool. There was only one car in the parking lot—although it was likely that anyone staying at the motel was probably out at FunJungle or some other tourist attraction for the day.

"Wow," Xavier said. "This wasn't too far from the ranch."

"Makes sense," Dad told us. "If everyone from the dig needed to grab a place to spend the night in a hurry, they probably wouldn't want to go too far. Or spend too much, given that most of them are volunteering for this as it is." He got out of the car.

So did Xavier and I. The blackest rain clouds had moved on, but the day was still blustery.

"How'd you know this was here?" I asked.

"I *am* allowed to go out on occasion," Dad teased. "And sometimes it's nice to go someplace that isn't part of FunJungle." He led the way to the front door of Ruby's.

"What's wrong with FunJungle?" Xavier asked, slightly confused. Xavier revered FunJungle so much, he seemed surprised that anyone might have a problem with it.

"Everything there is themed," Dad explained. "It's all pretend. Fake safari lodge. Fake outback camp. Fake Caribbean resort. It can be fun, but . . . it can also be a bit too much. This place just is what it is."

A sign on the door of Ruby's listed the hours, *Noon–2:00 a.m.*, along with a note saying, *No Minors Allowed after 10:00 p.m.* There was also a boot scraper by the door, which we put to good work, knocking all the mud off our shoes.

Our clothes were damp and dirty, but we were still presentable. The mud in my pants had dried up so that it was only moderately annoying rather than terribly uncomfortable. I was eager for a shower, but even more eager to find out whether the alibi for Dr. Chen and all the other diggers was legitimate. Xavier seemed to feel the same way, so once our shoes were clean, we followed my father inside.

Ruby's was a U-shaped dining area arrayed around a smaller U of a bar. The booths along the walls had red fake leather seats. The decor was all neon beer signs and mounted deer heads. Xavier grimaced at the sight of them.

Although it was lunchtime, only two of the booths were taken. A family sat at one: two harried-looking parents, two young children, and a toddler in a high chair. They had the look of tourists who had just finished a long road trip; I guessed maybe it was their car parked at the motel.

The other booth had three old men who looked like they might have sat in the exact same places for lunch every day for the past thirty years.

A teenage girl was manning the hostess stand, idly looking at her phone. "Yes?" she asked curtly, as if we were imposing on her personal time.

"Three for lunch," Dad said.

The girl grabbed three menus and led us through the restaurant.

"By any chance, were you working here last night?" Dad asked.

"Can't," the girl said. "I'm not old enough to be here after ten. Ask Gladys, your server. I think she was on last night." She plunked the menus on a table and slouched back to the hostess stand.

Dad, Xavier, and I made a beeline for the restroom, where we used the facilities and thoroughly washed all the mud off our hands. When we returned to our table, Gladys was waiting for us. She looked to be in her seventies, if not older, but was spry and far friendlier than the hostess had been. "How are you gentlemen doing today?" she asked.

"Doing fine." Dad gave Gladys his most charming smile as we took our seats. "How are you?"

"Better, now that three handsome men like you are here," Gladys said teasingly. "Looks like you got caught in that storm."

"We did," Dad agreed. "The hostess said you might have been working here last night."

"You got that many words out of her?" Gladys asked. "Congratulations. That might be a record."

We looked back at the hostess, who was riveted to her phone again.

Dad went on. "The three of us are here to join up with a paleontology dig. We were supposed to get in last night, but our plane was delayed due to the weather. I *think* we're at the right motel, though. Do you know if there's a paleontology group staying there?"

"They definitely were last night," Gladys answered. "In fact, they were practically staying *here*. They didn't head home until closing time. And I thought construction workers could drink."

"Oh," Dad said, like this was news to him. "It was a big group? Nine people?"

"Nine exactly," Gladys said. "I served them myself. Though we had to send the two girls home after a while due to bar hours."

I jumped in then, so it wouldn't look like Dad was being nosy. "And they were here all night?"

"Just about. They came in around eight, right before the storm started, had dinner, then dessert, and then kept right on going. But enough about them. Can I get *you* folks anything to drink? The lemonade's delicious. Fresh-squeezed today."

Xavier and I took her advice and ordered lemonades while Dad asked for an iced tea.

"Coming right up." Gladys started to go, then looked back to Xavier and me. "Just so you know, those teenage girls you'll be working with are awfully cute. I'm sure they'll be pleased to learn some handsome young gentlemen will be joining them." She gave us a wink and headed for the kitchen.

Xavier turned red around the ears and quickly changed

the subject. "Sounds like Officer Brewster was right. Every-one from the dig was here."

"*Nine people* were here," Dad corrected. "We're still not sure if it was everyone from the dig or not."

We discussed how to go about investigating from there. Dad had taken photos of everyone from the dig with his cam-era, but we couldn't show those to Gladys without revealing that we had lied to her about just arriving in town. So we figured that, for the moment, we had to assume everyone from the dig had been at the restaurant from 8:00 p.m. until closing time around 2:00 a.m. Six hours. Which made the possibility of any of them spending up to ten hours stealing the skull in the rainstorm impossible.

Not that we had any better ideas about how the skull could have been taken. We all ended up ordering burgers, which were really good, and discussing possibilities all the way through lunch, but failed to come up with anything reasonable.

We were polishing off our lunches when three cars pulled into the motel parking lot at once.

The people from the dig had finally returned from the site.

As Officer Brewster had said, they had been caught in the storm. It didn't appear that taking cover in the trees had protected them much. They were all bedraggled and soaked to the bone. Every one of them looked miserable as they climbed out of their cars and headed for their motel rooms.

The four older people were in a high-end luxury SUV. The ponytailed guy was driving a small camper. The mom and the two teenage girls were in a much older SUV; it had quite a collection of dings on the doors and the bumper.

As I watched the girls climb out, I suddenly remembered what I'd seen at the dig. "One of those girls took something from the site!" I exclaimed.

"You're sure?" Dad asked.

"Not a hundred percent, but close. She was definitely up to something suspicious. While Summer was out on the rocks."

"And you didn't say anything to Brewster?" Xavier asked.

"I forgot! There was a lot going on!"

Dad dropped some money on the table to cover the bill, then snapped to his feet and headed for the door. Xavier and I followed him.

"We need to catch her before she gets to her room," Dad said. "If she did swipe something, it's probably still on her." He shoved out the door and then broke into a run, rounding the corner of Ruby's and racing into the motel parking lot.

I ran after him. I had managed to forget about the mud in my pants during lunch, but now I found it had congealed on my rear end, which was yet a new level of discomfort.

"Hey!" Dad yelled to the girl I had pointed out. "I need to talk to you!"

The members of the dig all paused on the way to their rooms and stared at Dad. Some seemed to be having trouble placing him while others seemed surprised he was there.

However, the teenage girl's eyes went wide with fear at the sight of him. Although she dressed a lot like her friend, I could now see marked differences between them. She had long dark hair that was dyed with streaks of blond, and she definitely resembled the mother more than the other girl. While everyone else kept looking at Dad, she turned away and hurried toward her room.

"You!" Dad yelled at her. "Stop! You're who I need to talk to!"

The girl glanced back over her shoulder at us—and then ran.

BITTEN

The teenage girl darted across the motel parking lot. Her mother stared after her, surprised. "Caitlyn!" she yelled. "Come back here!"

Dad, Xavier, and I raced after the girl. The older couples and the guy with the ponytail all watched us run past. Caitlyn's mother and her friend fell in behind us.

We rounded the end of the motel in pursuit. Behind the motel was a drainage culvert, a grassy ditch that was dry 99 percent of the time, but today had two feet of water churning through it.

Caitlyn ran down into the culvert, slogged through the water, and scrambled back up the other side.

Dad and I followed her. Behind us, Xavier slipped in the

wet grass and tumbled down the steep hill, splatting into a slick of mud by the edge of the water.

I paused to check on him.

"I'll be okay!" he yelled, like a downed soldier in a war movie. "Go on without me!"

Dad and I charged into the water.

My jeans had almost dried out. Now they got soaked again. The runoff was colder than I had expected and a chill shot through my body.

We clambered up the far side of the culvert. My shoes and socks were now saturated and squelched with every step.

There was a barbed-wire fence at the top of the culvert with nothing but woods on the other side. Someone's private property. A ranch like the Bonottos', maybe. For all I knew, it might have even been an extension of the Bonottos'. The fence wasn't really designed to keep anyone out; it was simply there to let you know someone owned the property—although it would have stopped a cow. There were only four sagging strands of barbed wire, so rusty they were probably decades old. It was extremely easy to slip through the strands.

Caitlyn had already done this. We could see her ahead of us, dodging through the trees on the fenced property.

Dad and I slipped through the fence and continued after her.

"Caitlyn!" her mother yelled behind us, sounding exasperated. I glanced back to see her on the far side of the culvert. She seemed to be really hoping that her daughter would come back and save her the annoyance of having to follow through the water.

Caitlyn's friend had stopped to tend to Xavier.

Caitlyn kept on running. Either she hadn't heard her mother, or she was ignoring her.

Dad and I continued chasing her.

The forest undergrowth was thick and wet, the branches bowed under the extra weight of the water on their leaves. I caught a few branches to the face and slipped twice.

Still, we were gaining on Caitlyn. It was much easier to follow someone through the woods than it was to figure out a path through them.

We were about twenty feet behind Caitlyn when she suddenly yelped in surprise and dropped out of sight. A second later, she cried out in pain.

Dad and I shared a look of concern, then hurried through the woods. We slowed down as we came to the point where Caitlyn had disappeared and cautiously pushed through a curtain of branches.

A stream cut through the forest. Most days, the streambed probably would have been dry, but now there was a foot of water in it. It wasn't moving nearly as fast as the water in the culvert had been. And yet, it was still strong enough to erode its banks, which was what had just happened.

The bank of the stream, saturated and weakened by rain, had collapsed under Caitlyn's feet and she had fallen into the water. The bank had only been about two feet high, and now a sizable chunk was missing. White tree roots poked out of the side, seeming almost startled to find themselves in the open air.

Caitlyn was sitting in the creek, wincing in pain and clutching her side. She looked at us defeatedly, aware that she wasn't going to be able to run away again.

"Are you okay?" Dad called to her.

"Not really," she replied through gritted teeth.

Dad and I cautiously climbed down the collapsed bank into the water and waded to her side.

"What's wrong?" Dad asked. "Did you break anything?"

"No," Caitlyn answered. "I kind of got bitten."

I looked around us nervously. The Texas Hill Country was home to plenty of venomous snakes, although given our location, I was most worried about water moccasins. "By what?" I asked worriedly. "A snake?"

"No. A tyrannosaur." Caitlyn held open her jacket. An eight-inch-long conical brownish object had torn through the interior pocket and was jabbing her in the left side through her T-shirt. The tooth of a tyrannosaur.

I assumed this was what she had stolen from the dig that morning. And now, she had been wounded by it.

Dad knelt by Caitlyn's side. "Can you stand up?"

"I don't know," Caitlyn said. "It really hurts."

Dad put an arm around her back and gave me an expectant look that indicated I should do the same. So I did. With our help, Caitlyn stood, although she winced in pain.

There was a small island in the middle of the stream with the trunk of a fallen oak tree stretched across it. "Over there," I suggested.

Caitlyn's legs turned out to be fine. Supported between us, she easily made it to the fallen tree and sat down on it.

Blood had slowly seeped from her wound into her shirt, staining it red.

"How much do you care about this shirt?" Dad asked. "Can I tear it?"

"Sure," Caitlyn said. "Mom only bought it for the dig. We were gonna toss it afterward anyhow."

Dad tore the shirt from the bottom, taking care to only go as high as the wound in Caitlyn's side.

Now that I could see the injury better, I realized it wasn't too bad. The tooth had jabbed her between the ribs, but hadn't gone too deep, maybe only a quarter of an inch, and the wound appeared to be quite clean. Yes, there was blood, but not too much, indicating that no major veins or arteries had been hit.

Caitlyn kept her eyes locked on my father, not wanting to look at her injury. "Is it bad?"

"No," Dad said reassuringly. "In fact, it looks awfully good, considering you're the first victim of a tyrannosaur bite in sixty million years. Mind if I try to remove the tooth?"

"Do you think that's a good idea?" Caitlyn asked.

"I think your biggest risk is from infection," Dad said. "So the sooner we get this out, the better."

"All right." Caitlyn clenched her teeth, preparing for more pain.

"Is that a baby deer over there?" Dad asked suddenly.

"Where?" Caitlyn asked, looking around excitedly.

While she was distracted, Dad quickly yanked the tooth out of her side. It came out so easily, Caitlyn didn't even feel it. She kept scanning the forest. "Where's the deer? I don't see it . . . Oh." Understanding of what Dad had done dawned on her.

Now that the tooth was in his hands, Dad couldn't help staring at it. "Holy cow," he said, amazed.

"Can I see it?" I asked.

Dad handed it to me. The sensation of holding it was surreal; it seemed impossible that I could be touching part of an animal that had lived millions of years before I had. The tooth was bigger than my hand, and heavier than I had expected. It made me realize how large the skull of a tyrannosaur was, and how powerful the dinosaur must have been to support it.

The tooth was not in pristine condition. It was chipped and scarred and there was still a good amount of rock and dirt stuck to it after hundreds of millennia in the ground. But it was still in good enough shape to slice through skin, as Caitlyn had discovered the hard way. I could make out small serrations along the tip, which would have allowed the dinosaur to saw through meat—and the tooth itself was big and thick enough to punch a hole through bone. I delicately ran my thumb along the serrations, imagining that the last time this tooth had been used, it might have been to kill an iguanodon or an ankylosaur.

"What were you planning to do with this?" Dad asked.

"I don't know," Caitlyn admitted, sounding upset—although I couldn't tell whether she was upset with herself or upset about being caught. "I know we're not supposed to take anything from the site—and I *hadn't*. I'd done everything exactly the way we were told to, even though it was really tempting and *way* hotter and harder working out there than anyone thought it was going to be. But then we showed up there today and the skull was gone—and Dr. Chen said that without the skull, everything else was pretty much useless . . ."

"I don't think that's exactly what she said," I corrected.

"Well, whatever it was, it wasn't good," Caitlyn retorted

defensively. "So I figured, maybe it wouldn't matter if I took something. Because I'd been working my butt off out there for two weeks already. And besides, all I took was a tooth. The other person made off with a whole skull! That's way worse than what I did!"

"Maybe so . . . ," Dad began, trying to calm her down.

"And anyhow," Caitlyn protested, "if you want a *real* criminal, you ought to be looking at Jeb!"

"Who's Jeb?" I asked.

Caitlyn looked at me like I was an idiot. "Weirdo ponytail guy. From the dig. He's cousins with Harper Weems!"

Dad and I shared a look of surprise.

Harper Weems was one of the wealthiest people in the United States. She was very young for a self-made billionaire, only in her thirties. She had first struck it rich at twenty-two by selling a website she had created while she was in college, but her real fame had come as a businesswoman. Harper was one of the big players in developing private space travel, but she was also involved in other ventures, like large-scale 3-D printing, and had even produced some movies. Harper loved the spotlight and was particularly well-known for her love of science fiction. Her office was designed to look like the bridge of the USS *Enterprise* from *Star Trek*, and she conducted meetings from the captain's chair. She often dressed as famous movie heroes, like Wonder Woman or Ellen Ripley from *Aliens*, and she was rumored to be fluent in Klingon, Wookiee, and Dothraki.

Harper was also known to be obsessed with *Jurassic Park*. It was her favorite book, and she had often stated that she thought bringing dinosaurs back from extinction would be fun—even though this was the complete opposite of the book's message. The grounds at her mansion had been modeled after the theme park in the book, with animatronic dinosaurs throughout. Harper had even claimed, on several occasions, that "a *real* Jurassic Park would blow FunJungle out of the water." (To which J.J. McCracken had replied, "Go ahead and try. But don't come crying to me when you get eaten by one of your own velociraptors.")

So it wasn't too hard to imagine that, if *any* billionaire really wanted a tyrannosaur skull, it would be Harper Weems.

"They're cousins?" Dad repeated.

"*First* cousins," Caitlyn stressed. "Jeb is Jebediah Weems. He's spent the whole dig going on and on about how close they are. Dr. Chen was even worried about it. We all had to sign these nondisclosure thingies, promising to keep the dig a secret, and she made Jeb sign a whole bunch of extra ones, but I *know* he told Harper."

"How?" I asked. "Did he tell you that?"

"No, but I'm sure he did it. The whole dig, he's been like, 'I just talked to Harper this morning,' and, 'Harper and

I were texting all last night.' He couldn't possibly have kept Minerva a secret."

Caitlyn had been so intent on pointing the blame at Jeb that she seemed to have forgotten all about her wound—which indicated it wasn't nearly as bad an injury as she had first let on. I was sure it had hurt, but wondered if maybe Caitlyn had played up the pain so we wouldn't be too angry at her for stealing the tooth.

Dad seemed to be thinking along these lines as well. "Looks like your injury isn't bothering you anymore," he observed.

"What?" Caitlyn asked blankly, and then realized that she hadn't been acting like she was wounded. "Oh, it's definitely still hurting." She made an agonized wince to sell us on this. "I've just been trying to fight through the pain."

Dad didn't call her on it. "I think we should get you back to the motel. Your mother's probably worried about you."

"Sure." Caitlyn looked to the tooth in my hands. "Can I have that back?"

"Better let me hold on to it," Dad said. "In your weakened condition, we don't want you to fall on it again. Next time it might stab one of your internal organs. I'd hate for you to be the first person ever killed by a *T. rex*."

Caitlyn seemed to realize there was no point in arguing. She stood up and made a show of limping back the way we had come, even though the wound was nowhere near her leg.

We found her mother back by the barbed-wire fence. She had waded through the culvert and was pacing frantically along the edge of the woods, searching for any sign of her daughter. She was at first relieved to see Caitlyn, then concerned about her wound, and ultimately embarrassed and angry when Dad revealed what Caitlyn had done. "Oh, Caitlyn," she said. "I am sooo disappointed in you."

We all crossed back through the culvert together. Caitlyn no longer seemed to be bothered by her wound at all. Now she just seemed embarrassed as well.

Caitlyn's friend, who was named Madison, was still tending to Xavier on the other side of the culvert. Xavier had gotten a bloody nose as a result of his fall, and Madison had fetched some ice from the motel for him. The blood appeared to have stopped long before we returned, but Madison was still by Xavier's side; she was fascinated that he worked at FunJungle and was listening with rapt attention as he described his adventures there.

"You get to see the giant panda every day?" Madison was asking.

"There wouldn't even *be* a giant panda at FunJungle if it wasn't for me," Xavier said proudly. "I helped Teddy track it down when it got stolen."

The four older members of the dig were gathered by the

edge of the motel, gossiping about what was going on. I would later learn that they were the Brocks and the Carvilles, and that they had been friends for over forty years and went on a different adventure together every summer. As we got closer, I could hear them all talking about how they always knew Caitlyn was trouble, even though Caitlyn was now easily within earshot of them.

"What'd she do?" one of the women asked my father.

"Nothing," Dad said diplomatically. "It was only a case of mistaken identity."

The Brocks and the Carvilles didn't look like they believed this at all and started gossiping again; still, Caitlyn seemed pleased that Dad had concealed what she had done.

Jeb Weems was nowhere to be seen. I figured he simply wasn't interested in what was happening with Caitlyn—or had maybe been desperate for a shower.

But then we rounded the corner of the motel and saw that his camper was no longer in the parking lot.

Dad turned to Caitlyn. "What room is Jeb in?"

Caitlyn pointed to a room on the first floor. The door hung open and the housekeeping cart sat in front of it. "That one, I think."

We hurried to the room. The housekeeper was exiting with a load of dirty towels.

"Is this Mr. Weems's room?" Dad asked.

"It *was*," the housekeeper replied. "But he checked out."

"How long ago?" I asked.

The housekeeper shrugged. "Fifteen minutes, maybe."

We all turned toward the highway. Fifteen minutes was plenty of time to get far away from the motel.

Jeb Weems was gone.

PLAN OF ACTION

For once, I was in a hurry to go home.

The trailer park that served as FunJungle employee housing was sandwiched between the employee parking lot and a construction site where the newest thrill rides at FunJungle were being built. I loved FunJungle itself—there were always plenty of amazing things to see and do there—but our house was small, cramped, and uncomfortably hot in the summer.

Still, it had a shower. And on that day, I wanted a shower more than I ever had in my life.

I was chilled from my repeated soakings, my feet were clammy, and my toes were puckered after wearing wet shoes for hours. Plus, I had mud caked onto my private parts. Even the saunalike heat of the trailer was a blessing given how cold I was. I stayed in the shower for a good fifteen minutes, scrubbing every last inch of myself clean and getting my core temperature back to normal.

Then I got the heck out of the trailer again.

Dad had work to catch up on, having been gone all morning, so I headed to Mom's office at Monkey Mountain to borrow her computer. The office had much better air-conditioning than the trailer, plus a window that looked out onto the gorillas. Mom wasn't there; she was at the veterinary hospital with a young macaque who had gotten into a bad fight with a dominant male. She texted me that day's code to access the offices; I already knew her computer password, as I was the one who had set it up in the first place.

A web search quickly confirmed that Jeb Weems was the first cousin of Harper Weems, and that they were at least in contact. There were several photos of the two of them together, all posted by Jeb himself on his various social media accounts. The most recent one was from three weeks earlier. Jeb was tagging along on Harper's tour of a rocket launch site at the Kennedy Space Center in Florida. There were multiple selfies of Jeb with Harper in the back-ground, and one in which Harper and Jeb were actually right next to each other, although Harper was distracted by something and didn't even seem aware that the photo was being taken.

I found a blog of Jeb's called WeemsWorld. Half of it

was devoted to detailing Jeb's travels around the country in his camper, and half was playing up his connection to his famous cousin. The travelogue from the past three months showed Jeb slowly working his way down the east coast of the United States to Florida and then along the gulf to Texas, stopping at sites ranging from the Smithsonian museums in Washington, DC, to the Okefenokee Swamp in Georgia to the Alamo in San Antonio. The most recent entry was about FunJungle. There was even a photo of Jeb at Monkey Mountain, which was a little weird to look at given that I was inside Monkey Mountain while I was looking at it.

The blog posts about Harper mostly seemed to be cataloguing whatever Harper was doing and then Jeb's thoughts on it, which were inevitably in favor of whatever Harper was doing.

Jeb had also posted some photos of the dinosaur dig. He never gave away the location—or revealed what had been found—but I still assumed the photos had been posted without Dr. Chen's permission. Anyone following the blog could easily piece together that Jeb was in central Texas, given that the dinosaur dig post was bookended by posts on the Alamo and FunJungle.

Jeb didn't appear to have a job. Although he owned the camper, he usually seemed to be staying in motels. If they were anything like the one I had seen that day, they weren't expensive, but still, I figured the costs of living for months on the road would add up quickly. I wondered how Jeb paid for everything and if his rich cousin helped out.

I sat back, doing the math on Jeb's recent timeline. He had traveled slowly down the east coast of the United States, taking over two months to get from Washington to Florida, but then, after meeting up with Harper at the Kennedy Space Center, he had moved across the southern US much faster, covering Florida to Texas in less than a week before starting the dig.

I made a mental note to try to find out when Jeb had signed up for the dig. If he had done it after meeting Harper in Florida, that might have been suspicious. Perhaps Harper had heard about the skeleton and asked Jeb to go check it out.

I wondered why Jeb had taken off so suddenly and where he might have gone. Had he really been scouting the dinosaur for Harper and become worried that we were onto him? Was he even more closely connected to the theft, and fleeing the scene before we figured it out? Or was there another, less incriminating reason?

That was about as far as I could go with Jeb, so I turned my attention to the other members of the dig.

Since the dig was a secret, the full names and contact information of everyone on it weren't available online. I really only knew how to locate one person: Dr. Ellen Chen.

I found her on the University of Texas faculty website. There was a photo of her out on another dig, in virtually the same clothes she had been wearing that day: jeans, a long-sleeved button-down shirt, work boots, and a floppy hat. Since it was a sunny day in the photo, she was also wearing sunglasses. She was kneeling by some bones protruding from the ground and examining them. The photo caption said she was directing the excavation of a predator called a tarbosaurus in Mongolia. It had been taken eight years earlier. Apparently, the University of Texas didn't update its faculty photos very often.

Dr. Chen's official university biography was surprisingly brief. All it said was that she was from San Francisco, had gone to the University of Texas for undergrad and graduate school, and now specialized in therapod dinosaurs. I had to look up what "therapod" meant.

It turned out to be the suborder of dinosaurs that included tyrannosaurs—as well as the spinosaurus, the giganotosaurus and the tarbosaurus, which was regarded as the tyrannosaur of Asia. I googled the tarbosaurus. It looked an awful lot like a tyrannosaur. So did the giganotosaurus, although the spinosaurus was bizarre. It had a skinnier body with a large frill down its back and a long, thin snout full of sharp teeth, making it look vaguely like someone had mated a crocodile with a duck.

My phone rang. According to the caller ID, it was Summer, wanting to video-chat. I answered it quickly. "Hey! How are you?"

"Clean, thank goodness." She was in the back of her car, wearing a new shirt and shorts.

"Me too."

"So, have you done any more investigating into this stolen dinosaur?"

"A lot." I gave her the lowdown on everything that had happened after we had split up, except for the part about Officer Brewster suspecting her father, which I knew would only upset her. Besides, if Dad was right and Brewster was only telling me so that I'd tip Summer off and provoke a response from J.J., I wanted to do the exact opposite.

It took quite a while to share all the rest of the information, as Summer rarely let me say more than a sentence without interrupting to express surprise or ask a question. It was never annoying, though, because Summer really listened carefully, and her questions tended to be good ones. When I finally wrapped up with an explanation of what I had found about Jeb Weems and Dr. Chen online, Summer thought for a few seconds, then said, "I think we need to go back out to the dig site. With Sheriff Esquivel and all those people there today, we didn't really get a chance to look around. I'll bet there's still a clue or two out there."

"Yeah," I agreed. "I don't think the police did much snooping themselves."

"Can you reach out to Sage and see if we can visit again?"

"Sure. Hold on." I switched from video-chat to messaging, although I hesitated for a moment before sending the text.

"This won't be dangerous," Summer said, sensing my trepidation.

"It *could* be," I argued. "What if whoever stole the skull wants more of Minerva? They might come back."

"The skull's the most important piece—and they were lucky to get it out of there. There's no way they're going to tempt fate by coming back for some crummy old ribs."

"I guess." I texted Sage, asking him if we could come by again, then shifted back to the video. "Done."

"Good. Now here's where we are with the anaconda investigation . . ."

"*We?*" I repeated, surprised. "I didn't agree to investigating the Barksdales."

"I'm not talking about *you*. You're not the only person around here who can investigate a crime. While you were busy with the dinosaur, I called Violet and asked for her help."

Violet Grace was one of our friends from school, the head cheerleader and a classmate of Summer's. "You dragged Violet into this?" I asked.

"I didn't *drag* her. She's excited to do it. We're going to do exactly what you suggested: visit the Barksdales and question them about where they got the snake."

"I didn't suggest that," I reminded her. "Xavier did."

"Well, it's still a good plan. When Violet called the Barksdales and told them she'd heard they had a new anaconda, they invited her over in like two seconds."

"She already called them?!"

"I told you she was excited. I'm going too, so I can help with the questioning."

"I don't like this," I said. "The Barksdales are bad news."

"That's why I need *you* to come," Summer told me. "And Dashiell and Ethan too. You guys can all hide outside. Violet and I will call you before we go in and you can simply eavesdrop over the phone. If anything goes wrong, you can be our backup."

I swallowed hard, thinking about that. If Tim and Jim Barksdale wanted to cause trouble, there wasn't much I would be able to do about it. Dashiell and Ethan would be much more help. They were star athletes at school and pretty much the only people Tim and Jim were afraid of. Plus, both Dashiell and Ethan had gone through growth spurts recently. They were significantly taller and more muscular than they'd been when I had met them six months earlier. And yet, I still was concerned. "Maybe we should leave this to the authorities . . ."

"We've already tried that. Have you heard anything from Tommy Lopez or the FunJungle reptile guys?"

"The reptile guys said they were going to visit the Barksdales," I reported. "But I don't know what happened—or if they've even gone yet. We haven't given them much time and I'm sure they have other things to do . . ."

"For all we know, it could take weeks for the adults to do anything. We can learn where the Barksdales got the anaconda *today*. They're expecting us in half an hour."

"That soon?!" I exclaimed.

"Yes. What were we supposed to do, wait until tomorrow?"

"Yes! Or maybe never go over there. The Barksdales are psychos."

"Well, we're going. With or without you. So are you in or out?"

I weighed my options. I didn't like this plan much, but I knew Summer was going to go ahead with or without me. I didn't want her to end up in danger. I wasn't sure if I could handle the Barksdales, but if anything went wrong with the anaconda, I knew a thing or two about snakes.

"Okay," I said. "I'm in."

"Good. Because I'm here." Summer turned her phone around to reveal that the car was approaching the front gates of FunJungle. "So come meet me. We have a case to solve."

THE STING

We ended up getting to the Barksdales' later than
Summer had hoped, because I had to call my parents to let
them know I was leaving the park—and as I was about to do
that, Sage texted back. He was thrilled that I wanted to visit
the dig site again, and he suggested that we make up for our
failed attempt to camp out the night before and camp by the
dig that night. I told him that I was about to see Summer
and Violet, and maybe Dashiell and Ethan too, and he said
everyone could come if they wanted; obviously, there was
plenty of room to camp on the ranch.

So then I had to ask my parents if it was okay to camp
out at Sage's. I had thought they might balk at the idea, but
they were okay with it. In fact, Dad was extremely enthusi-
astic; I think he wanted to find out what had happened to

Minerva even more than I did. Still, that meant I had to go back to my trailer to pack clothes for the next day, and then we had to go collect Violet. By the time we arrived at the Barksdales', it was half an hour after Summer had said she and Violet would be there.

The Barksdales lived in a small house a quarter mile from our middle school, on the outskirts of town. It had been Tim and Jim's grandparents' house and had passed down to their family. At one point, it had probably been kind of nice, but the Barksdales hadn't taken very good care of it. This was partly due to laziness, but also because the Barksdale parents had trouble holding jobs. They were renowned throughout town as troublemakers—and had been since *they* had been in high school—so the local business owners were wary of hiring them to do anything that required skill or morals. The Barksdales eked out a living by doing sporadic work like digging ditches and stringing up barbed wire fences, and they hunted for meat to eat as well. (You were allowed to hunt for sustenance if you followed certain laws, although it was suspected that the Barksdales often violated them.)

Thus, the Barksdale home wasn't in good shape. The front porch sagged, several windows were patched with duct tape, and the chimney tilted at a precarious angle. The front yard was merely a weed patch strewn with broken appliances. I could only guess why the appliances were there: Maybe the Barksdales had bought them for spare parts, or had attempted to repair them and failed, or had broken them and never got around to hauling them to the dump. Eventually, someone had used them for target practice. There were two washers and dryers, a stove, an ancient television, and a stack of microwaves, all perforated with bullet holes.

However, the Barksdales' pickup truck was in perfect condition. It seemed to be the only thing they had spent any money on. It wasn't new, but unlike the house, it was lovingly cared for, recently washed, and even polished since that day's rainstorm. It had a large crew cab with a back seat, and like many pickups in central Texas, it was jacked up to accommodate oversize tires, which would allow for better four-wheeling.

Behind the house was a decrepit chain-link dog run. Three mangy dogs paced back and forth in it, barking and snarling as our car approached. They reared up on their hind legs and placed their front feet on the fence, looking like they wanted to climb over and rip our throats out. I had rarely ever met an animal I didn't like, but the Barksdale dogs instantly put me on edge.

Dashiell and Ethan were later than we were.

They had agreed to come help with the sting; they were always happy to do anything that could result in causing trouble for the Barksdales. The plan was for them to hide with me in Summer's car while the girls went inside, but as Tran parked in front of the Barksdale home, Dash texted to say they were running behind. Ethan's older brother had volunteered to drive them over, but he hadn't shown up to get them yet.

"We have to wait for them," I said.

"I don't think we can," Summer told me. "The Barksdales know we're here."

Sure enough, the dogs had tipped them off. Tim and Jim emerged onto the sagging porch. To my surprise, it appeared that they had tried to dress up for the girls. Normally, the boys wore almost nothing but camouflage hunting gear or clothes from the army surplus store, but both had put on polo shirts and slacks and even combed their hair. They looked to Summer's car a bit too eagerly, indicating that they had been waiting impatiently for the girls to arrive.

"Look at them," Violet said. "They actually think this is, like, a double date. Like we'd ever forget how awfully they've behaved."

Summer dialed my phone with hers. "I'm going to leave my phone on speaker," she said, "So that you can hear everything. Just don't make any noise."

I ignored the ringing. "You can't go in before the other guys get here! What if you end up in trouble? *I* can't beat up the Barksdales!"

"You won't have to," Violet assured me. "These guys are going to be putty in our hands."

"We'll be fine," Summer said. "If there's any trouble, Tran's here to back us up too." She looked to her driver. "Right?"

"Sure," Tran replied. He was already opening his book to start reading and didn't seem nearly as concerned as I was.

Summer returned her attention to me. "See? Nothing to worry about. So answer your dang phone."

I did. Summer then got on her phone, even though she was sitting right next to me. "Agent McCracken ready for action. Do you copy?"

"I copy," I said.

"Good." Summer gave me a kiss on the cheek. "Now hide so they don't see you when we get out."

I slumped behind the driver's seat. Summer tucked her phone into her pocket and both girls climbed out of the car.

The Barksdales grinned expectantly. Until recently, the two of them had been indistinguishable from each other, but Tim had developed a virulent case of acne that he made worse by scratching until it became infected, so his face was now as scaly and red as that of a Gila monster. He made a last-ditch attempt to smooth his cowlick into place while Jim waved to the girls and spoke as cordially as he could manage. "Hey, ladies! What took you so long?"

"Sorry," Summer said. "We got stuck in traffic." Her voice was muffled, since her phone was in her pocket, but the system still worked decently.

I sat up again and peeked through the window. I figured this was safe, as the glass was darkly tinted, and I was pretty sure the Barksdales' attention would be riveted to the girls anyhow.

Summer and Violet wound their way through the obstacle course of bullet-pocked appliances, acting like this was a perfectly normal thing to have in one's front yard.

"Thanks for having us over!" Violet said. "I'm really excited to see this snake of yours!"

"Oh, we've got plenty more to show you than that." Tim held open the door to the house.

"More?" Summer asked, intrigued. "Like what?"

"Wait and see." Tim grinned knowingly at Jim as the girls passed between them. Then the boys followed them into the house and shut the door.

The moment the girls were out of my sight, I grew nervous. I didn't like the idea of them being inside the Barksdales' house at all. I glanced down the street, hoping to see Dashiell and Ethan arriving, even though I knew they were still probably several minutes away at best.

Another voice came through the phone. It was extremely faint, as whoever was speaking seemed to be at the far end of the house from Summer. "Tim! Jim! Who's here with you?"

"Just some girls from school, Mom!" That voice was much clearer, as it was closer to Summer, although I couldn't tell if it was Tim or Jim.

"Girls?" another distant voice asked. Pa Barksdale. "What girls?"

I grew even more nervous. I had forgotten that the Barksdale parents' sporadic employment meant they might be home in the middle of a workday. While most adults could have been counted on to curb their children's bad behavior, the Barksdale parents were prone to behaving badly themselves.

"Summer and Violet," Tim or Jim answered quickly, like they didn't want to deal with their parents.

"Your father and I are going out!" Ma Barksdale yelled. "You know I don't like you having strangers in the house when we're not home!"

"They won't be here long, I promise!" Tim or Jim yelled back. "They only came by to see our new pets!"

There was the sound of a door opening, followed by a startled cry from Violet. "What is *that*?"

"A baby alligator," Tim or Jim said proudly.

That got Tran's attention. He set his book down. "Those morons have an *alligator*?"

"Ain't it cool?" Tim or Jim asked.

"*So* cool," Summer replied, although it sounded like she was trying hard to sell this. "Can I take a video of it?"

"Sure!" Tim or Jim said.

A few seconds later, I got a notice that Summer wanted to switch to a video call. I realized what she was doing; she was only pretending to film while actually allowing me to see what was going on. I had to smile; my girlfriend was awfully clever.

I accepted the call, and suddenly, I had a handheld view of the Barksdales' bathroom. It was as rundown as the rest of the house, with chipped tile, rust stains, and a shower curtain that was black with mold. But Summer was directing my attention toward the bathtub, which was half-full of water and had a young alligator submerged in it.

It was hard to judge its size on the phone, but it seemed to be about eight inches long and was black with yellow stripes. It was so delicate, it looked more like a toy than a live animal.

I snapped a few photos of it from the video call, in case we needed them as evidence.

"It's so cute!" Violet said, despite herself.

"Her name's Snappy!" Tim or Jim said, and the camera shifted to them.

"Want to feed her?" Jim asked. "She eats hot dogs. She'll jump up and take them right out of your hand." He held up his hand, and I saw that three of his four fingers had Band-Aids on them, indicating that the baby alligator might have taken bits of fingertip along with the hot dogs he'd been feeding it.

"Where'd you get her?" Summer asked.

"It's a secret," Jim said.

"Awww," Summer said, in her coyest voice. "C'mon. You don't have to keep secrets from us."

"All right," Tim said. "We got it from—"

Jim punched him in the arm before he could finish. "Dude! We said we'd keep it a secret!"

Tim punched him back. "Don't hit me!"

"Then don't go blabbing our secrets!" Jim punched him again.

Tim then slugged his brother in the jaw.

Suddenly, the Barksdale boys were in a full-on fight, trying to throttle each other in the tiny bathroom. The camera shook as Summer and Violet scrambled out of the way, obscuring my view of everything.

"Stop it!" Violet yelled at the Barksdales. "You're being idiots!"

I heard more punches being thrown, a couple curses, and what might have been the sound of someone whacking their head on a toilet.

Tran had now turned around in the front seat to watch

the video with me. "These guys ought to have their own reality TV show," he said under his breath.

My phone buzzed as a text came in from my father. Normally, I might not have switched over to it, but I couldn't see what was going on anyhow.

Heard from reptile guys. They just got back. Barksdales didn't have any exotics on property. Even showed the whole house. Call me.

That confused me. The Barksdales obviously had a baby alligator, which I had just seen—and they seemed to have an anaconda as well, as they had promised the girls they'd show it to them. Maybe they could have hidden the alligator, as it was small, but it was hard to imagine how anyone could conceal a fifteen-foot snake in such a small house.

I couldn't call Dad back, though, as I still needed the phone to follow what was happening. I switched back to the video call. Summer had now steadied the phone, although she was trying to hide the fact that she was still filming and was holding it by her side.

The Barksdales were really pounding on each other, writhing around in the bathroom, ignoring Violet's pleas for them to stop. Jim shoved Tim's head down onto the toilet bowl and slammed the toilet seat in his face. Then Tim sucker punched Jim below the belt and flipped him into the bathtub. There was a splash, and Jim screamed in pain. The camera shook a bit, and when it steadied once more, Jim was up on his feet again, although the baby alligator had sunk her teeth into his ear. While Jim wailed and whirled around, the poor little reptile clung on like a living earring.

"Get her off me!" Jim wailed. "Get her off!"

"Don't hurt her!" Summer warned.

Footsteps boomed in the hallway and the camera shifted to show Pa Barksdale storming toward the bathroom, red-faced with anger. "What in high heaven is going on in here?" he demanded. "You two dingbats had better not be fighting again, or so help me, I'll punch both your lights out!"

There was another, more final scream of pain. The camera shifted back toward the bathroom. Snappy was no longer latched on to Jim's ear. She—and a small portion of Jim's earlobe—were gone. Jim quickly clamped a wad of toilet paper over his ear to stanch the blood.

Pa Barksdale moved into the shot, blocking my view of everything. "What's happening?"

"Nothing," Tim or Jim said.

"That's more like it," Pa told them. "Now, your mother and I have to go see about a job. You dummies are already on thin ice after letting your stupid snake eat the cat. If we come back and find there's been any more roughhousing, I'm flushing that darn gator down the toilet. Got it?"

"Yes sir," Tim and Jim said meekly.

"Good." Pa stormed back down the hall, clearing the shot again and allowing Summer to keep filming surreptitiously.

A few seconds later, through the car window, I saw the Barksdale parents emerge from the house and head for their pickup.

On the video, Tim turned to Jim and said, "You're such a tool."

"You're the tool," Jim retorted.

They might have started fighting again if Violet hadn't said, "You're *both* tools. And if either of you throws one more punch, Summer and I are leaving."

The boys stopped arguing immediately.

"Now," Violet said sternly, "where's the anaconda?"

"It's not here," Tim said.

"What?" Summer asked. "You told us you had one!"

"We *do*," Jim assured her. "But we had to move it."

Outside the house, the Barksdale parents climbed into their truck and backed out of the driveway, coming very close to Summer's car. I could see Pa Barksdale reflected in the side-view mirror, studying the car closely.

On the video, Summer asked, "Why did you move the snake?"

"'Cause these reptile guys from FunJungle came snooping around," Tim explained. "That dork Teddy probably tipped them off that we had an anaconda."

"We didn't want to get in any trouble," Jim continued. "So we hid our pets. We put the little gator in an ice chest, but the anaconda was too big for anywhere in the house."

At that very moment, Pa Barksdale put his truck in gear and punched the gas. His rear tires squealed on the ground, kicking up a spray of gravel that ricocheted off Summer's car. He was obviously doing it on purpose, being a jerk for no good reason. Then the truck rocketed down the road.

"What the . . . ?" Tran yelled.

I was worried that Tim and Jim would hear him over the phone, but they were too preoccupied by the girls.

"So where'd you hide the anaconda?" Violet asked.

"In the back seat of our parents' truck," Tim said proudly.

"Your parents just left in their truck!" Summer exclaimed.

Tim and Jim looked to each other with horror.

There were a pair of screams from the Barksdales' truck. Screams of abject terror. Even though the truck was several dozen yards away from me, they were still loud enough to hear.

I was well aware that there was an innate, primal response most humans experienced upon coming across a snake. I had stumbled upon plenty of snakes in the wild, and even though I really liked them and knew that most of them were harmless to humans, I had inevitably felt a moment of fear and panic. On each of those occasions, I had screamed in surprise and possibly even sprung back a startling distance, fueled by an instantaneous spike of adrenaline.

So I could imagine that suddenly finding an enormous anaconda slithering around in a confined space with you was bound to be scary. Even if it was your own snake.

The truck swerved wildly, veered off the road, flattened the neighbor's mailbox, and then smashed into an oak tree. The front end of the pristine vehicle crumpled like tinfoil, and the airbags deployed.

Thankfully, the Barksdales hadn't been going too fast yet, but I was still worried they might have been hurt. I forgot all about hiding in the car and leaped out to see if they were okay.

I was focused on the truck, rather than anything else around me. So I hadn't seen the other person coming alongside Summer's car until I almost clocked them with the car door as I flung it open.

"Sorry," I said, and then discovered I knew the person I had nearly run into.

It was the person who probably hated me more than anyone else on earth.

Vance Jessup.

THE SQUEEZE

The reason Vance Jessup hated me so much was that I had helped bust him for a crime. As a result, he had been sent to juvenile hall, and he blamed me for it—even though *he* was the one who had broken the law. He was supposed to go for six months, but I had just discovered—a bit too late—that he had been released a few weeks early for good behavior.

I would learn later that his old friends, the Barksdale twins, had invited him over to see their new pets as well, which explained what he was doing outside their house. But all that *really* mattered at the moment was that Vance had spent the last several months imagining how he would get his revenge if he saw me again—and now I had practically dropped into his lap.

Given that Vance was a meathead and a thug, the entire plan he had come up with for revenge was: "Hit Teddy really hard. A lot."

I had the exact same reaction to seeing him that Ma and Pa Barksdale had to finding an anaconda in their truck. I screamed in terror.

"You!" Vance snarled. And then he tried to clobber me.

I ducked away and ran.

Tran was already out of the car too, having planned to check on the Barksdales. "Hey!" he yelled at Vance, and chased after us.

At the same time, Tim and Jim barged out onto their porch, having heard the crash. They were so worried about their parents—or possibly their snake—that they didn't even register surprise that I was there, not to mention being pursued by Vance. "Oh no!" they exclaimed, upon seeing the truck, and then ran toward it as well.

Summer and Violet expressed much more concern upon seeing Vance and me. They both stopped on the porch and gaped in surprise at what was going on. "Vance!" Summer yelled. "Leave him alone!"

Vance ignored her and kept right on after me.

I ran through the maze of abandoned appliances, trying to put any obstacle I could between Vance and myself. Unfortunately, there was lots of junk hidden in the weeds that made running more difficult than I had expected. I nearly tripped over an old blender, the remains of an ancient lawnmower, and the guts of a washing machine. The good news was that Vance was less agile than me and had trouble avoiding those things too. He stumbled over the lawnmower and went down hard, smashing headfirst into an eviscerated dishwasher.

Sadly, that barely slowed him down. If anything, it made him angrier. Vance was built like a bull, right down to the thick, impervious skull. He sprang back to his feet and howled with rage as he charged after me again.

Tran was also having trouble getting through the yard. I heard him cry out in pain as he bashed his toes on an ancient toaster oven that was lurking in the weeds.

Meanwhile, down the road, the Barksdale parents emerged from their truck, unharmed but furious. Tim and Jim stopped running toward them and started running away in fear. Their parents set after them in the same way that Vance was after me.

"You morons wrecked our truck!" Pa Barksdale yelled.

"It was an accident!" Tim yelled back.

"I'm gonna kill both of you!" Ma warned.

Back at the house, Violet tried to intervene on my behalf. "Vance!" she said sternly. "If you lay so much as a finger on Teddy, I will never even *look* at you again!"

Vance paused for a moment, as surprised to see Violet there as she was to see him, but then resumed chasing me. "He put me in juvey!" he yelled as a defense.

"You put *yourself* in juvey!" Violet informed him, but Vance didn't listen.

The minor distraction *had* given me at least a little time to formulate a plan, though. The Barksdales had a clothesline, which made sense, seeing as their dryer was disemboweled in the front yard. It was a jury-rigged length of rope sagging between two trees. As Vance came for me again, I yanked hard on it, snapping it taut in his path. Vance literally clotheslined himself, catching himself right in the face, and went crashing down on his back.

Once again, this barely slowed him down.

"Stop trying to hurt him!" Summer yelled to me. "You're only making him angrier!"

"What else am I supposed to do?" I yelled back in desperation. "Let him catch me?"

I stumbled over a jettisoned toilet and decided to abandon the yard before I impaled myself on something. I shoved the tower of bullet-pocked microwaves into Vance's path, hoping it might slow him, and then ran down the road in the direction of the Barksdales' pickup.

The microwaves didn't slow Vance much.

Summer and Violet leaped off the porch and ran after

us. Summer screamed to Tran, who was hopping around on one foot, clutching his wounded toes. "Don't just sit there! Do something!"

"Like what?" Tran shouted back.

"Get the car and run him over!" Summer suggested. "Maybe that will stop him!"

Ahead of me, the Barksdale parents were still chasing their sons around. Ma Barksdale was so angry that, unable to catch Tim, she simply yanked off one of her boots and flung it at him, catching him in the back of the head with such force that she knocked him down.

Despite the bonks to his head, Vance was still gaining on me. He was much bigger and stronger than me and motivated by revenge. I could hear the thudding of his feet on the road behind me and hear the heaving of his breath. It was like being chased by a rhinoceros. Except that rhinos are generally good-natured.

I ran toward the Barksdales' pickup, giving it everything I had, thinking that maybe, if I could get there fast enough, I could lock myself inside. Yes, I'd be trapped in a truck with an anaconda, but even that seemed safer than being out in the open with Vance. Unfortunately, I didn't make it. I was three feet from the truck when Vance caught the neck of my T-shirt and yanked backward, nearly strangling me and pulling me off my feet at once.

I tensed my body, fearing that I was in for a world of pain, but to my surprise, Vance didn't throttle me. Instead, he made a startled gasp.

I risked a look back at him. His face was white as the fur of a polar bear and his eyes were as big and wide as a bush baby's.

I then looked where he was looking—at the pickup.

The front left end of the truck was crushed against the oak tree. The hood had folded so that it was peaked in the middle. Steam billowed from the engine, while a faint smell of gunpowder from the airbags still hung in the air.

In his haste to throttle his sons, Pa Barksdale had left the driver's side door wide open. Julius Squeezer was now slithering out of the truck. About four feet of the snake had emerged so far. Upon seeing us, it had stopped moving forward and now looked our way, its forked tongue flickering.

Even though I had known the snake was going to be big, I was still astonished by the size of it.

I had seen the anaconda at FunJungle plenty of times. That one was longer than Julius, but it was always coiled up at the back of its exhibit, so I had never seen its unspooled body. Now Julius had slithered over the front seats of the truck to the open door, so his massive length and girth were on full display. He was as thick and wide as a palm tree, although there was a watermelon-size lump in his midsection which I recognized as the current location of Griselda. The snake was definitely beautiful, with a bright yellow body mottled with dark patches, although its dark, beady eyes, set in the great wedge of its head, were unsettling. As was the flickering tongue.

The real reason snakes flick their tongues is to help them smell. Most snakes have crummy eyesight and poor hearing, but their sense of smell is excellent, in part due to something called the Jacobson's organ, which is located in the roofs of their mouths. Snakes collect odors from minuscule moisture particles on their tongues, then stick the forked ends into the Jacobson's organ, which transfers the images to the brain. Even though I knew all this, it still *looked* freaky. A shiver went down my spine.

Julius didn't scare me nearly as much as he scared Vance, though. Tim and Jim apparently hadn't told him what their new pet was, and Vance looked terrified by the sight of it. He released his grip on my shirt and slowly shifted his weight to make sure that I was between him and the snake.

"Wh-wh-wh-what is that?" he whispered.

My own fear was quickly replaced with elation. I *knew* Julius wouldn't be too dangerous. He wasn't quite big enough to try to eat me, and besides, he had already consumed Griselda that morning, meaning he probably wouldn't be hungry again for another few days. However, there was no need for me to share any of that with Vance.

"That's a Mongolian death adder," I whispered back, doing my best to sound equally terrified. "The biggest one I've ever seen. It escaped from FunJungle last week."

"Is-is-is-is it dangerous?" Vance stammered.

"Extremely," I said. "It has the most powerful venom of any snake on earth. If it so much as touches you with that tongue, you'll drop dead. This one has already killed six people and nine dogs since it escaped."

Vance gave a little whimper.

I heard the distinct sound of water trickling onto the ground behind me. "Did you just wet yourself?" I asked.

"No!" Vance said, a little too quickly, shifting back into full-on jerk mode.

"Shhhh!" I told him. "They're drawn to loud noises—and the smell of urine."

Vance whimpered again. "What do we do?" he asked.

"The Mongolian death adder is extremely fast," I warned with mock sincerity. "Hopefully, we can move faster. Are you ready to run?"

"Definitely," Vance said.

"All right. On the count of three. One . . . two . . ."

Vance ran before three. Which I had been expecting. Like most bullies, Vance was a coward at heart. If the snake had truly been dangerous, he would have been leaving me to get attacked. Now he fled back the way he had come as fast as his feet would carry him.

"It's coming for you, Vance!" I screamed after him. "Run!!!!!"

The girls took my lead. "It's right behind you!" Summer yelled.

"Whatever you do, don't look back!" Violet added.

Vance was quite fast normally, and now he had fear propelling him as well. He shot down the street like an Olympic sprinter and kept on going until we couldn't see him anymore.

Tran came hobbling along, laughing at Vance's flight. "What scared that guy so much?" he asked.

"Only a snake," I said.

"He was that scared by a snake?" Tran laughed even harder—until he noticed Julius. I got the sense Tran had no idea that a snake could possibly get that big. He stopped laughing, made a tiny gasp of terror—and passed out right in the street.

"Thanks for all your help," I told him.

Julius flicked his tongue a few more times, then began to slither out of the truck again.

I realized that I had to stop him from going any farther. Snakes were notoriously hard to track down. A year before, a black mamba had escaped at World of Reptiles and had never been seen again, despite the mobilization of the entire reptile squad. True, Julius was much bigger, but we were right on the edge of the forest, where there was a lot of room for him to hide, and a snake that size could wreak havoc on the local wildlife. Plus, for all I knew, Julius Squeezer might have really been a Juliet—and pregnant. Which could have led to a whole crop of anacondas loose in the woods.

Summer and Violet arrived at the truck and saw Julius for the first time. Both were as unsettled as I was by the sight of the snake.

"Whoa," Violet said. "That is *big*."

"Bigger than I expected," Summer agreed.

"I'll need some help here," I told them. "I'm going to grab the snake, and his instinct is going to be to grab me right back. So keep him from wrapping around me, okay?"

"Uh . . . okay," Summer agreed, although she didn't sound happy about it.

I cautiously approached Julius. Six feet of the snake was now out of the truck. I reached down and grabbed him right behind the head with both hands.

Julius immediately became far more animated. He opened his mouth, revealing his thin, hooked teeth, and hissed angrily. His body writhed, trying to coil around mine.

Summer and Violet both rushed to my aid, grabbing Julius farther down his body. They kept him from wrapping around my arms and legs, although he was powerful enough to pull us all together. I was quickly smashed up against both girls as we fought to control the snake.

"This is not how I thought this day was going to go," Violet gasped, straining to control the anaconda.

"Welcome to my life," I told her.

Meanwhile, the Barksdales had settled their differences—sort of. The parents had grown tired of chasing the boys around and given up on clobbering them. Both were bent over, hands on their knees, gasping—although they still had enough breath to yell at their sons. "I want that snake out of my truck—and out of my house!" Pa Barksdale ordered.

"What?" Tim whined. "But we just got him!"

"And he's already eaten our cat and destroyed our truck, you moron!" Ma yelled. "You're taking him back to Snakes Alive today and that's final!"

The girls and I all shared a look of interest, although it quickly shifted back to concern, as we were still wrestling with the anaconda. The entire snake was now out of the truck. Its tail whipped around my right leg like the vine of a strangler fig.

"But they said no refunds!" Jim protested.

"I don't care," his father replied. "You either take it back—or I'll gut it and make you two eat every last inch."

The twins seemed to realize there was no point to arguing

and sadly returned to the truck, where they were surprised to find the girls and me grappling with Julius.

"Hey!" Tim exclaimed. "That's our snake!"

"We know," Violet said. "Can you give us a hand here?"

The boys came to help—although both looked slightly disappointed that *I* had gotten wrapped up with two of the most beautiful girls from school instead of them. With their added muscle and extra hands, it was much easier to control the anaconda, and we began to extricate ourselves from its grasp.

"You got him at Snakes Alive?" Summer asked, trying not to sound too accusing.

Tim and Jim looked at each other, as if considering denying this, but then realized the secret was already out.

"Yeah," Jim admitted sullenly. "But now it sounds like we've got to give him back."

"Maybe that's for the best," Violet said, unwinding a coil of anaconda from her left arm. "Having a snake this big doesn't seem like such a great idea."

"You don't think it's cool?" Tim asked.

"Not at all," Summer said, stepping out of a loop of snake.

"What about a cobra?" Jim inquired. "Would you think *that* was cool? Because they had some cobras for sale too."

"No!" both girls exclaimed at once.

"Really?" Tim seemed surprised by the vehemence of their reaction.

"Cobras are incredibly dangerous!" Summer explained.

"Exactly!" Jim agreed. "That's what makes having one so awesome!"

"That's what makes having one idiotic," Violet argued. "You guys have had an anaconda for one day and look what it's done so far. If you got a cobra, you'd probably be dead by sundown."

Tim and Jim exchanged another look, wondering if this was true. Then they looked back at the girls. "The alligator's still cool, though, right?" Tim asked.

"No!" the girls exclaimed again.

"That alligator might be cute now," I said, "but what happens when it doesn't fit in the bathtub anymore? In a few years, it'll be six feet long and need a lot more to eat than hot dogs. What are you going to feed it then?"

"Stray dogs?" Jim suggested.

The girls both made faces of disgust.

By the truck, Tran had regained consciousness. He seemed embarrassed to have passed out—but he made no attempt to help us either. Instead, he kept his distance and looked ready to flee at any moment.

Summer, Violet, Tim, Jim, and I had now uncoiled the snake and stretched it out into a straight line. Or as straight as you could get an anaconda. I was still holding it behind the head as tightly as I could, which wasn't easy, as the snake didn't appreciate it. It was wriggling in my grasp and hissing angrily. My hands were starting to cramp up. "How'd you get this snake here in the first place?" I asked.

"It was in a big old plastic tub," Jim explained. "It's still on the porch."

"I'll get it!" Violet volunteered, and quickly ran back to the house.

Without her, it was a slightly greater struggle to control the snake.

"Snakes Alive just sold this to you?" I asked the Barksdales. "Without any questions?"

"What do you care?" Tim asked.

Summer sighed, aware that she would have to unleash her feminine wiles again. I could tell this annoyed her, but she knew it would be the fastest way to get an answer. She fluttered her eyelashes and spoke in her coyest voice. "We just want to know how you got it. It's important."

The boys instantly cracked, desperate to impress her. "There's this guy there," Tim said, doing his best to sound cool. "Rick. He can hook you up with anything you want. It's on the down low, though. You have to ask to see him and use the code word 'erotic.'"

"*Exotic,* you dimwit," Jim corrected.

"Right!" Tim agreed. "You ask to see something exotic."

"Rick has all kinds of amazing stuff," Jim told Summer. "Including things even you would think were cool, I'll bet."

"I doubt it," Summer said.

Violet came running back across the yard with a plastic storage tub. It was three feet wide and two feet deep, with plastic clamps to hold the lid down. "Got it!" she announced breathlessly, then set it on the ground and popped the lid off.

I slipped Julius's head inside and finally let go. Tim, Jim, and Summer quickly crammed the rest of the snake into the tub. It wasn't easy, although it wasn't quite as hard as I had expected, either. Julius didn't seem too upset; it was as if being wound up in a confined space was comforting to him. Anacondas often denned in small spaces, so maybe it felt natural.

I set the lid back in place and used the clamps to lock it down.

As I did, I caught a glimpse of my watch. It was getting late in the day. "I have to get to Sage's ranch," I told the girls. "Before it gets dark."

Violet considered the snake in the tub, then looked to Summer and me. "Maybe we shouldn't leave Julius here. Could we take him back to FunJungle?"

"No way!" Tran exclaimed. "I'm not putting that thing in the car!"

"You're not taking him period," Jim said. "We paid for

Julius fair and square. He cost us six months of lawn-mowing money. If you take him from us, that's stealing!"

"We're returning him to Rick first thing tomorrow and getting our money back," Tim added.

"Tomorrow?" Ma Barksdale came around the truck, finally having got her breath back. And her boots as well. "I don't want that thing in my house one more minute."

Pa Barksdale was now inspecting the smashed-up front of his pickup. I thought I heard him sobbing softly.

"Snakes Alive is closed right now," Tim argued. "But I promise, we'll keep a close eye on Julius until then."

"Darn straight you will," Ma Barksdale warned. "Or I'll sell both of *you* to Snakes Alive."

"What if Rick won't take the anaconda back?" Violet asked.

"Oh, he'd better," Tim said. "If he doesn't, we'll kick his butt."

"Maybe we'll kick his butt anyhow," Jim said. "For what the snake did to Griselda."

"Great plan," Summer said. She was obviously being sarcastic, but the Barksdales didn't catch this. Instead, they beamed at her praise.

"We'll let you know what happens," Tim told her.

Summer, Violet, and I stepped away and headed back to Summer's car, glad to be done with the Barksdales and Julius.

I still had the musty smell of anaconda all over me.

Summer slipped her hand into mine and said, "You were very brave with that snake."

"Which one?" I asked. "Julius or Vance?"

Summer laughed, then said, "Julius."

"Running away from a bully doesn't exactly count as bravery," Violet informed me.

"I punched his lights out once," I reminded her. "You weren't so snarky then."

"Touché," Violet conceded.

"How'd you even know how to handle a snake like this?" Summer asked.

"There were plenty of snakes in the Congo," I explained. "Most were a lot smaller, but the venomous ones were still dangerous. If you grab them behind the head, they can't bite you."

"Growing up in the Congo must have been crazy," Violet said. "It's so dangerous there."

"Actually, my life here has been far more dangerous," I said, glancing back toward Tim and Jim. "In the Congo, I never had to worry about guys like the Barksdales, or Vance Jessup. And I've ended up in a lot more danger at FunJungle than I ever did in the actual jungle."

Tran was waiting for us beside the car, looking embarrassed about how he had behaved around the anaconda. He looked to Summer. "You won't tell your father about how I, uh . . ."

"Passed out when we needed you?" Summer asked. "Don't worry. Your secret's safe with us."

"Thanks." Tran opened the door of the car. "I just had no idea there were snakes that big!"

The three of us climbed into the back seat. "Back to the Bonotto Ranch," Summer informed Tran. "We're dropping Teddy off there."

"I'll let Dash and Ethan know we're done here," I said, already texting them.

"And let them know we handled everything perfectly fine without them," Violet added.

We headed down the road, passing the Barksdale family. Ma and Pa were berating Tim and Jim again, while the boys clutched the plastic tub with Julius between them.

Violet mused, "Would it really be stealing if we took the anaconda to FunJungle? And the baby alligator too? I mean, they were both probably stolen from the wild already, so really, the Barksdales are the ones who broke the law. We'd be setting things right."

Summer sighed. "I don't think the Barksdales would agree with that. And Daddy's not going to risk bad publicity by taking someone's pets away from them."

"Even if those pets are dangerous to them?" Violet asked.

"Jim just had part of his ear bitten off! When that gator gets bigger, it could *kill* one of them."

"I can definitely see that happening," I said.

"Plus, it seems wrong to let them give Julius back," Violet went on. "Rick will just sell him to someone else. And maybe that person won't know how to take care of an anaconda either."

"That sounds likely," I agreed.

Violet looked at Summer and me. "There must be something we can do to keep that from happening."

"I'll bet there is," Summer said, with a determined look in her eye.

"Maybe," I said. "Although, right now, I have a dinosaur to find."

PALEONTOLOGY

Dashiell and Ethan ended up coming on the camping trip too. They called a few minutes after we had left the Barksdales' to apologize for not showing up; Ethan's brother had busted the axle of his truck while four-wheeling. When they heard I was going camping at Sage's ranch, they asked if they could join us. After a quick round of calls, everyone's parents agreed. So Tran swung by Ethan's place to pick them up.

Summer and Violet both wanted to come as well, but none of their parents were keen on the idea of them camping with a bunch of teenage boys, and their requests were rejected. So Summer was annoyed when she had to drop the rest of us off at the Bonotto Ranch.

"My parents suck," she said grumpily as we climbed out

of her car. "If I was a boy they wouldn't think twice about letting me do this."

"It's not that they think you can't handle it," Dashiell explained. "It's that they don't think we're trustworthy. And to be honest, they're probably right about Ethan."

"You're hilarious," Ethan said.

Summer ignored them and looked to me. "Maybe tomorrow we can go to Snakes Alive and find out who Rick is."

I wasn't sure that this was a good idea, but Summer was already in a foul mood, so I said, "Yeah. Maybe. If my parents say it's okay."

Summer brightened a bit at that. "All right. Don't have too much fun without me."

"I won't," I said, then hugged her good-bye, which Dashiell and Ethan responded to by making kissy noises and chanting, "Teddy has a girlfriend."

Sage was waiting for us by the front gate with his car. It took far less time to go back up the driveway than it had after that morning's rains, but we still had to go slower than usual due to the mud and the occasional giant puddle. Sage had already packed up all the gear for camping in a small trailer that hitched to an ATV, but by the time we rode out to the dig site, there was only about a half hour of daylight left.

Camping at Sage's ranch was a lot different from camping outside my trailer. At my home, we were still close enough to hear all the residents of employee housing inside their trailers, and we weren't allowed to build campfires because J.J. McCracken owned the property and he didn't want us burning the place down. So we usually ended up eating dinner in my trailer, then maybe watching a movie, and merely sleeping in the tent.

However, at Sage's ranch, we were really in the wilderness—or at least as close to it as our parents would allow us to go. Sage's family camped a lot, so they had a lot of top-quality gear for us: nice tents, bedrolls, and a full set of pots and pans to make our dinner. And since it was a working ranch, the Bonottos provided us with a cooler full of steaks so fresh, they had probably been walking around the day before. There were also homemade sausages and freshly laid eggs for breakfast. The only thing the Bonottos didn't provide for us was firewood, as there was plenty of that out by the campsite—although they did give us some hatchets and saws to collect it, with the stipulation that we not chop any of their trees down. We were only to hack up trees that had already fallen.

We decided to camp atop the small bluff that overlooked the dinosaur dig, rather than down by the river. It didn't look like it was going to rain again, but we didn't want to risk getting flooded out.

We set up the tents as fast as we could. Then, while

Dashiell and Ethan went off to get firewood and Sage set up the camp kitchen, I took advantage of the remaining daylight to check out the dig site.

Dr. Chen and her team had used dozens of plastic tarps to protect everything from the rain. The tarps were staked over sensitive areas of the dig, draped over piles of equipment, and wrapped tightly around what I presumed were pieces of Minerva that hadn't been stolen. Given the violence of the storm, the tarps hadn't all worked perfectly. A few had blown off in part—or entirely—exposing some of the sensitive areas and equipment to the elements. In addition, an entire canopy had blown away and lay crumpled by the edge of the river. Luckily, that one hadn't been sheltering as many artifacts, and the gear that had been stored beneath it had secondary tarps as cover, but much of it had gotten drenched anyhow.

To my surprise, the tools the paleontologists were using were very low-tech. I had expected to find some sort of fancy device that x-rayed the ground for fossils, like the one shown at the beginning of the original *Jurassic Park* movie, but there was nothing so advanced. Instead, the entire dig looked like it had been outfitted at a hardware store. There were picks, shovels, trowels, and levers to get the artifacts out of the ground, although those didn't look nearly as well used as the more delicate instruments: brushes, chisels, rock hammers, and tweezers. For wrapping the fossils, there were bundles of burlap and two wheelbarrows in which plaster had been mixed. The act of excavating dinosaur bones didn't seem to have changed much since it had first been practiced in the 1860s.

I knelt by one of the artifacts that had been bundled up, and carefully unwrapped the tarp. Encased in burlap and plaster, the artifact was a white, misshapen blob, one and a half feet high, two feet long, and more than a foot in diameter. Someone had written on it in Sharpie: *T. rex ulna,* along with the date. I knew the ulna was an arm bone—in humans and dinosaurs alike. In a *T. rex*, the arms were comically tiny compared to the rest of the animal, but given the size of the bundle, I realized that they were actually quite big when compared to, say, my own arms. Which indicated that Minerva was a very large dinosaur.

I checked a few of the other bundles. According to the labels there were several vertebrae, a pelvic bone, and a lot of metatarsals, which I thought might be parts of the feet or hands but couldn't remember for sure. The ulna was the biggest bundle, which meant that either the large bones of the legs like the femur and tibia hadn't been dug up yet—or maybe they hadn't been found at all. As Dr. Chen had said, no one had ever located an entire dinosaur.

I wrapped the bundles back up in their tarps and turned

my attention to the bones that were still in the ground. All of those had tarps pulled tightly over them and staked around the site. I cautiously untied one tarp and pulled it back, taking care to make sure that any water that had collected on it ran away from the bones.

What remained of Minerva didn't look like much.

If I hadn't known that these were the bones of a tyrannosaur, I probably would have walked right past them. As I had noted earlier that day, the ribs were all broken and thus not particularly rib-shaped; they merely looked like shards of rock. Many of the other bones were still mostly buried, and the parts that protruded from the earth gave no indication that there might be an entire femur or pelvis underneath. It made me realize there must have been a real art to telling whether something was a bone or a rock; it was possible that thousands of dinosaur fossils hadn't been discovered, just because people simply hadn't recognized what they were. Maybe I had even walked right by one myself at some point.

I was also struck by how painstaking the work of removing the fossils was, and amazed that someone could not only find them all, but also figure out how to reassemble them into a skeleton. It would have been like doing a 100,000-piece jigsaw puzzle after someone had buried all the pieces in the mud— and without a picture of the finished object to guide you.

The sun had disappeared behind the trees, and the clouds

to the west were starting to turn pink and red. It wouldn't be long until the light was gone.

There was a loud pop behind me.

I turned around, startled, then realized it was only the sound of damp wood beginning to burn. Sage had gotten the campfire started. Dashiell and Ethan had brought the first loads of wood and then gone to get more. Sage had built a fire ring out of rocks, then made a teepee of sticks and filled the gap beneath it with kindling. Given the faint smell of butane in the air, I could tell he had also doused it with lighter fluid to get it started.

Steam and smoke rose from the wood, which popped again and again. That, I knew, was from tiny pockets of water inside the wood, heating up from the fire. Steam would build up inside, the same way it did inside a popcorn kernel, and then make a tiny explosion.

I looked down the river, toward the boulders Summer had been playing on that morning. The river had risen another few inches with that afternoon's rains, so that most of the big rocks were completely submerged. Downstream, Dashiell and Ethan were hacking the limbs off a dead tree that lay along the riverbank.

I returned my attention to the dig site while there was still light remaining to see it, focusing on the large gouge in the bluff where the tyrannosaur skull had once been. No one had made any attempt to protect this area from the rain as there was nothing left to protect. The small bluff had been weakened when the skull was removed, so part of it had collapsed in the storm, filling the gouge with several new inches of dirt.

The mud in the area around the gouge had been saturated in the storm, so that even the deep footprints that Sheriff Esquivel had made that morning were barely visible anymore. They had been reduced to wide, shallow divots.

The mud had baked a bit in the afternoon heat, but it was still quite soft. My shoes sank two inches into it as I approached the gouge.

Which meant no one had been back to that site since the rains had come. They would have left footprints.

I studied the gouge carefully but couldn't deduce anything from it. If there had been any clues there, they had probably washed away or been buried in the mud. So I turned to leave, retracing my footsteps.

Metal glinted at the bottom of one of them.

I figured the object must have been dropped a few days before, then buried in mud by the rains; when I had walked through, the mud on top of it had stuck to the bottom of my shoe, exposing it to the light once again.

I reached down into the footprint and plucked the metal object out.

It was a ballpoint pen. It was sort of fancy, like the kind

J.J. McCracken used in his office, rather than the cheap plastic ones my parents bought in bulk at the office store. There was a little round symbol on it with the initials *WA*.

I knew I had seen that symbol before, but couldn't remember where.

It was getting dark down by the river. I started back toward the campfire, wanting to be away from the river before it got too hard to see. The last thing I wanted to do was take a spill and end up with my pants full of mud again.

Ethan and Dashiell were coming along the riverside, each with a large bundle of wood in their arms. They were walking quickly, also trying to get back to the fire before it got too dark to see.

"Thanks for all your help," Dashiell told me sarcastically. "If we freeze to death tonight, it's all going to be your fault."

"Like that'll happen," I replied, equally sarcastic. It was hot enough in the humid night that we were still warm in only T-shirts and shorts. I held up the pen so they could see it. "You guys recognize this?"

"It's a pen," Dashiell teased. "You write with it. Jeez, Teddy. I thought you were supposed to be smart."

"I mean *this*," I said, pointing to the WA logo.

"Dude," Ethan said, like I really *was* dumb. "Everyone knows that. It's the logo for Weems Aerospace."

THE CAMPOUT

"There was a tyrannosaurus skull right down there and you'd never noticed it?" Ethan asked Sage, incredulous. "Even though it was the size of a boulder?"

Night had fallen and we were gathered around the campfire to cook dinner. We had all found thick logs to sit on and then arrayed them in a circle around the flames. Sage had set a grill rack on top of some stones by the fire and was tending to four steaks. I had dumped a few cans of baked beans into a cast-iron pot and was heating them up.

Except for a few clouds by the western horizon, the sky was clear. We were far from the light pollution of civilization, so a million stars shimmered above us. The moon was a mere sliver, looking like a heavy-lidded eye, and Venus glowed brightly to the east.

While prepping to cook, Sage and I had brought Ethan and Dashiell up to speed on the Minerva investigation.

"First of all, it wasn't like the skull was just sitting out in the open," Sage said, sounding a bit offended. "It was barely poking out of the bluff. And it probably hadn't been like that very long. There was some loose dirt piled nearby, so Dr. Chen figured there had been a little landslide only a couple days before to reveal it."

"What'd your parents think when you told them about it?" Dash asked.

"They thought I was playing a joke," Sage replied. "Even after I showed it to them, they still couldn't believe it."

"They thought you buried a fake dinosaur skull way out here?" Ethan asked skeptically.

"Actually, that *would* be a pretty great practical joke," Dash said. "Like, you bury some old steak bones and shark's teeth out in a field and then try to convince someone it's a dinosaur? I'll bet the Barksdales would fall for it in a second."

Ethan said, "If you buried a LEGO *Star Wars Millennium Falcon* in a field and told the Barksdales it was a UFO crash, they'd probably believe it."

"We should do that," Dash said.

I stirred the beans a bit more and asked Sage, "Did you guys call the university right away?"

"Pretty much." Sage shifted the steaks on the grill. "My

folks didn't know what to do, so they just googled 'Texas paleontology,' and the university came up. I think they talked to an assistant or they left a message, and Dr. Chen called back that night, super excited. She came out to see Minerva the next morning, and then arranged everything else. The crew and all the logistics and everything."

"Why's the dinosaur even called Minerva?" Ethan asked.

"Dad named her after Mom's mother," Sage said.

"To honor her?" I asked.

"That's what he told Mom," Sage replied. "But he says it's really because Grandma is even meaner than a *T. rex*. And they have the same overbite."

I debated posing the next question for a moment, not sure if it was a good idea to ask it or not. "Did you ever hear about J.J. McCracken wanting to buy Minerva?"

"Of course." Sage wasn't upset by the question at all. Instead, he seemed excited. "That was my idea."

"It was?" I asked, surprised.

"Sure. One night, my parents were talking about how much Minerva would be worth and wondering who could afford to buy it, and I suggested J.J. Because he already had the whole dinosaur display at World of Reptiles. So they reached out to him."

"How?" I asked.

"The ranching community out here is pretty small," Sage

said. "We sold J.J. most of the original cattle stock for his ranch when he started it up. It's not like my folks are best friends with him, but we've got his number. And I was right. He was *really* interested."

Dash and Ethan were staring across the fire at Sage, extremely intrigued now. Ethan asked, "Exactly how much *is* a *T. rex* skeleton worth?"

Sage said, "There was one named Sue that was found up in Montana. It sold to a museum for over eight million dollars."

Dash gagged on a sip of water, spraying it into the campfire, where it instantly burst into a cloud of steam. "Did you say *eight million dollars?*"

"That's right," Sage agreed. "And Dr. Chen said Minerva might have been even more valuable than Sue." His features suddenly clouded. "Although, I guess we'll never know now."

He looked beyond the campfire, toward the expanse of his property. In the almost moonless night, we couldn't see much. Even the river, despite being close enough to throw a rock into, was lost in the darkness. But still, the great mass of shadow, unbroken by any lights, attested to the enormous size of the ranch. Sage sighed heavily. "Without that dinosaur, I guess we're going to have to start selling this place off."

"What?" Dash asked, startled. "Why?"

"The ranch isn't making that much money anymore,"

Sage told him. "We're pretty deep in debt. Minerva could have saved us. But without her, the only way we can get by is to sell off part of our land."

"You mean, to developers?" Dash frowned, upset. "So they can tear all this down and build more subdivisions and Pizza Huts?"

"I guess," Sage admitted sadly.

Ethan poked at the fire with a stick, unhappy to hear this as well. "Every time you turn around, another developer has destroyed a piece of land out here. They just tore up this whole stretch along Decker Road so they can put in another stupid outlet mall."

"And the Turners sold their whole ranch," Dash added. "It's gonna be one giant subdivision. Some of the best turtle-catching ponds in the whole state, gone."

I said, "It's a good thing Summer talked her father into making the rest of the property around FunJungle a wildlife refuge. Or else that would have all been golf courses and resorts."

"Yeah," Ethan said, "but the McCrackens have done plenty of damage out here already. I mean, FunJungle might have a big environmental message and all, but they still took out plenty of forest to build it."

"The parking lot alone is, like, forty acres," Dash observed. "And they're still expanding to build all those theme park rides. That's got to be another ten acres right there." He paused thoughtfully, then said, "Although I *am* kind of excited about the rides."

"Especially the roller coaster," Ethan agreed. "That thing's going to be awesome."

Which was the whole problem with humans in a nutshell. None of us liked when our wilderness was destroyed, but then we all wanted the places it was being destroyed to build. Some of us wanted theme parks; others wanted outlet malls. And we all needed schools and roads and places to live.

Sage flipped the steaks over on the grill. "It's not like my parents *want* to sell off our land. It's actually the last thing they want to do. But without Minerva, we don't have a lot of options left." He looked at me pointedly. "You don't think J.J. would have stolen her, do you?"

"No way," I said, and I truly meant it. "J.J. wouldn't destroy your family's livelihood for a *T. rex*. If he really wanted Minerva, he could afford eight million dollars."

"Besides, Harper Weems is obviously the one who stole Minerva," Dash suggested. "I'll bet she sent a whole team of people out here to get the skull last night, and one of them dropped that pen."

"Oh please," Ethan said dismissively. "That pen was way too obvious a piece of evidence. If anything, it was left at the crime scene to frame Harper Weems."

Dash shook his head. "You and your conspiracy theories. No one leaves evidence behind to frame someone else. The simplest explanation is always the best. If there's a pen from Weems Aerospace, it means Harper's involved."

"Unless someone simply happened to drop the pen out here by accident," I said. "One of the guys on the dig was Harper's cousin."

The others looked at me, surprised. "Who?" Sage asked.

"The guy with the ponytail," I said.

"I *knew* that guy looked suspicious!" Sage exclaimed. "And he was really weird, too. He never hung out with the others. He was always off by himself, making notes in this little book he carried."

Dash beamed proudly at Ethan. "There you go. Harper sends her cousin in to check on the dinosaur and figure out the lay of the land. Then they swipe the skull, but accidentally drop the pen in the process."

"Who brings a pen with the logo of their own aerospace company to a theft?" Ethan argued. "And how did they get Minerva out, anyhow?"

"I don't know," Dash said. "But if *anyone* could figure out how to pull off this crime, it's Harper Weems. She revolutionized the aerospace industry. So she can certainly steal a dinosaur skull."

All of which made me wonder what had happened to

Jebediah Weems and where he had run off to again.

"Steaks are done," Sage announced.

"Great!" Ethan said. "I'm starving."

"Beans are ready too," I said, pulling the pot from the fire.

We each had a tin plate, silverware, and a cup, courtesy of Sage's family. We all set about loading our plates with food.

"Whoa there," Dash warned Ethan, watching him ladle beans onto his plate. "Not so many of those. Or this place is gonna be Toot City tonight."

"I'll be fine," Ethan replied.

"Yeah, right," Dash teased. "Last time you ate beans, it sounded like the D-Day invasion. And the smell! Every canary for twenty miles dropped dead."

I moved around the fire to get a steak off the grill—and as I did, I noticed something inside the fire itself. Among all the dead branches was a plank of wood. The sides were planed smooth, indicating it had come from a lumberyard. It had been in the fire for a while, so much of it had burned, but I could still make out the general shape. It was about eighteen inches long, six inches wide, and two inches thick. I might not have thought anything of it, but there were two holes bored through its width. Each was about a quarter inch across, and they were definitely man-made, far too big and straight for an animal to have done.

I grabbed a stick and poked at the plank, toppling it out of the fire. It fell to the ground with a shower of sparks.

"Watch it, Teddy!" Sage warned. "Or you'll set this whole place on fire!"

"Sorry." I leaned closer to the plank to inspect it. It was charred black most of the way around, but I saw some faint thin strands of something that had burned around the holes. "Who found this piece of wood?" I asked.

"Me," Ethan said, his mouth full of beans. He had already dug into his dinner.

"Was there anything going through this hole when you found it?" I asked.

"Yeah. A thick piece of rope. But it was all wet from the rain, so I chucked it."

"Where'd you find it?"

Ethan pointed in the direction of the river. "Downstream from here a ways. Why? It's just some wood. Probably part of an old plank bridge over the river."

"We've never had a plank bridge over this river," Sage informed him.

"You think it's a clue?" Dash asked me.

"Maybe." I stared off toward the river, listening to it, even though I couldn't see it. It was still running hard enough to be quite loud. "If I had wanted to get rid of some evidence, the easiest thing to do would be to throw it in the river and let it sink or get washed far downstream. Maybe this piece just didn't float as far as the thief had hoped."

"We got plenty of other wood," Dash said, pointing to the pile he and Ethan had collected. They had gathered enough to keep the fire going for hours.

I examined all of it more closely. There wasn't anything as obvious as another plank of wood with holes bored through it, but another log caught my eye. It was from the trunk of a young tree, about three inches in diameter and a foot long. While one end of it had been chopped through with an axe, the other was neatly cut, as though someone had used a chain saw on it.

I pulled it out of the pile and found that someone had also removed the small branches from the log. They were sheared extremely close to the trunk, probably with a chain saw as well.

Meaning someone had taken time and effort to sculpt the log exactly the way they wanted. And then someone else had come along and chopped it in half.

"Did one of you gather this?" I asked Ethan and Dash, presenting it to them.

"Oh yeah," Ethan said. "That was me too."

"Where did you find it?" I asked.

"Down by the river. Close to where I found that plank."

"And you chopped it up?"

"Yeah. It was way too big to carry otherwise."

"How big?"

"Like three feet long. Maybe four."

I pointed to the cleanly shaved end. "Was the other end like this too?"

"I think so."

"Dude!" Dash exclaimed. "You didn't think there was anything weird about that?"

"It's not weird," Ethan said defensively. "I figured a beaver might have done it."

"A beaver?" Sage asked. "What kind of beaver would cut a log that cleanly?"

"A very neat one," Ethan replied.

"Beavers don't have obsessive-compulsive disorder," Sage informed him. "A human did that."

"That doesn't mean it's suspicious," Ethan said defensively. "Like, maybe it was part of the dig somehow."

"If it was," I said, "then it would have been by the dig site, with all the other supplies. But it was downriver, which indicates that someone tried to get rid of this, too."

"What use would a three-foot-long log be?" Ethan asked. "Or a plank with holes in it?"

"I don't know," Sage said. "But I suppose that—"

"Shhhh!" Dash hissed.

The rest of us instantly fell silent. I stared out into the darkness, listening intently for whatever had caught Dash's attention. For a while, all I could hear was the crackle of the fire and the rushing of the river.

And then I heard something else.

Voices in the distance.

We weren't the only people out at the crime scene.

THE SUSPECTS

We all tensed in fear, wondering who else might be out there.

"Oh my god," Ethan moaned quietly. "Do you think it's the chupacabra?"

Even though Dash had just warned us to be quiet, he groaned. "You and your stupid chupacabra," he muttered.

The chupacabra was a mythical creature that was rumored to suck the blood out of goats—and possibly humans. As ridiculous as it sounded, Ethan wasn't the only person who believed it existed. Some people thought it was a reptilelike creature that hopped like a kangaroo, while others thought it was more doglike in appearance.

"The chupacabra isn't stupid," Ethan whispered back. "It's extremely wily and as smart as a chimpanzee."

"That makes one of you," Dash said. "That's not a chupacabra you hear. It's obviously humans talking."

I was trying to focus on the voices. Between the fire and the river and my friends arguing, there was too much noise to hear what was being said. It was hard enough to even pinpoint where the voices were coming from, but they seemed to be downstream somewhere.

"The chupacabra can make itself sound human," Ethan argued. "To trick unsuspecting campers into dropping their defenses."

Well down the river, a flashlight beam suddenly cut through the night, as though whoever was carrying it had just emerged from a stand of trees.

"Do chupacabras carry flashlights?" Dash asked pointedly.

"They do after they kill humans who were carrying them," Ethan said ominously.

Several other flashlight beams joined the first. All were aimed in our direction.

They weren't very strong beams, probably the type of small flashlight that you could strap to your forehead. The newcomers were merely using them to light the path directly ahead of them. We were too far away for them to see us clearly . . .

But they could easily make out our campfire.

There was nothing we could do to hide it. In the pitch-black night it might as well have been a spotlight.

The flashlight beams froze suddenly as the intruders stopped. Then the beams spun around and disappeared back into the trees.

"They're getting away!" Dash exclaimed, and took off after them.

Before I even knew what I was doing, I was running after him as well. Sage was right next to me, although Ethan hung back by the fire. "You idiots!" he yelled. "What if it's a chupacabra?"

"Don't be such a chicken!" Dash yelled back.

Ethan sighed and joined the chase. There was nothing worse for a teenage boy than being labeled a chicken. Even getting attacked by a chupacabra.

Dash and Ethan were both extremely good athletes and very fast, but they didn't know the terrain nearly as well as Sage did, so they had to wait for him to lead the way. Sage found the safest place to descend the small bluff to the riverbank in the darkness, and then brought us along the edge of the water.

Ahead of us, the flashlight beams were gone. Either they had vanished into the woods, or the people we had seen had turned them off so that we couldn't follow them.

We also couldn't hear the people anymore. The river was too loud beside us to pick up any voices.

We kept on running anyhow. "This had better not be a chupacabra," Ethan grumbled under his breath.

I briefly wondered if the intruders might be planning an ambush, but decided that didn't make much sense. They had obviously been surprised to see us there, and they had immediately run, which meant they weren't looking for a fight. Instead, they were probably trying to get away fast before we could see who they were. Ambushing us would require coordinating a counterattack on the spur of the moment, and it would be hard to do without revealing their identities.

But still, all that was guesswork. I kept my guard up as I ran.

Now that we were away from the campfire, my eyes were adjusting to the light. The night was no longer a field of black, but was instead shades of darkness. The stars had come out in force above. The Milky Way was a great white slash across the sky, and it was reflected in the river to our right as well.

I could make out a path along the river, the reeds trampled by a dozen feet going over them every day. It must have been the route that the paleontology crew took back and forth to their camp—and the road.

The great shadow of the woods loomed just ahead, which was the point where our surprise guests had turned and fled.

From deep in the forest, I heard a thud, followed by a yelp of pain.

It sounded as though someone had run straight into a tree, although I couldn't tell from the yelp whether it was a man or a woman.

But it was definitely an indication that the others were running away from us, rather than lying in wait, and that one of them was now injured.

"C'mon!" Dash urged us, then yelled out, "You'd better run, you losers! Because we're coming for you!"

We reached the woods.

It was darker in the trees, without the stars above. A trail had been cut through, but it was hard to pick out. We had to slow down for fear of suffering the same fate our targets had and hurting ourselves. And yet, even then, I kept smacking into branches and getting facefuls of cedar needles.

Ahead of me, Ethan suddenly shrieked in terror.

"What happened?" I asked worriedly. "Are you okay?"

"I just ran into the biggest freaking spiderweb of all time!" Ethan howled. "Ugh! I think I got dead bugs in my mouth!"

"Sucks to be you!" Dash laughed, and then cried out as he tripped over a tree root and crashed to the ground.

Up ahead of us came the sound of a great splash.

Dash snapped back to his feet, wiping mud and dead

leaves out of his hair. "What was that? Think one of them fell in the river?"

"It was too loud to be a person," Sage said, then forged ahead through the woods.

We finally emerged from the trees into a large expanse of grassland.

Five large canvas tents were pitched there, each big enough for at least four people, set a good distance from the river to be safe from flooding. They were arranged in a ring around a central area where the grass had been trampled flat and a large fire pit was filled with the damp remains of campfires.

"This is the paleontologists' camp?" I asked Sage.

"Yes," he replied, then pointed across the river. "The way to the road is over there . . . Oh crud."

"What's wrong?" Ethan whimpered. He looked around skittishly, as if expecting the chupacabra to pounce on him any second.

"This is where the log we used as a bridge to cross the river was," Sage said. "But it's gone."

The river narrowed ahead of us, which meant it was running deeper and faster, and the water funneled through the gap. There were some big rocks in the middle of it that created a short series of rapids. The white foam from their churning gleamed in the dark night.

"That's what the big splash must have been," Dash observed. "They shoved the log into the river."

Sure enough, we found a deep gouge in the riverbank not far ahead, indicating that the end of a log had nested there for quite some time. A rope stretched across the river, four feet above the water, tied to a tree on each bank.

"We used that as a handrail," Sage explained. "To steady ourselves while crossing."

I gauged the river. At the rate it was flowing, trying to wade across it in the middle of the night would be suicidal. "Is there any other place to cross close by?"

"Not when the water's like this," Sage replied sadly. "We'd have to go another mile downstream until there's a safe enough ford."

I looked to the opposite bank. Far in the distance, well across a field, the intruders had turned their flashlights on again. They were no longer running full tilt, but were moving at a more leisurely, careful pace. Obviously, they knew we were no longer a threat to them.

Without the bridge, there was no way we could catch them. They had gotten away clean.

SNAKES ALIVE

The billboards for Snakes Alive began to appear along the interstate twenty miles before we got there. SEE THE WORLD'S MOST DEADLY SNAKE! SEE THE WORLD'S MOST VICIOUS CROCODILE! SEE A REAL LIVE MAN-EATER! Each had a lurid painting of an animal next to it: a king cobra, a saltwater crocodile, and a Bengal tiger. Each mile or so, we passed another sign. At the bottom of each was the inevitable phrase: MORE FUN THAN FUNJUNGLE—AND A WHOLE LOT CHEAPER!

"It should say 'a whole lot sleazier,'" Summer grumbled.

It was late in the morning after my campout at the Bonotto Ranch. The rest of the previous night had been uneventful after our mystery guests had escaped. Our presence there had scared them off for good. I had fallen asleep shortly after returning to the campsite with Sage, Dash, and Ethan; it had been a very long day.

I had woken early and searched for any clues I might have missed in the fading light the night before. Downriver, I found the footprints of our mystery guests, but they were from the kind of hiking boot that pretty much everyone wore. I didn't find anything new around the dig, not that I really expected to come across anything else as blatant as the Weems Aerospace pen. But it was still incredible to be in the middle of a real dinosaur dig, surrounded by honest-to-goodness tyrannosaur bones.

We had to strike camp early. Sage needed to help out around the ranch, Dash and Ethan had to get to their summer jobs, and Summer had lined up more investigating for us to do. Once again, I hadn't agreed to this so much as been thrust into it. I had turned off my phone when I went to sleep, and when I turned it back on, I found a long text chain from Summer saying that she was heading to Snakes Alive in the morning to question Rick, and she was doing it with or without me.

I also found a series of e-mails that I had been included on between Summer and Tommy Lopez.

Summer had written to Tommy with an update about what had happened at the Barksdales' and our lead to Rick at Snakes Alive. Tommy had responded that this was great work, but then said he was still going to be out of town on business at least another day, at which point Summer had suggested approaching Rick with me, posing as normal kids who wanted to buy a snake. To my surprise, Tommy had been supportive. He even thought there might be an advantage to having Summer and me to talk to Rick before he did; no one would expect two teenagers to be running a sting operation. If Rick took the bait and offered to sell us something illegally, then Tommy could use that as evidence to argue for investigating Snakes Alive to his boss.

We weren't being asked to do anything dangerous, Summer pointed out. We were merely going shopping. Except, instead of looking for books or clothes, we were looking for snakes.

Put that way, it didn't sound too bad.

Even Mom, who was always looking out for my safety, had been in favor of the plan. She had picked me up at Sage's ranch and spent most of the ride home ranting about how upsetting the illegal animal trade was. This was a particular concern to her, as reptiles weren't the only victims; there was also a booming illegal trade in birds, tropical fish, and Mom's area of specialty: primates. Mom reminded me that she had even thwarted a trafficker herself on one occasion, when she had boarded a plane in the Congo and found a man trying to smuggle a baby De Brazza's monkey.

"He wasn't even trying to hide it!" Mom exclaimed, still just as angry about the event ten years after it had happened. "He had the poor thing in the pocket of his jacket and was showing it off to the other passengers!" Mom had promptly alerted the airline staff, who hadn't been too concerned until Mom claimed that the monkey could be carrying a deadly disease that would make all the passengers' brains dissolve. That was an exaggeration, but it got the attention of everyone on board, who were upset to learn their lives were in danger. The pilots had radioed ahead to the authorities, who were waiting to arrest the smuggler when the plane landed.

Mom was less pleased about my involvement with the stolen *T. rex*, though. When I told her about what had happened the night before, her face creased into a frown. "Why on earth did you chase those people? You should have called the police."

"By the time the police showed up, the bad guys would have been long gone. And besides, Sheriff Esquivel doesn't even care about this case."

"That's no excuse for putting yourself in danger. You ought to call the police right now, let them know what happened—and then be done with this."

"All right." I looked up the number for the sheriff's department, then called and asked for Officer Brewster. She wasn't in, which was fine with me, as I didn't really feel like talking to her again. The dispatcher put me through to her voicemail and I left a message detailing what had happened.

When I hung up, Mom said, "Maybe you ought to let that paleontologist—Dr. Chen?—know what happened as well. I'm sure she'd want to know about it too."

It took me a little bit longer to track down Dr. Chen's number, but after some searching, I found her listing in the Department of Vertebrate Paleontology at the University of Texas at Austin. It was located at—of all things—the J. J. Pickle Research Campus.

I giggled at this. "J. J. Pickle? Really?"

"Believe it or not, J. J. Pickle was a respected congressman from Texas," Mom informed me. "I believe Summer's father is named for him."

"Good thing they went with the 'J. J.' and not the 'Pickle,'" I observed, then called the number. I got a receptionist who informed me that Dr. Chen was out in the field. I asked if I could have her number and he told me that wasn't allowed, but offered to take a message. So, for the third time that morning, I gave the details of what had happened at the dig site the night before. The receptionist sounded very concerned, said he would let Dr. Chen know immediately, and thanked me for my help.

By that time, we were almost home. Mom and Dad both had to work that day, so Mom took off right after getting me back to our trailer. I quickly showered and changed, then met Summer and Tran in the employee parking lot and headed out again.

The billboards became more common as we got closer to Snakes Alive. They began to announce how far it was:

ONLY HALF A MILE TO THE WORLD'S MOST INCREDIBLE COLLECTION OF REPTILES!

ONLY 1,000 FEET TO THE GREATEST ZOO ON EARTH!

EXIT HERE FOR THE MOST EXCITING TOURIST ATTRACTION IN TEXAS!

We pulled off onto the access road. Snakes Alive was located just beyond the exit.

The billboard in the parking lot was the biggest one yet, a full two stories promoting wild animals, refreshments, and souvenirs.

Even FunJungle might not have been able to live up to so much hype, but at first glance, Snakes Alive was extremely unimpressive. It appeared that they had spent far more on billboards than buildings. The main structure was a long, drab cement bunker with a gravel parking lot. Someone had attempted to sculpt the head of a giant venomous snake atop the building, with the mouth open and fangs bared, but they hadn't done a great job.

"Looks like a vampire beaver," Summer observed. She was in her standard outfit she wore when she didn't want to be recognized: baseball cap, sunglasses, and a nondescript shirt.

Despite its dreary appearance, however, Snakes Alive was attracting customers; the parking lot was full. Tran parked by the giant billboard and stayed in the car with the air conditioner running.

After a day of rain, the summer heat had returned with a vengeance. Summer and I wilted as we crossed the parking lot.

Snakes Alive was so close to the highway that we could hear the constant roar of semitrucks rushing by. Directly to the right side of the tourist attraction was a recreational vehicle dealership, a two-acre parking lot filled with RVs. On the left side was an enormous convenience store called Jerk-ee's.

There were several Jerk-ee's in Texas; all were located on the highways halfway between major cities, where travelers would need to make pit stops. Each was the size of a Walmart. They lured customers by claiming to have the biggest and cleanest bathrooms on earth; the men's rooms had up to eighty urinals. Not surprisingly, they specialized in beef jerky, which they sold over a hundred types of, but you could also buy thousands of other snacks and drinks, as well as a surprising array of other things, like clothing, toys, kitchenware, and, since this was Texas, hunting supplies. Jerk-ee's didn't sell guns, but they had almost anything else you needed for a hunting trip, and thus, it was a very popular spot for hunters.

This created an odd juxtaposition of businesses. Snakes Alive, while it might have been tacky, was trying to attract customers who wanted to see living animals, while Jerk-ee's was trying to attract people who wanted to kill them. The cars in the parking lot of Snakes Alive were mostly rental cars and minivans, the kinds of things tourists and families would drive, while the parking lot of Jerk-ee's (which was much better paved and significantly larger) was full of pickups with gun racks in their rear windows.

Summer and I entered Snakes Alive. A bored girl not much older than us sat at a ticket counter beside a turnstile. Over her head, a large banner proclaimed that Snakes Alive was a great place to have your child's birthday party; it featured a crudely drawn cobra looking excitedly at a cake.

The price to visit Snakes Alive was twenty-one dollars a person, which wasn't that cheap as far as I was concerned (although it *was* considerably cheaper than FunJungle). Summer had already volunteered to cover the cost, though, and I let her. If this had been a date, I would have felt weird about it, but she had railroaded me into this, after all.

"How many different kinds of snakes do you have here?" I asked.

The girl shrugged. "I don't know anything about the snakes. I just work the register."

"Thanks for your help," Summer said, in a way that didn't

sound too sarcastic, and we passed through the turnstile.

The first thing we entered was the reptile room, which was long, narrow, and windowless, drably lit by fluorescent lights. On one side were three shelves, each lined with aquariums. On the other side, the wall was taken up with larger exhibits, all built from plywood and fronted with plexiglass.

The aquariums on the shelves held the smaller animals; in addition to snakes, there were also lots of lizards, tortoises, and frogs. There were actually some pretty fascinating snakes, like Gaboon vipers and green mambas, though there wasn't much to their exhibits; each had some dirt, a few plants, water, and heat lamps. Fake plastic human skulls had been placed in with some of the venomous snakes, as if to give the impression that the snakes had killed someone—but still, none of the tourists seemed remotely interested in any of them. Instead, they were quickly drawn to the bigger exhibits, which held larger animals like alligators and water monitors—although at the moment, most of the visitors were gathered around a guy holding an albino Burmese python.

The python wasn't as big as Julius Squeezer, but it was still at least ten feet long. The guy holding it had a name tag that said LAMAR. To his credit, Lamar seemed to be doing a decent job educating the people around him about the snake.

There was a cluster of young children in the group who were all obviously part of a birthday party, as they were wearing conical paper hats strapped to their heads with thin elastic bands.

"A lot of people think a snake like this kills by crushing you to death," Lamar said. "But that's wrong. Instead, it kills by constriction." He looked the birthday boy in the eye. "If she was gonna eat you, she would wrap around you and squeeze you so hard that you couldn't breathe anymore—so you'd die by suffocation. And then she'd swallow you whole!"

The snake flicked her tongue at the birthday boy.

He screamed in terror and fled down the hallway. "Don't let it eat me!" he wailed. "I don't wanna die!"

The parents shot Lamar dirty looks and ran after the kid. "Johnny, wait!" the mother cried. "He was only joking!"

"Happy birthday!" Lamar called after them.

"Does this mean we don't get cake?" one of the other kids asked.

"Beats me," Lamar said. "It's not my party." He glanced toward us, then did a double take, and his eyes went wide in shock.

He had recognized Summer, despite her outfit.

Normally, Summer might have been bothered by this, but at that moment, she seemed to realize she could use her fame to her advantage.

Lamar ditched the rest of the crowd and came right over to us, trying to look as suave as someone could with an albino python draped over his shoulders. "You're *her*, aren't you?" he asked.

"I am," Summer said. "Nice snake."

"Want to touch it?" Lamar asked. "Or hold it? I could take a photo of you holding it! That'd be amazing."

"She's beautiful," Summer said. "Where'd you get her? I'd love to have a snake like this."

"Oh, she's not for sale," Lamar said, then looked around furtively to see if anyone else was listening. He lowered his voice and leaned in closer than I thought was necessary. "But if you *are* interested in a snake, you should talk to Rick."

Summer flashed him a smile that made him weak in the knees. "Where's Rick?"

"Out back by the hyenas," Lamar said. "If you want to wait a few minutes while I put this snake back, I can take you out to him . . ."

"That's all right," Summer said. "I'm sure we can find him."

Lamar seemed to be giving serious consideration to simply abandoning the python on the floor so that he could accompany Summer, but we slipped out the door before he could act on it.

Behind the reptile building, there was a surprisingly large plot of land. It held two dozen animal enclosures, all quite spacious, albeit extremely simple in design: They were merely large, fenced-in tracts of grass, some with a tree or two, and a small building for their residents to take shelter in. In one, two American bison wallowed in the mud. A family of capybaras rooted around in another. A petting zoo butted up against the parking lot of Jerk-ee's; it was mostly goats and sheep, although there was also a potbellied pig and a llama in it. Another birthday party was gathered there, with even younger children, one of whom was crying because the llama had spit on him and then eaten his party hat.

A sign indicated that a few of the goats in the petting zoo were fainting goats, which is a strange domesticated breed that has seizures and passes out when startled. Although the sign warned that it wasn't kind to induce this behavior, the park employees weren't discouraging it. In fact, one was actively showing some children how it worked. He snuck up behind some goats and yelled "Boo!"

The goats promptly collapsed, as though they had fallen asleep in one second. The children laughed hysterically. So did some of their parents.

"That's not cool at all," Summer commented.

We found the hyenas by their sound. They were toward the back of the property, yipping excitedly while Rick tossed chicken parts to them through the chain-link fence.

Rick was in his forties, squat and bald, with the type of muscular build that could only come from using steroids.

He'd had to tear the sleeves off his official Snakes Alive shirt so that he could fit his arms through it; the veins along his biceps bulged like earthworms. He carried a bucket full of raw chicken, and the hyenas were hungrily racing back and forth along the other side of the fence, then rearing up onto their hind legs to catch the pieces he threw. A small crowd of tourists had gathered to watch, snapping photos and shooting videos with their phones.

I wasn't so pleased. Begging for food wasn't a natural animal behavior. At FunJungle, the animal keepers worked hard to deliver the food to the animals in more realistic ways: hanging it from trees, or hiding it in logs, or luring the carnivores on a hunt. They never merely handed the food to the animals, and they certainly didn't make them do tricks for it.

Rick chucked the last piece of chicken into the jaws of a male hyena. "That's all folks!" he announced to the crowd. "Though I'll be feeding the lion in half an hour."

The tourists groaned, disappointed the show had ended, then wandered off to look at other animals. Rick started back toward the reptile building, happily swinging his chicken bucket.

Summer stopped right in his path, and I followed her lead.

"Hi," she said. "Lamar told us you're the one to talk to about getting a snake."

Rick paused, looking at Summer. "Do I know you? You look familiar."

"I don't think we've met," Summer said.

Rick shrugged. Like Tommy Lopez had hoped, he didn't seem suspicious of us at all. Instead, he looked excited to make a sale. "What kind of snake are you thinking of?"

"Something exotic," Summer told him.

"Exotic things ain't cheap."

"I've got money." To my surprise, Summer opened her purse, revealing a wad of cash inside.

Rick broke into a big smile. "It's your lucky day. I just got an anaconda in this morning. He's a beauty."

I figured it was Julius. Tim and Jim had probably returned him first chance they got. And now Rick was trying to sell us a used anaconda.

"An anaconda's way too big," Summer said. "Don't you have anything smaller?"

"Come with me." Rick led us back to the reptile building. As we passed the petting zoo, the fainting goats had regained consciousness—and the Snakes Alive employee was startling them again. Rick chuckled appreciatively. "That never gets old," he said, then took us through a back door marked EMPLOYEES ONLY. DO NOT ENTER UNDER PENALTY OF DEATH.

We ended up in a room separate from the rest of the building. It seemed to serve two purposes: storage for the animals that weren't on display and food preparation. Several refrigerators and freezers were lined up against one wall. Along the other wall was a row of shelves that were filled with plastic storage tubs like the one Julius Squeezer had come in, but in a great variety of sizes. I estimated there were at least sixty, although since they were opaque, I couldn't tell how many had animals inside them.

In the middle of the room was a baby pool filled with turtles.

A teenage girl was chopping carrots and lettuce at a small counter.

"Beat it," Rick told her brusquely. "I've got customers."

The teenage girl scooped the vegetables into a bowl and scurried out with barely a glance at us.

Rick returned his attention to us and smiled, like he hadn't just been a jerk to the girl. "I bet you'd like an emerald tree boa. Folks love those. They're gorgeous." Rick took a medium-size plastic storage tub off the shelves, set it on a table, and popped the lid off.

Sure enough, there was an emerald tree boa inside, lying on a bed of sawdust. Like Rick had said, it was a gorgeous animal, with iridescent green skin, save for a spot on its tail where it had a white scar.

"Can I take a picture of it?" Summer asked, reaching for her phone.

Rick caught her hand. "No photos." There was an edge to his voice as he said it, a warning that disobeying him would be a bad idea.

That was a bummer, because it would have been nice to have photos as evidence for Tommy. Summer was shrewd enough not to show her disappointment, though. "All right," she agreed, then returned her attention to the emerald boa. "It's nice," she said thoughtfully, like she was considering a pair of shoes, rather than a live reptile. "But it's not quite what I'm looking for. What else do you have?"

Rick slapped the top back on the tub, returned it to the shelf, and perused the other options there. "Ooh. How about a Mangshan pit viper?"

"A pit viper?" I exclaimed, despite myself. "Those are venomous!"

"So?" Rick asked, in a tone that indicated I was being a weenie. "A real man doesn't mind a little danger."

"It's a *lot* of danger," I said.

Rick took a somewhat larger tub off the shelf, set it on the table, and despite my concerns—or perhaps to make fun of them—casually removed the lid.

Inside this tub was a snake that was perhaps even more beautiful than the emerald boa. It was about two feet long and its skin was marbled with gorgeous green and black bands. Like the last snake, this one also had an injury to its tail, a slight kink near the end where it angled to the right. It didn't react at all to the movement of its tub, remaining almost completely inert.

"Trust me," Rick told us, "there is no greater feeling of power than to own a snake like this. To be able to control something so deadly. It's a rush. I've sold plenty of these— and no one has ever complained. Or gotten hurt. If anything, they come back wanting more."

"You've sold lots of these Mangshan vipers?" Summer asked.

"Well, not Mangshans in particular. That beauty there is *rare*. But venomous snakes in general. Rattlers, cotton-mouths, mambas, cobras . . ."

"Aren't all of those hard to care for?" Summer asked.

"Nah." Rick made a dismissive gesture with his hand. "They're easier than a dog. You have to walk a dog, get it shots, clean up its poop all the time. A cobra only eats once every few weeks and poops even less."

"But they eat live food, right?" I asked. "That's not so easy to get."

"You can train them to eat dead stuff," Rick informed me. "And then I can handle that for you too. I've got plenty of food." He opened one of the big freezers, revealing that it was crammed full of dead animals.

Summer, who had been doing a decent job of being non-chalant so far, made a gasp of surprise.

The upper shelves were stacked high with the frozen corpses of rats and mice, while the lower shelves were mostly rabbits. It looked like a Beatrix Potter story that had gone horribly wrong.

"See?" Rick asked proudly. "I can hook you up with all the frodents you need."

"Frodents?" Summer and I asked at once.

"Frozen rodents," Rick said. "I'm thinking of trademarking the term." He shut the freezer, then returned to the Mangshan viper, whose tub he had carelessly left open. "So? You want her?"

Summer pursed her lips thoughtfully, then shook her head. "It is pretty, but . . ."

"You want a cobra, don't you?" Rick asked. "I can see it in your eyes."

"Maybe," Summer said coyly.

"Good choice. At least one of you has some guts." Rick gave me a pointed look, then put the lid on the tub with the Mangshan viper and returned it to the shelves. "Only, I don't have a cobra . . . at the moment. But that's about to change. As you might have noticed, I'm a little low on merchandise right now. But I've got a shipment coming in soon."

"How soon?" Summer asked.

"Hard to say." Rick picked up a hand strengthener and squeezed it methodically, making his muscles bulge. "Should be within the next few days. Maybe even tomorrow. But I never know with these things until right before they happen. That's how the business works. If you're interested, though, give me your number. I'll give you a heads-up the moment I know anything."

Summer made a show of considering this, then asked, "What kind of cobra are we talking about here?"

"I put in for some Egyptians, some monocleds—and a few kings." Rick grinned at our surprised responses. "That's right. The king of cobras. The most amazing snake on earth. And one could be yours by the end of the week."

"How much?" Summer asked.

"A thousand dollars," Rick said.

"I'll give you half that," Summer said.

Rick countered with nine hundred dollars, and they began to haggle about price. Summer made sure that Rick's back was to me, so I turned my attention to the other animals in storage.

Some of the plastic tubs had labels, but many didn't. Most of the smaller tubs appeared to hold snakes, who, being generally lethargic, didn't seem to be too cramped by their small spaces. In the largest tub, I could see the coils of an extremely large snake pressed up against the opaque sides; I figured that was the recently returned Julius Squeezer.

Meanwhile, the lizards were much more active than

the snakes. In some of the larger tubs, they were scrabbling against the plastic walls, trying their best to get out. One of the most active lizards was in a tub simply marked $$$$.

I glanced back at Summer and Rick. Rick's back was still to me. Summer met my eyes and gave me a slight nod, letting me know she would try to keep distracting him.

I took out my phone, shifted it to the camera, and cautiously opened the tub with the dollar signs. I was extremely careful to not make a sound, because the last thing I wanted was a steroid-enhanced mass of muscle like Rick getting angry at me.

There was a big iguana inside the tub, although it was a type I didn't recognize. It was stocky and mostly yellow, but with a few red patches on its skin. It looked much more banged up than any of the snakes had, with scabs and scars all over its body.

I quickly snapped a few photos of it, then closed the lid again.

Rick and Summer were still discussing price.

I opened another tub. There was a young crocodile in this one. I snapped a photo of it, too, then replaced the lid.

I felt terrible, keeping the animals trapped in their tubs. I wanted to yank every tub off the shelves, open them, and set all the animals free before Rick could sell them. But I knew that would be foolish. The animals probably wouldn't survive—and Rick would pound me into hamburger meat. I was lucky to have gotten the photos I had.

Behind me, Summer and Rick settled on a price of seven hundred dollars for a king cobra. Rick didn't seem the slightest bit surprised that a teenage girl had that kind of money. Maybe he had recognized Summer but hadn't let on. Maybe he had noticed us arriving in a private car with a chauffeur. Or maybe he was used to teenagers with plenty of cash showing up looking for exotic pets.

He dutifully typed her number into his phone. "What's your name?" he asked.

"Holly," Summer lied, not wanting to give out her real name.

Rick dutifully entered that into his phone as well, indicating that he didn't recognize Summer after all. "Here's how it works," he explained. "I'll call you when the shipment has arrived and set up a time for you to come back and get your snake. All sales are in cash—but with every purchase of an exotic from me, you get three free frodents. Also, I'll give you the proper paperwork, in case anyone starts asking questions, proving that this is all on the up-and-up."

"Is there a chance it's not?" Summer asked suspiciously.

"Of course not!" Rick said quickly. "But there are various agencies out there who police the illegal reptile trade, and in case one of them comes snooping around, you just show them the documentation, okay?"

"Okay," Summer agreed.

"Then we've got a deal. Now, I hate to rush a good customer like you, but I've got to prep lunch for the lion. So if you don't mind . . ." Rick opened the door that led back into the makeshift zoo.

Summer and I stepped back outside.

"Pleasure doing business with you," Rick said. "I'll be in touch." Then he shut the door behind us.

In the petting zoo, another child had lost her party hat to the llama.

Summer gave me a wide-eyed look. "Can you believe that guy? He just sold me a freaking cobra!"

"And he didn't even seem the slightest bit concerned that it might be dangerous. There's got to be like fifteen laws against that."

Summer bit her lip thoughtfully. "How do you think he has official documentation for them, though? Think he forges it?"

"I think we need to talk to Tommy Lopez," I said.

16

REPTILE LAUNDERING

While Tran drove Summer and me home, I texted Tommy the photos of the reptiles I had taken at Snakes Alive. He called back two minutes later.

I answered him on speakerphone so Summer could hear too. "That was fast," Summer said teasingly. "I thought you had important stuff to do."

"This just became my number one priority," Tommy said. "That lizard you took a photo of? It's a Galapagos land iguana."

"Really?" I gasped. "Aren't those endangered?"

"Extremely endangered," Tommy confirmed. "There might be only a few hundred of them left on earth. Zoos don't even have them."

"So how does Rick from Snakes Alive have one?" Summer asked.

"My question exactly," Tommy said.

"And who's going to buy it?" I added.

"Taco Cabana!" Summer exclaimed, so suddenly that I almost dropped the phone.

"What?" Tommy asked, sounding horrified. "Taco Cabana doesn't serve iguana."

"Sorry," Summer apologized. She pointed through the windshield so I would understand what she meant. Sure enough, there was a Taco Cabana by the access road ahead. It was a chain that sold cheap fast food, and Summer loved it. "There's one up the road and I'm starving. I didn't want to eat at Snakes Alive. That place probably *does* put all the old animals in the hot dogs." She leaned over to the front seat and asked Tran to pull off the highway.

I told Tommy, "Rick had all kinds of animals that he wouldn't let us take photos of. Like emerald tree boas and Mangshan pit vipers. He also said he'd sold lots of cobras already and has more coming in. . . ."

"Believe it or not, it's legal to deal all those snakes," Tommy said sadly, "assuming they've been captive-bred and not stolen from the wild."

"How would I know if they've been stolen?" I asked.

"What condition were the animals in?" Tommy said. "Did they seem to be in perfect condition, or did they have scrapes or scars?"

"They had scrapes and scars," I reported. "And the Mangshan had a kind of bent tail."

"Then they were probably caught in the wild," Tommy said. "A reptile that has been born and raised in captivity has been coddled. It hasn't been forced to deal with natural elements or survival of the fittest. But reptiles in the wild get banged up. It's part of life. And quite often, someone poaching them illegally and then smuggling them will bang them up as well."

Tran pulled off the highway and headed for the Taco Cabana. Summer sat back next to me. "So someone hunted down all these reptiles out in the wild and then shipped them all the way across the world to Snakes Alive, just so people can have them as pets?"

Tommy said, "The illegal pet trade is a lot bigger than most people realize. After drug smuggling, it's the biggest criminal business on earth. A person in a third world country can sometimes make more money poaching a Mangshan viper or a parrot or a pangolin than they can make in an entire year of honest work."

"Did you just say a pangolin?" Summer asked. "Like, a scaled anteater?"

Tommy said, "They're the most trafficked mammals in the world. We estimate that a hundred thousand might be getting poached every year. Most of them are being killed for their hides, but the pet traders are taking some too. Heck, the pet traders are taking *everything*: monkeys, lemurs, hedgehogs, tigers. And they'll do almost anything to sneak them into the country. About a year ago, some idiot on a passenger plane got caught with Asian cats stuffed in his backpack and pygmy monkeys in his underwear. Unfortunately, for every idiot who gets caught, there's at least a hundred smarter people who don't. Most of these animals aren't being smuggled in airplane luggage. They're being hidden in shipping containers and things like that."

"So why aren't you searching all the shipping containers?" Summer asked.

"Because that would cost billions of dollars a year and no one wants to give the Fish and Wildlife Service that much money," Tommy explained. "If we're lucky, we can search one container out of a hundred, and it'll be a cursory search at that."

Tran pulled into line at the drive-through for Taco Cabana.

"But compared to mammals or birds," Tommy went on, "it's easier to smuggle reptiles. They can go for days without eating and they like to den in small spaces, so they don't need much room. Smugglers pack them in shipping crates full of just about anything else and they sail right through customs. Although sometimes people still bring them on airplanes, in some of the craziest ways you can imagine. A couple years back, one guy actually stuffed his prosthetic leg full of Fiji iguanas."

"That's insane," I said.

"And yet it worked. In fact, the guy had done it dozens of times. The only reason he got caught was that he fell asleep with the leg sticking in the aisle and the flight attendant hit it with the drink cart. The leg came off and the iguanas started running loose all over the plane. They had to make an emergency landing."

We reached the order box for the drive-through. "Hold on," I told Tommy, and then Summer and I ordered tacos to go.

Once we had done that, Summer said, "Here's what I don't understand: Rick told us that he would give me documentation that these snakes had been acquired legally. How can he do that if these animals were smuggled into the country?"

"They've obviously been laundered," Tommy said.

Summer and I shared a look. Both of us knew what laundering was, more or less. It was the process of disguising something illegal so that it looked legitimate. I had generally heard of it being done with money; for example, a criminal might have a fake business to cover up the money he received from breaking the law. But I had never heard of it in this context before. "How do you launder a reptile?" I asked.

Tommy said, "The United States has pretty stringent laws about what animals can be brought in and out of the country, which is done to discourage smuggling. However, that's not the case with a lot of other countries. For example, Germany has much looser laws. So sometimes, a smuggler might send animals to a dealer in Germany, who will make official documentation claiming that the animals were captive-bred, and then ship them into the US. If we catch something at the border with documentation like that, there's nothing we can do, no matter how sure we are that the animal was really stolen from the wild. I'm betting your pal Rick is getting his animals from some source like that."

"He's *not* our pal," Summer said coldly.

We pulled up to the drive-through window. Summer handed over her money and we got our tacos. Tran pulled back onto the highway as we dug into our food.

"So what do we do now?" I asked, doing my best to be understood with my mouth full of taco. "How do we bring this guy down?"

"If he really has documentation for these animals, it might be hard to make something stick," Tommy said. "But maybe we can nail him for having that Galapagos iguana. I might be able to get a warrant based on the photo Teddy sent me. Although, to be honest, that might take a little while."

"Even though this guy's illegally selling an incredibly

rare, endangered iguana?" Summer asked, aghast. "What if he sells it to someone today?"

"Or what if an anaconda eats it?" I asked. "Rick's basically keeping those snakes in Tupperware. I'm surprised one hasn't escaped yet."

"Who says one hasn't?" Tommy replied.

"That'd be awfully bad for business," Summer said, and I found myself imagining several birthday parties at Snakes Alive going horribly wrong with the sudden appearance of a king cobra.

"The wheels of justice don't move that fast," Tommy explained. "There's a huge backlog in the courts. It's not easy to get a warrant, period—let alone quickly—especially not for something like reptile laundering. As far as the judges are concerned, it's not a priority. No one's life is in danger."

"The reptiles' lives are," Summer said, sounding offended.

"I'm on your side here," Tommy told her. "I wish things were different. But maybe there's a way to move things faster. You texted me that Rick has a shipment coming in soon?"

"In the next few days," I said.

"If we can catch the delivery in progress," Tommy said, "then the reptiles aren't technically in Snakes Alive, which means we don't need a warrant to get on the premises. Maybe, if it's a big shipment, the smuggler won't have documentation for *every* animal. Something might have slipped through the cracks. And, to be honest, I wouldn't mind nailing the smuggler in addition to Rick. I mean, you take Rick out, and our smuggler will find someone else to deal to. But if you take out the smuggler, then you've stopped a major pipeline of illegal animals."

"Rick's going to call me when the shipment's coming in!" Summer exclaimed. "If you're in the area, I can tip you off and then you can bust them!"

"Perhaps." Tommy didn't sound nearly as excited as Summer. "Assuming that Rick lets you know ahead of time, rather than after the fact."

"I'll bet I can get him to alert me beforehand," Summer said confidently. "I've offered seven hundred dollars for this cobra. That has to be more than most of his other clients are paying."

"Seven hundred?" Tommy echoed. "That's pricey all right. Okay, see what you can do."

"How much advance warning would you need?" I asked.

"The more, the better," Tommy replied, then told us, "Hold on." Someone was talking to him. He muted the phone for a few seconds, then came back on. "Sorry guys, but something has come up."

"Ooh!" Summer said. "What's going on? Are you busting some smugglers?"

"Nothing that exciting. But still, I've gotta go. Let me

know the moment you hear anything from Rick!" Tommy hung up.

I tucked my phone back into my pocket and started on my second taco. At the same time, Summer was taking her phone out. She barely had glanced at it before she sighed, "Oh no."

"What's wrong?" I asked, mouth full.

"There's been another zebra spanker copycat."

I looked at her blankly. "What are you talking about?"

"You haven't been paying any attention to the news?"

"I've been kind of busy lately. With trying to find a stolen tyrannosaur skull and getting attacked by an anaconda and all."

Summer gave a mock sigh of exasperation "You *really* need to go online more often." She handed me her phone. On her Twitter feed, the very first tweet was about someone else who had tried to spank a zebra in a zoo, this time in Cleveland.

I clicked on the link and quickly read the story. The perpetrator was a twenty-year-old college student who had been inspired by the original Zebra Spanker. While his friends filmed him, he had jumped into the zebra exhibit, intending to smack a male on the butt. However, he made one serious mistake that the original spanker had never made: He approached the zebra from the rear. Before he could even spank the zebra, it reared up and kicked him in the face, resulting in the loss of sixteen of his teeth—and all of his consciousness. Since the criminal was out cold, he didn't give Cleveland zoo security much of a chase when they came to arrest him. His friends had then posted the video on You-Tube anyhow, where it already had over a million hits.

"Wow. Just when you think people can't get any dumber." I handed Summer her phone back, then thought of something. "Did you say there was *another* copycat?"

"There have been at least eight so far. The original guy sparked a whole trend. And it's not only zebra spanking." She consulted her phone for details. "There's also been a rhino spanker in Omaha, an okapi smacker in Seattle, an aardvark tickler in Philadelphia, and a kangaroo puncher in Miami. Although that last one might not have been a true copycat. The guy was drunk and thought the kangaroo made a face at him. Apparently, this sort of thing happens a lot in Florida."

"What on earth are these people thinking?"

"They're seeing that the original guy got famous doing this, and they want to be famous too."

"And every time we watch the videos, we feed the beast," I said.

"Hey, it's not our fault this is happening," Summer said, sounding slightly offended. "It'll run its course, just like all fads do."

"And in the meantime, zoos all over the country will have to ramp up security and hope none of these idiots sue them because they got their teeth kicked out." I sighed sadly and looked out the window, thinking about all the awful things people did to animals.

We were approaching the motel where the volunteers for the dinosaur dig were staying. I could see the sign for it up ahead, beyond all the fast-food joints and Ruby's Taphouse. I must have reacted in some way, because it caught Summer's attention.

"What are you looking at?" she asked me.

"All the people from the dig are staying up here," I said.

"At that place?" Summer's voice was full of disgust. "Ugh."

"Not everyone can afford the Ritz-Carlton," I reminded her.

I kept my nose pressed to the window as we passed the motel. Since it was a warm day, Caitlyn and her friend Madison were sitting on deck chairs by the pool, wearing bikinis and working on their suntans. The only other person at the pool was Caitlyn's mother, who was reading under the shade of the lone patio umbrella. I could see them easily since the pool was right next to the access road, and Caitlyn was recognizable by the medical patch she had on her abdomen, covering her tyrannosaur bite. "The girls are still there!" I said, then turned to Summer. "Any chance we could stop to talk to them?"

"You want to stop to talk to some cute teenage girls in bikinis, and you think I'm going to be okay with that?" Summer asked, although I could tell she was only teasing.

"I just want to ask them some questions about Minerva," I said. "Well, really, I want to ask their mother some things."

"I thought your parents didn't want you investigating this any further."

"My mother told me not to chase after any more bad guys. All I want to do now is talk to some people by a swimming pool out in plain sight of every car on the highway. How much trouble could we possibly get in?"

Summer grinned. "I wouldn't mind talking to them too. Tran, take the next exit. We're making an unscheduled stop."

THE DIGGERS

Since the access roads only ran in one direction along the highway, we had to make a big loop to get back around to the motel, passing five fast-food restaurants, three gas stations, two convenience stores, an auto dealership, a go-kart track, and the future sites of four more businesses that were under construction.

Once again there were only a few cars in the motel parking lot. There wasn't much to do there during the day except use the pool, and the pool didn't seem that great. It hadn't been cleaned after the previous days' storms; dead leaves floated on the top and were piled in sunken clumps on the bottom. The roar of the cars passing on the highway was loud and constant. Caitlyn's mother looked as though she was there under duress.

She and the girls eyed our car suspiciously as we parked beside the pool.

Summer started to get out of the car, then changed her mind. She took off her baseball cap and shook out her hair.

"You want them to recognize you?" I asked.

"It's probably gonna happen anyway," Summer said with resignation. "Might as well take advantage of it. It's served us well so far." She pasted a smile on her face and stepped into the motel parking lot.

Caitlyn and Madison didn't seem very pleased to see me again, but they were downright thrilled to see Summer. They sat up in their patio chairs as she approached.

"No way," Caitlyn said. "You're Summer McCracken!"

"Hey," Summer replied. "I was out at the dig with you two yesterday morning."

The girls' jaws both dropped in shock.

"You were the one out on the rocks!" Madison exclaimed. "The one Dr. Chen had a cow about! We totally didn't recognize you!"

"That was the point," Summer admitted.

"I'm Madison," Madison said. "And this is Caitlyn."

"I'm Caitlyn's mom," Caitlyn's mom said. She seemed kind of starstruck by Summer too. "Call me Julie."

"Hi, Julie," Summer said brightly. "I know you've all met Teddy here."

I asked Caitlyn, "How's your bite doing?"

Caitlyn reddened, like she was embarrassed I had brought this up in front of Summer. "I had to get a few stitches, and the doctor says I can't swim for a day. Which stinks because it's *hot.*"

"So hot I might actually go into that pool," Madison said. "Even though there's stuff growing in it."

"We weren't sure what we were supposed to be doing today," Julie said, by way of explanation. There was a hint of frustration in her voice. "The original plan for this week was that we were going to be working on the dig every day. But now everything's been thrown out of whack. Dr. Chen told us she would get back to us this morning about what we're supposed to do, but . . . we still haven't heard from her. Which is why we're just sitting here. If I'd known we were going to have the whole day free, we would have gone to FunJungle."

"What's it like, owning that place?" Madison asked Summer excitedly.

"I don't own FunJungle," Summer replied. "My father does."

"But, like, it'll still be yours someday, right?" Madison pressed. "So, can you do anything you want there? Like ride the elephants?"

"I don't ride the elephants," Summer told her. "They're zoo animals, not my pets."

"Can you go on all the rides whenever you want?" Caitlyn asked. "And not even have to wait in line?"

"Not really," Summer said, although the truth was, if she had ever wanted to cut the lines, she could have.

While the girls were distracted hounding Summer with questions, I turned to Julie. "How did you end up on this dig?" I asked.

"We applied for it," Julie replied. She seemed excited to talk, like she was bored after sitting by the pool all day. "Although we didn't apply for *this* dig in particular. Because until a few weeks ago, this dig didn't even exist. We thought we'd be going to Montana. That's where most of the dinosaur fossils are."

"What did you have to do to apply?"

"Oh, it was easy. The University of Texas has it all set up online. We simply filled out some forms and sent in a deposit. Anita—that's Maddy's mother—and I thought the girls would love it. They've been friends since kindergarten and have always been crazy about dinosaurs. They used to pretend they were a stegosaur and an ankylosaurus who were best friends—"

"Mom!" Caitlyn snapped. "Too much information!"

"Sorry," Julie said, though she gave me a wink to know she found her daughter's embarrassment amusing.

"So the university just accepted you for this dig?" I asked.

"Not quite. At first, we were wait-listed. Turns out, this is a very popular program. The girls were very upset. We figured we'd be out of the running until next summer. But then, a couple weeks ago, out of the blue, we got a call from Dr. Chen. She told us that this tyrannosaur had just been discovered and that it was a huge find and that we were next on the dig list, so we had dibs if we wanted to come. Unfortunately, due to the timing, Anita couldn't make it, but I was still available, and the girls were so excited. We had never expected we'd get to excavate a *T. rex*! So we decided to move things around and come for a few weeks."

"Is that what happened with the other people on the dig too?"

"That's the case with the Carvilles and the Brocks. Those are the older couples. They've all known each other since college! They said they try to volunteer for a different thing every year: building houses for the poor, protecting sea turtles after they hatch, that sort of stuff. But they were on the wait list too, until Dr. Chen called. It was easy for them to come on the spur of the moment, because they're all retired and they don't live too far from here. Fort Worth, I think."

A semitruck roared past on the access road, going well above the speed limit. The pool was so close to the road that we could feel the slipstream as the truck went by.

"How about Jebediah Weems?" I asked.

"I'm not sure about him," Julie said. "He kept to himself. Talked to himself too. To be honest, the guy was kind of creepy."

"*Kind of* creepy?" Madison interjected. "The guy was a full-on skeeve."

"I don't think he came off the wait list," Julie clarified. "But given that he's Harper Weems's cousin, maybe he could simply buy his way onto any dig he wanted to."

I asked, "What did he talk to himself about?"

"I don't know," Julie replied. "To be honest, I didn't want to be close enough to listen. The dig wasn't that social anyway. I had expected that we'd all be talking the whole time we were out there and then sitting around the campfire at night, but the days were long and hard. And the heat! It would just drain you. We were always too tired to do much after dinner except go to bed. So I mostly spent my time with the girls. I didn't really even get a chance to know the Carvilles and the Brocks that well until two nights ago, when we all had drinks at Ruby's during the rain."

"But not Jeb?" I asked.

"He wasn't there," Julie said.

"Oh?" I did my best not to sound too suspicious. According to everyone at Ruby's, there had been nine people in the group at the bar that night. "I'd heard the whole dig was there."

"Not Jeb," Julie reported. "He said he wasn't feeling well and stayed in his room. Not that it was any big loss. It was probably better without him there. I think he made Dr. Chen a little uncomfortable too."

"Why's that?"

"I don't know. Maybe, like the girls, she thought he was a skeeve. Or maybe Dr. Chen was just more relaxed at the bar because we'd all had a few drinks. I mean, she was in top form that night, telling us all these crazy stories about her paleontology expeditions. It was fascinating. I wish the bar would have let the girls stay to listen to her, seeing as she was a little late to dinner."

"Late?" I repeated.

"She stayed behind at the site to make sure everything was prepped for the rain. We all had our concerns, leaving her there, but Dr. Chen's probably tougher than all of us put together. She demanded we all go on ahead so we wouldn't get caught in the rain. And I guess it didn't take her that long. After all, she was probably only an hour or so behind us, if that."

I frowned, despite myself. I had been thinking it was suspicious that Dr. Chen had been late to dinner, but an hour wouldn't have given her a chance to steal the skull, even if she'd had an entire team of helpers lurking in the bushes.

Meanwhile, Jeb Weems had been missing the entire night, which *was* suspicious. . . .

"Is something wrong?" Julie asked, noticing the look on my face.

"Er . . . no," I said. "What kind of stories was Dr. Chen telling?"

"There was one about her having to chase off some bone thieves in Australia with a boomerang . . . I can't really do it justice. I'm sure she'd be happy to tell you if you got to see her again. I tell you, the woman is incredible. She probably knows more about theropod dinosaurs than anyone else on earth."

As Julie talked, I noticed her hands. They had taken a beating during her time on the dig. Her fingers were covered with Band-Aids, as well as white patches of what I figured was plaster from the bone casts that she hadn't been able to scrub off. Her fingernails were worn down to the nubs. It was all a testament to the hard work she had done.

I glanced over at Madison's and Caitlyn's hands. They looked the same.

Caitlyn was grilling Summer about a famous singer that she was rumored to have dated. "You swear you two weren't a thing? Because all the websites said you two were a thing."

"I've never even met the guy," Summer said, sounding a bit exasperated. "So we couldn't have even remotely been a thing."

Summer never told anyone that she was my girlfriend,

because then it would drag me—and her private life—into the spotlight, and she didn't want either one of those things to happen. At times like this, I could see why that was a good idea.

But Summer's fame was certainly working to our advantage now. I had noticed that people tended to offer up information very quickly around her, eager to create a bond with her. I doubted the girls—or Julie—would have been quite so quick to talk to me had I shown up alone.

Given that, I decided to press Julie a little harder about how many people had actually been at the bar that night. "So, Dr. Chen was just hanging out, telling all those stories to only you and the Brocks and the Carvilles?"

"Oh, she had the whole bar listening to her," Julie replied. "The woman can really spin a story. Although I think half the men wanted to ask her out. I know the Brocks' son did."

"The Brocks' son?" I asked, a little quicker than I had intended.

Julie didn't seem to notice. "Yes, I think his name was Robert. He works in moving and storage down in San Antonio. When he heard that his parents weren't camping for the night, he came up to meet us all for dinner. And I'm sure he was glad he did. He was looking at Dr. Chen the way these two girls look at the high-school quarterback."

"Mom!" Caitlyn exclaimed. "Please stop talking."

Julie made a face at me that indicated she might have pushed things too far.

I tried to think of a way to ask more questions about Robert Brock without it seeming odd, but couldn't. So instead, I asked, "So what happens with the dig now?"

"I don't know," Julie replied. "I'm not sure Dr. Chen knows herself, the poor thing. She was devastated by that theft. Her room is right next to ours, and the walls in this place might as well be tissue paper. You can hear right through them. She was bawling last night. I hope we'll end up excavating the rest of Minerva. I mean, why leave a dinosaur in the ground? But if the skull is the most important part for science, then maybe excavating all the rest is just a waste of time." Despite the sadness in her voice, Julie's eyes lit up a second later as she noticed someone behind me. She waved and said, "Hey there!"

I turned to see the Carvilles and the Brocks crossing the parking lot from Ruby's, headed back to their motel rooms after lunch.

One of the older men was now on crutches. He was hobbling along, keeping his right leg off the ground.

"Afternoon!" the other man called back as the women waved hello. "Getting a little pool time in, I see!"

"Might as well," Julie called back. "Doesn't seem like we're digging today. Have you heard anything from Dr. Chen?"

"Not a word," one of the older women said. "If we don't hear from her by tonight, I think we'll go to FunJungle tomorrow."

"Sounds like a good idea," Julie said.

"How's your leg, Mr. Brock?" Caitlyn asked.

"All right," the man with the wounded leg replied. "The doctor said it ought to be as good as new in a few days. Guess I chose the right day to wound myself, though. I wouldn't be able to get out to the dig on these crutches."

"Speaking of which," his wife said, "you ought to get back to the room and elevate that leg a bit."

Everyone said some friendly good-byes, and the Brocks and Carvilles kept on going to their rooms.

Once they were out of earshot, I asked Julie, "What happened to Mr. Brock?"

"He tripped over a curb last night," she replied. "While leaving a restaurant."

I pointed to Ruby's. "This restaurant?"

"No," Julie said. "I don't know which one. Some place in San Marcos, I think. I guess he wrenched his ankle pretty bad. They had to take him to an urgent care facility."

"Do you know what time that happened?" I asked.

Julie's eyes narrowed suspiciously, like she was wondering why I would ask something like that. "Dinnertime, I guess."

"It was night," Madison offered helpfully. "They said he didn't see the curb in the dark."

"And it was late when they got back from the doctor," Caitlyn added. "Like midnight. We watched two movies in the room last night and we were almost done with the second when we heard them come back."

"Did you see Dr. Chen last night at all?" Summer asked.

"I know she watched a movie kind of late too," Madison said. "We could hear it."

"Like I said, the walls in this place are awfully thin," Julie explained. "We might as well be camping." She didn't seem nearly as suspicious about Summer asking questions as she was about me. The effect of Summer's fame again.

Summer probably could have kept questioning them for hours, but it seemed like we had bothered them enough. Plus, neither of us really had anything else to ask.

"Thanks for your time," Summer told them. "It was nice meeting you."

The girls seemed thrilled that Summer McCracken had said this to them. "Any chance we can get a selfie with you?" Caitlyn asked.

"Sure," Summer agreed.

Rather than selfies, I ended up taking the photos with their cameras. Julie even joined for a few of them. Summer dutifully posed and smiled with everyone, and then we said our good-byes and got back into the car.

"Mr. Brock hurt his leg last night," I said as we pulled back onto the access road. "When the guys and I were chasing the prowlers out by the dig site, one of them hurt themselves badly. We heard it."

"And you think it was *Mr. Brock*?" Summer asked. "He's old."

"That doesn't mean he can't be a criminal. He was in awfully good shape for an old person. All of them are."

"You're proposing they're a gang of geriatric dinosaur thieves?"

"It's possible. His son was here the night of the theft— and he works in moving and storage. Maybe he could have helped. Like providing a moving van."

"They would still have had to get the skull to the van in the first place," Summer reminded me. "And they were all at dinner the night Minerva was stolen. Everyone from the dig was—except Jeb Weems. So really, he was the only one who *could* have been involved."

"Unless Julie was lying about him not being there to make him sound guilty."

"And why would she do that?"

"To hide her own guilt, maybe . . ."

"So now you think the mom and the girls stole Minerva? Even though they have an airtight alibi?"

I shrugged. "I don't know what to think."

"Well, I do. Jeb Weems is the only one without an alibi for the night of the theft, and he's the cousin of Harper Weems, who is rich and smart enough to figure out how to pull off a crime like this. Plus, you found a pen from Weems Aerospace at the dig site, Jeb vanished mysteriously right after the crime was revealed—and everyone says he was a weirdo."

I considered all that, then nodded in agreement. "All right. He's definitely our best suspect."

"We ought to call Sheriff Esquivel and let him know what we've found."

"I don't think Sheriff Esquivel wants to hear from us."

"What about the other police officer, then? Officer Brewster?"

"She doesn't want to hear from us either."

Summer gave me a disappointed look. "Well, we have to tell *someone.*"

"I'm only saying they won't listen to *me.* Esquivel doesn't even think a crime has been committed, and Brewster has her own theories."

"Like what?"

I considered whether or not to reveal who Brewster's

number-one suspect was, but didn't want to upset Summer. So I lied instead. "I don't know. She wouldn't share them with me."

Summer took out her phone. "I'm calling anyhow. Maybe they'll . . ." She trailed off, noticing a text she had missed while we were at the pool. Her face immediately soured. "Oh."

"What's wrong?"

"I just found out who the police really suspect: They've issued an arrest warrant for my father."

THE WARRANT

A showdown was taking place in front of the FunJungle administration building when Summer and I arrived.

The admin building was in the employee section of the park, which tourists couldn't access. It was eight stories, which made it the tallest building for miles in any direction. J.J. McCracken's offices were on the top floor, although the building also housed executives for everything from park design to public relations to the legal division.

FunJungle security was blocking the front doors to the building, facing off against Sheriff Esquivel, Officer Brewster, and eight other police officers, which was probably the entire force for the county. It occurred to me that if the local criminals knew about this, they could be robbing the town blind.

Chief Hoenekker, who ran FunJungle security, stood directly in front of the doors, flanked by his team. Beside him was Pete Thwacker, the head of public relations, and Marge O'Malley. Hoenekker was rumored to be ex-military, and he certainly looked it, from his meticulous uniform to his perfect crew cut. Pete Thwacker was dressed for the TV cameras, as usual, in a bespoke three-piece suit. Marge O'Malley's arm was in a cast, due to her fall into the otter pit the day before.

The local press was also there. FunJungle was the biggest tourist attraction in that part of Texas, and virtually anything that happened there made the news, whether it was the birth of a new monkey or a rise in the price of soft drinks. So of course they had shown up. There were four camera crews and a dozen local reporters.

A large crowd of FunJungle employees had gathered, eager to see what was happening: maintenance staff, food service workers, veterinarians, keepers, and a few of the people who acted as FunJungle mascots. The actors had ditched the heads of their costumes so that they could see better; the disembodied heads were lying on the ground nearby, like someone had guillotined an elephant, a zebra, and an exceptionally large koala.

Summer and I had come there directly after hearing the news about her father. She had tried calling J.J. directly, but he was understandably busy, so she had then tried her mother, who had told us the story: Sheriff Esquivel's entire case against J.J. was based upon two pieces of evidence: (1) J.J. had known about Minerva and been in contact with the Bonotto family about buying the skeleton, and (2) J.J. had been in contact with a shady fossil dealer named Dmitri Kleskovich.

This last piece of evidence was news to Summer—and to her mother as well. Both assumed it had to be wrong.

As we arrived, Pete Thwacker was in the midst of making an official statement to the reporters, reading off a press release. "While it is true that we at FunJungle Wild Animal Park have been trying to obtain a dinosaur skeleton to enhance our award-winning immersive dinosaur experience at World of Reptiles, J.J. McCracken has never engaged the services of any criminal fossil dealers . . ."

"Oh boy," Summer said to me. "I guess Minerva's theft isn't a secret anymore."

"Then how do you explain this phone record from two weeks ago?" Sheriff Esquivel demanded, holding up a piece of paper. "It clearly shows a call from J.J. McCracken's offices to Dmitri Kleskovich, who has been accused of multiple counts of fossil smuggling!"

If Pete Thwacker was unsettled or caught off-guard by this, he didn't show it. Instead, he maintained his usual cool gravitas for the cameras. "Thousands of calls are made from

J.J. McCracken's offices every day. That is not proof that J.J. McCracken spoke to Mr. Kleskovich and it is definitely not proof that Mr. Kleskovich's services were engaged—"

"It's proof enough for us to issue a warrant for J.J. McCracken's arrest!" Esquivel yelled, waving the warrant in the air for the cameras.

The crowd erupted in excitement. Suddenly, everyone was talking at once.

Summer glared at Sheriff Esquivel hatefully. "Yesterday, he acted like this might not have even been a crime. But today, when he can make a big scene in front of the cameras, he's Sherlock Holmes. What a hypocrite. I'll bet he doesn't even believe Dad did this."

"Really?" I asked. "Then why . . . ?"

"He's never liked Daddy," Summer told me. "They went to high school together here and Daddy stole his girlfriend."

Sheriff Esquivel attempted to lead his officers into the administration building, but Chief Hoenekker and his security team refused to budge.

Hoenekker stepped directly into Esquivel's path and announced, "You do not have any jurisdiction here. Fun-Jungle is its own municipality and has its own police force."

"We're the law here!" Marge added. "Not you!"

Hoenekker grimaced at this, obviously displeased by Marge's attempt to help.

Before I knew what was happening, Summer was heading toward the admin building. She hadn't bothered to put her baseball cap and glasses back on, so word quickly spread that Summer McCracken herself was there. The crowd parted to let her through. Lots of people took out their cell phones to take photos and shoot video of her.

Summer made a beeline for Sheriff Esquivel. "If you *really* care about justice, then why are you hounding my father and not Harper Weems?"

The name of the young billionaire quickly rippled through the crowd; everyone was surprised and intrigued by the mention of her name.

"What's Harper Weems got to do with any of this?" Esquivel asked.

"Plenty!" Summer declared. "She was even more interested in buying that dinosaur than my father, her own cousin was working as a spy for her at the dig—and my friend found *this* at the scene of the crime!" She triumphantly held up the pen I had discovered the night before.

I grimaced, worried that Summer was making a mistake. After all, we didn't have any concrete proof that Jeb Weems had been spying for Harper, and the pen didn't really tie Harper to the crime at all. But Summer was obviously worked up about her father being accused of a crime, and determined to protect him.

The crowd ate it up. They all gasped at the sight of the pen—even though most of them couldn't possibly have been able to tell what it was from a distance.

Sheriff Esquivel couldn't tell either. "What's that?" he asked.

"Evidence!" Summer exclaimed. "Evidence that you didn't find because you didn't even bother looking for it!" She turned to the TV cameras and said, "Yesterday, Sheriff Esquivel questioned whether the dinosaur had even been stolen at all! In fact, he accused the owners and the entire dig team of making the whole thing up!"

All attention shifted back to Sheriff Esquivel, who squirmed uncomfortably before coming up with a new, aggressive plan of action. "Well, it wouldn't have made much sense to accuse J.J. McCracken of theft in front of his own daughter. You could have tipped him off and then he'd have fled the country on one of his fancy private jet planes."

The crowd didn't seem quite sure what to make of that. On the one hand, there was some logic to it; on the other, J.J. McCracken paid the salary of almost everyone there, so no one wanted to be caught agreeing with Esquivel.

Pete Thwacker did his best to come to J.J.'s defense; after all, that was his job. "For the record, J.J. McCracken has *never* been accused of a crime in all of his decades of business."

"Maybe he just hasn't been caught," Sheriff Esquivel

pronounced, then squinted suspiciously at the pen Summer was holding up. "How do I know that even came from the crime scene? Or that you didn't plant it there to protect your father?"

"Why don't you ask Teddy Fitzroy that question?" Summer shot back. "He's the one who found it while you were twiddling your thumbs." She scanned the crowd, then pointed me out. "There he is!"

Every head in the crowd turned toward me at once. I felt like a squirrel facing an oncoming truck.

"Teddy's the one who figured out who killed Henry the Hippo when no one else could!" Summer told Sheriff Esquivel. "And he figured out who kidnapped Kazoo the Koala and who was trying to shoot Rhonda Rhino and who stole Li Ping the Panda. He's ten times the detective you are!"

The crowd cleared around me and everyone looked at me expectantly. The TV cameras all pointed my way. So did a lot of cell phones.

I gulped, uncomfortable to be at the center of attention. "Summer didn't plant that pen at the crime scene," I told the crowd. "I found it there last night."

The crowd murmured in response. All eyes shifted back to Sheriff Esquivel.

"And what were you doing poking around a crime scene?" he asked accusingly.

"Yesterday, you said it *wasn't* a crime scene!" Summer reminded him. "You didn't even think that a crime had been committed."

"Oh, I knew a crime had been committed," Esquivel said defiantly. "And I knew who was behind it. As far as I'm concerned, J.J. McCracken is guilty."

"Well, as far as *I'm* concerned," Marge shouted, unable to hold her tongue any longer, "you're an idiot!"

Quite a few FunJungle employees cheered this pronouncement, which encouraged Marge and exasperated Esquivel.

"You can't talk to me that way!" Esquivel raged. "I'm an officer of the law!"

"Then why can't you find a clue the way Teddy can?" Marge taunted. "He's doing a better job than you and he's only thirteen! Maybe we ought to elect him sheriff next time!"

The crowd was enjoying this. Now several people heckled Esquivel, which rankled him even more. "One more word out of you," he warned Marge angrily, "and I'll haul you into jail along with J.J. McCracken!"

"I'd like to see you try, you dipstick," Marge challenged, and the crowd hooted in response, which pushed Esquivel too far.

"All right, that's it!" he shouted, and came at Marge,

reaching for his handcuffs. If he didn't have the jurisdiction to arrest J.J. McCracken, then he probably couldn't arrest Marge, either, but he seemed too angry to care.

Hoenekker quickly stepped between the two of them, trying to maintain some sense of decorum, while Pete Thwacker tried his best to call for order, and Summer kept waving the pen about. The crowd roared with approval. Everyone who had gathered hoping for a spectacle was now getting one. They surged forward to see what was going on, swallowing me up in the crowd.

Esquivel and Marge were ignoring Hoenekker and shouting at each other. And then Esquivel lost his cool and tried to handcuff Marge. Marge responded by slapping him across the face, and then all heck broke loose. Esquivel's officers and Hoenekker's officers all jumped into the fray.

The crowd started chanting "Fight! Fight! Fight!" like we were in my middle-school cafeteria, rather than watching a bunch of adults. Everyone was pressing in so closely now, I was finding it hard to breathe, as it was hot and humid and I was being pinioned against Eleanor Elephant, whose costume reeked as though it hadn't ever been washed (which really might have been the case). I pushed backward through the crowd while everyone else was pushing forward, and finally broke through into daylight again.

I took a few steps back to get a better view of what was

happening. I still couldn't see much over the crowd, but I did catch a glimpse of Marge O'Malley taking a flying leap off the administration building steps onto Sheriff Esquivel.

I could also see Pete Thwacker at the top of the steps, by the front doors of the admin building. I couldn't hear him over the roar of the crowd, but it looked like he was making a plea for sanity that was being completely ignored.

Summer was by Pete's side, thankfully free of the chaos, looking a bit concerned by what she had helped start. She noticed me and, unable to say anything over the crowd, took out her phone and typed quickly.

A second later, mine buzzed with a text. Loading dock?

I knew what she meant. Given the mob scene in front of the administration building, I couldn't get to the front doors. But if I circled around to the loading dock, there was another entrance.

Sure, I wrote back.

Summer sent me a thumbs-up emoji, then slipped through the front doors of the admin building while everyone was distracted by the chaos.

I started for the loading dock, but was only halfway there before I got another phone call from the Barksdales. And this time, they were in even more trouble than they'd been in the day before.

19

THE COBRA

I almost didn't answer the phone. I didn't really want to talk to the Barksdales. But I figured it might be a lead in the Snakes Alive case. Maybe Tim and Jim had heard when Rick's new shipment was coming in.

So I took the call. I was walking through the alley between the administration building and FunJungle's veterinary hospital, leaving the crowd behind. "Hello?"

"Teddy! It's Tim. Jim and I need your help."

"Again?" I asked, wondering exactly how one family could cause itself so much trouble. "What now?"

"We lost a cobra," Tim said.

"A cobra?!" I exclaimed. "Where?"

"In our house."

I heaved a sigh of relief, thankful that they hadn't

managed to lose a venomous snake at a playground or a shopping mall, where the lives of innocent people would be at stake. The only people in danger at the moment were the Barksdales, who had brought this on themselves.

"How did you guys get a cobra?" I asked.

"We returned the anaconda first thing this morning and that jerk Rick wouldn't give us our money back. He said he didn't give refunds. All he would do was offer us another snake in exchange."

"And you took a *cobra*? Even though they're deadly?"

"Of course! That's the whole point. The only other things Rick had to offer were these lame little green snakes and lizards and turtles. No girl is going to be impressed by a *turtle*." Tim said this last word disdainfully, the same way he might have said "body lice."

"Summer and Violet told you they thought having a cobra was idiotic," I reminded him.

"Rick says they were lying," Tim replied confidently. "He said all girls are attracted to danger."

I recalled what Rick had told me earlier that day, about how owning a venomous snake gave you a feeling of power. If I knew any people who would have been susceptible to that pitch, it was the Barksdales.

I arrived at the loading dock, which was on the back side of the administration building. An office supply truck was pulling out. I slipped past it and climbed the stairs to the security door by the dock. "What kind of cobra was it?"

"I don't know! What's it matter? It's a cobra!"

"Here's a reason it might matter: If it's a spitting cobra, it can shoot venom into your eyes, which can blind you."

"That's a thing?" Tim asked, sounding worried. "Rick didn't say anything about it being able to blind us! He only said it could kill us by biting us!"

"And you were totally okay with that?" I asked, incredulous.

"He said it probably wouldn't do that, as long as we were careful and didn't do anything dumb, like poke it with a stick. Which we didn't do. But then that idiot gave it to us in this stupid old plastic tub where the lid didn't fit on right. Only we didn't realize that until we got it home. We were setting up the cage for it and we turned around and the lid was off and it was gone."

Summer opened the security door from the inside, allowing me access to the administration building. As I stepped into the blessedly air-conditioned hallway, she pointed to the phone and whispered, "Who's that?"

I made the stupidest face I could.

"The Barksdales?" she asked, immediately understanding. "What now?"

I flipped the phone to speaker as we walked through the hall. Tim was still railing on about how losing the cobra in the house was Rick's fault. "He should have put the snake in some sort of special cobra-carrying case, not just a dumb plastic tub. Or at least he should have warned us to shut the latches again if we opened it."

"There were latches for the lid and you didn't use them?" I asked.

"Well, how were we supposed to know the snake could open the lid from the inside?" Tim asked angrily. "It's not like they have hands. Or arms. They're just tails with heads."

Summer looked at me with astonishment as she rang for the elevator. "They lost a cobra?" she asked, as quietly as she could.

I nodded my head, then said to Tim, "You're sure the snake is in your house?"

"No, it's at the movies," Tim snapped. "Of course it's in my house! That's where it escaped, dummy."

I didn't appreciate being insulted by someone asking for my help. I had half a mind to hang up right then and let Tim and his family all deal with the cobra themselves. Only, as much as I disliked the Barksdales, I didn't want them to die. And I worried there was a decent chance that one of them might kill the cobra before it could attack any of them.

The elevator door slid open and I got in with Summer. "I meant, have you kept all the doors to the house closed so that it can't escape?"

"Oh. Yeah. We did that."

"And where are you?"

"We're outside, keeping an eye on the house. Can you get over here soon? Our parents went out for groceries and Jim and I really want to catch this snake again before they come home."

The elevator reached the top floor, and Summer and I got off. "You want *me* to help catch the cobra?" I asked, startled.

"Yeah. You grew up in Africa. So you know how to do this, right?"

"Sure. I also know how to wrestle crocodiles and hypnotize elephants."

"Really?" Tim asked, completely missing my sarcasm. "Great. The faster you can get over here, the better. Dad's already super angry at us for what happened to his truck yesterday. If he finds out we've lost a cobra in the house, he'll kill us."

With most people, I might have assumed that was an exaggeration, but the Barksdales were a brutal bunch. "Tim, I don't know how to catch a cobra," I said, following Summer down the hall to her father's office.

"But you just said . . ."

"I was joking."

"This is no time for jokes, Teddy! There's a deadly snake in my house!"

That you put there, I thought, although I didn't say it. Instead, I said, "Why don't you call Rick? I'm sure he knows how to handle a cobra. He's the one who put it in the tub in the first place, isn't he?"

"Rick can't come out until tonight, after his shift is over. And he said it'll cost a hundred bucks for him to help catch the snake. We don't have that kind of money! We spent everything we had buying that stupid anaconda from him!"

Summer and I entered the reception area for her father's office. Lynda, J.J.'s receptionist, was on the phone herself. She waved happily to us and pointed to the couch, indicating that J.J. was busy, so we should make ourselves comfortable.

The reception area always had food and drinks for guests. There was a big bowl filled with snack-size packets of pecans, which was another one of J.J.'s businesses, and two big crystal dispensers, one with iced tea, and the other with ice water with grapefruit slices and mint leaves in it to give it a little flavor. (J.J. disparagingly called this "spa water," and claimed he found it a little too fancy for his tastes, but Lynda insisted that J.J. could stand to use a bit more class and made it anyhow.) Summer and I helped ourselves to tea and pecans while I thought over what to do.

It didn't seem like a terrible idea to let the Barksdales wait for Rick and fork over another hundred dollars to him. It might make them think twice about buying an animal they had no idea how to care for next time. But two things gave me concern:

First, Tim and Jim probably weren't patient enough to wait. Or they might fear their parents getting home first. If they tried to find the cobra, they could end up getting bitten, which would be bad. Or they might resort to leaving the door open and flushing it out of their house, at which point there would be a cobra on the loose in their neighborhood.

Second, even if Rick did show up to get the snake, then either Rick or the Barksdales would still have a cobra. If the Barksdales kept it, it was only a matter of time until something like this happened again—and if Rick took it back, he would probably unload it on some other unsuspecting person.

So I came up with another plan. "Let me call the snake team here. Maybe there's someone who can get out there and help you catch the cobra." I knew FunJungle had a team of experts on call to deal with any venomous snakes on the FunJungle property itself, as central Texas was home to rattlesnakes, cottonmouths, copperheads, and coral snakes, any one of which might pop up in a public area, where it could threaten the guests—or one of the exhibits, where it could threaten an animal. (Plus, there was still the chance that someday, the escaped black mamba might show up again.)

Tim was so relieved by my suggestion, he actually

dropped his aggressive attitude for once. "Really? That'd be great."

"There's one catch," I told him. "If they recover the snake, they'll need to keep it."

"What?" Tim exclaimed, already back to his jerky self. "No way! That's *my* snake, not theirs!"

"Would you rather it stay loose in your house, then?" I asked. "I'm sure your parents will love that."

"All right!" Tim agreed. "Fine. Whatever. Send them over. Fast." He relayed his address to me, even though I had been there only the day before, and hung up.

Summer looked at me and said, "Details. Now."

"Rick wouldn't give them their money back for the anaconda. So they traded it for a cobra instead. And then they didn't keep it locked up tight."

Summer rolled her eyes. "Those guys are the world's biggest idiots. For all we know, Rick didn't even give them a cobra. It was probably a sock with googly eyes glued to it."

"If only. A sock puppet can't kill anyone." I turned to Lynda, who had just hung up the phone. "Do you have the number for whoever handles the venomous snake removals at FunJungle?"

"Sure thing," she said. "But if they find that cobra, they won't bring it here."

"Why not?" I asked.

"There's no room for it. Do you have any idea how many requests FunJungle gets every day to take exotic animals off people's hands?"

"Dozens?" I guessed.

"*Hundreds*," Lynda corrected. "The operator catches most of the calls, but at least once a day, one makes its way through to me. Like J.J. McCracken has nothing better to do than adopt some knucklehead's used alpaca." She put a call on hold, then said, "From what I understand, even normal zoos get at least a few calls a day, but we're FunJungle, the most famous zoo in the world. Everyone who has an exotic animal they no longer know what to do with calls us, thinking we can take it. And there's a lot of people out there with exotic animals."

"Oh," I said, surprised that I hadn't known this.

"Holy cow," Summer said, looking at her phone. "Another copycat."

"Zebra spanker?" I asked.

"Warthog kicker. Baltimore. Apparently, the guy didn't know warthogs could fight with those tusks. He ended up in the hospital with a gouge in his leg."

"Serves him right," Lynda said with a sigh. "Hopefully his wound will get infected."

"Can I go in and see Dad now?" Summer asked.

"*You* can," Lynda told her. "He's always happy to see you.

But as for you"—she turned her attention back to me—"this isn't the best time. He's on the phone with his attorneys. As you're probably aware, he's having a rough day."

"I understand," I said.

Lynda plucked a Post-it note off her desk. "While you're here, though, it saves me the trouble of calling you. A friend of J.J.'s asked me to pass this on to you." She held out the note.

I took it from her, surprised anyone would go through J.J. McCracken to get to me. If anything, it seemed like things would work the other way around.

I was even more surprised when I saw who the message was from. "This is serious?" I asked Lynda.

"I talked to her myself," she said.

"Who's it from?" Summer asked, intrigued.

"Harper Weems," I replied. "She wants to have dinner with me tonight."

THE OTHER BILLIONAIRE

"To be honest," Harper Weems said, **"my cousin** Jeb is a weirdo."

It turned out that lots of billionaires knew each other. They had summits and get-togethers in fancy resorts where they would all meet and hang out. Sometimes they talked about positive things, like how to best use their enormous resources to help poor people or the environment. And sometimes they talked about things that only billionaires could, like how to upholster the seats on their private jets or what might be a nice island to buy.

So Harper Weems and J.J. McCracken knew each other, which was why, when Harper Weems wanted to talk to me, she asked J.J.'s office to pass the message along.

Harper had a team of employees who handled her social

media presence. They ghost-wrote her tweets and her blog posts and monitored how she was trending throughout the day. Thus, when Summer had accused Harper of stealing Minerva on live television—and then named me as the one who had uncovered the evidence—Harper had gotten wind of it right away. She had then called J.J., who had been keeping tabs on the news as well. They decided that J.J. would talk to Summer about why Harper was innocent, but Harper wanted to talk to me herself.

As it turned out, Harper wasn't too far away at the time. She had been visiting NASA's Johnson Space Center south of Houston, where the astronauts trained and where the operations for the International Space Station and other missions were headquartered. From there, she was heading to Weems Aerospace's private rocket testing facility, which was in northwest Texas. So it wasn't a big detour for Harper to drop by FunJungle for dinner.

To many people's surprise, Harper Weems, the wunderkind who was revolutionizing the entire aerospace industry, was afraid to fly. (She was often asked how someone with aviophobia could build rockets that were designed to take people into space. She inevitably replied, "The mechanics of plane flight and rocket flight are completely different. I don't want to fly like a bird. I want to visit the stars.") Harper did have a private jet that she begrudgingly used when she had to go overseas, but for shorter jaunts, she traveled in a tricked-out recreational vehicle.

The RV was called the Eagle 5, a reference to the flying Winnebago in *Spaceballs*, which was one of Harper's favorite movies. It was painted jet-black, with a custom-designed web of lights sheathing it that allowed Harper to make the RV look like almost anything she wanted to at night: a spaceship, a herd of elephants, one of the giant carnivorous alien worms from *Dune*. The Eagle 5 was a cultural phenomenon. Harper's social media specialists would send out alerts when it was about to pass through a town, and people had been known to line up along the roads hours ahead of time, waiting to see it.

However, the interior of the Eagle 5 was kept a secret. There were plenty of rumors about how Harper had decorated it. Fans thought it looked like the inside of the *Millennium Falcon* from *Star Wars*, or the *Nostromo* from *Alien*, or even a 1970s disco. But only the few lucky people invited aboard knew what it really looked like—and all of them were sworn to secrecy.

My parents and I were among those lucky people.

I had thought my parents might balk at our having dinner with Harper. After all, she was a potential suspect in a crime. But to my surprise, Mom hadn't merely been okay with the plan; she had been thrilled. I had always known my mother was impressed by Harper Weems, but I had never realized how much until that night. She was a complete fangirl, so excited that she could barely sit still at dinner.

The Eagle 5 was parked in the employee lot for FunJungle, which was a five-minute walk from our trailer in employee housing. There were no dinner options for fifteen miles except the restaurants at FunJungle, most of which only served fast food. So Harper had invited us to dine on the Eagle 5.

Since Harper didn't want to attract attention, the running lights on the Eagle 5 were turned off, so that it looked like a normal RV in the night. In fact, thanks to its dark paint job, it barely looked like *anything;* it was almost invisible in the parking lot.

As for the top-secret interior, it was designed like . . . a recreational vehicle. There was nothing space-age or sci-fi about it. "Honestly, there's not much you can do inside an RV," Harper had explained. "My designers came up with a few cool ideas, but they would have made the interior even more cramped than it already is." So Harper had simply stuck with the original design. She had upgraded the furnishings, putting a nicer bed in the master bedroom and fancy wallpaper in the bathroom, but it was just lipstick on a pig. We were obviously inside an RV.

It was still as nice as an RV could get, though. The

Eagle 5 was the top-of-the-line model, with modules that could extend out from the sides while it was parked, greatly increasing the room inside. And Harper's staff, which included two butlers and a gourmet cook, had followed in a second RV, which was outfitted with a gourmet kitchen. Thus, my family and I were being treated to a dinner of sustainable poached salmon in a lemon piccata sauce, along with locally sourced vegetables and freshly baked bread.

"Jeb has always been the odd duck of the family," Harper explained during dinner. "If anyone was going to go to the dark side, it's him."

"So you think *he* stole the skull?" Mom asked excitedly, hanging on every word Harper said.

"Not a chance," Harper replied. "He might have *thought* about it, but there's no way Jeb could pull anything like that off. The guy screws up everything. He's a complete nerf herder. Which is why I'm now implicated in this crazy scheme."

"What do you mean?" I asked.

Harper popped a forkful of salmon in her mouth. She had short hair cropped in a pixie cut, and was casually dressed in ripped jeans and a vintage *Star Wars* T-shirt. Even though she was worth at least a billion dollars, it looked like she had spent less on her clothes than I had. "Look, it's no secret that I'm successful, right? While Jeb is not. The guy barely finished high school, flunked out of college, and can't hold a job. But I'm his cousin, so he figures I'm his ticket to success. And I'll admit, I've been generous with family. I'm the one who bought him that camper. But that wasn't enough for him. He's always doing things to try to curry favor with me. And somewhere along the line, I might have told him I was in the market for a dinosaur."

"You only mean a skeleton, right?" Dad asked warily. "Because you've talked about bringing dinosaurs back, like in *Jurassic Park*."

"I said it would be *fun* to bring them back," Harper clarified. "But I never said it would be a good idea. *Jurassic Park* definitely shows there's a downside to pushing science too far. So sadly, no real living velociraptors or allosaurs for me. But I would definitely love to have a skeleton. Preferably a large theropod. Because, one: Theropods are awesome. And two: I can't fit a brachiosaurus in my house." She took a last bite of her dinner and shoved the plate away.

One of her butlers was standing at the ready. He immediately stepped forward, took the dirty plate, and whisked it off to the other RV to be cleaned.

Harper went on. "Full disclosure: I did not go about trying to get a dinosaur the right way . . . at first. I didn't realize there were all these shady fossil hunters, and the first guy I tracked down turned out to be one of the shadiest: Dmitri Kleskovich."

"The guy the police say J.J. McCracken called?" I asked.

"One and the same," Harper agreed. "In my defense—and J.J.'s—the guy markets himself well. And there aren't too many people out there claiming they can get you a *T. rex.* Which should have been a red flag, I suppose. I reached out to the guy, and he gave me the hard sell, saying that whatever I wanted, he could get, but when I did a little more digging, a lot of what he'd told me didn't hold water. On the surface, Dmitri has kept his nose clean. He's never been officially busted for a crime. But he has close ties to a lot of people who *have* been busted. The whole fossil business turns out to be a treacherous hive of scum and villainy."

"*Star Wars,*" Mom said, recognizing the quote. "How's it so bad?"

"It's kind of been bad since the beginning." Harper held out her wine glass to her second butler, who promptly refilled it. "Back in the 1880s, there were these two rival paleontologists, Edward Drinker Cope and Othniel Marsh. Cope worked for the Academy of Sciences in Philadelphia and Marsh worked for the Peabody Museum of Natural History at Yale. They ran all around the American West, grabbing as many fossils as they could and screwing each other over as much as possible. They *hated* each other. They stole from each other, sicced tribes of Native Americans on each other, and blasted each other in the press. And those guys were the forefathers of paleontology in this country.

"Things calmed down a bit after a few decades. There was a general consensus that any big dinosaur discovery ought to go into a museum. But then rich folks started getting the idea that they would like a dinosaur too."

"Rich folks like *you*," Dad pointed out.

"Jack!" Mom exclaimed, looking embarrassed that Dad had just insulted our host.

Harper wasn't offended, though. She raised her hands above her head in surrender. "Charlene, Jack is right. I'm partly to blame. I'd heard of a few other people getting their hands on skeletons, so I made the mistake of publicly stating that I wanted one too. Only, I hadn't done my research yet. Turns out, this influx of new cash has upended the whole system. Suddenly, fossils are worth big money, and when money is at stake, people start behaving very badly. Like this guy Kleskovich. He and other fossil raiders go into countries with far weaker laws than the US, bribe everyone they can, and make off with everything. Or worse, they let some other poor schmoes do the hard work digging the bones out, and then simply steal them."

"But Minerva wasn't in another country," I said. "She was right here. Are these thieves operating here, too?"

"Until Minerva vanished, I didn't think so," Harper said. "Generally, the fossil hunters in America work more legitimately: They buy a property in an area known for being rich in fossils, and then basically mine it for parts. Technically, anything you find on your property belongs to you, even if it's a dinosaur. Now, I'd heard of some small-time thefts: thieves getting into established sites and making off with a bone or two. But nothing like what happened with Minerva. I mean, a theft like that takes some serious guts—and some major brainpower."

"How do you think they did it?" Mom asked.

Harper shrugged. "Beats me. I haven't been out to the dig site, but I got the skinny from Jeb, and . . . man, it sounds impossible. I mean, I'm a certified genius and I can't figure out how this happened."

"Jeb told you about the site?" Dad asked. "I thought you said he was acting on his own."

"He *was*. But when he called to tell me he'd stumbled across a *T. rex*, I had to listen. Ooh! Dessert!" Harper sat up excitedly as the first butler entered the RV bearing a warm apple pie and a tub of vanilla ice cream. "You guys left room for dessert, didn't you?"

"I did," I said quickly.

"Serve the young man," Harper told the butler, then launched back into her explanation. "Jeb tracked down Minerva on his own. He had called a bunch of paleontology departments, looking for openings on digs, and this one was in the right place at the right time. He was told there was a wait list, but he dropped my name to jump the line. Universities tend to like to work with the cousins of people who can make big donations. I guess this Dr. Chen called him back and invited him on board, so he made a beeline across the country to help out. The moment he heard it was a *T. rex*, he flipped. He sent me like a dozen emails a day. I didn't believe him at first because, well . . . Jeb gets a lot of things wrong. He once thought he was buying the original time-traveling DeLorean from *Back to the Future* and ended up with a Ford Pinto with vacuum cleaner parts welded to it. But after Dr. Chen and her team excavated the skull, Jeb sent me some photos, and . . . it was a *T. rex*, all right. So, I cracked. I called the Bonottos to ask if Minerva was on the market."

"You called the Bonottos?" I asked, surprised. Neither Sage nor his parents had mentioned that to me.

"Oh yeah. And they told me that J.J. McCracken already had an interest in her. But they claimed they hadn't made a deal yet, so if I wanted to make a higher bid, I was welcome to."

"So what happened?" Mom asked.

"I called J.J.," Harper said. "There's no point in getting into a bidding war with a friend. I thought maybe we could work out some kind of arrangement."

"Like what?" I sat back from the table so the butler could place a slice of apple pie à la mode in front of me.

"Don't let that melt," Harper told me. "Dig in."

I didn't need to be told twice. It was delicious.

"You mentioned an arrangement?" Dad asked, not about to let Harper change the subject.

Harper's mouth twitched, like maybe she wasn't happy Dad had caught her. It took her a moment to collect her thoughts. "It never happened. J.J. and I talked, but then something came up and he had to go. And then I got all wrapped up in this rocket test I'm on my way to. Before I knew it, a week had slipped by. And then, suddenly, Minerva disappeared."

"And so did Jeb," I added. "The very next day."

"Yes," Harper said, resigned. Her butler started to place pie in front of her, but she pointed to Mom and Dad, indicating they ought to get served first. "Like I said, he's a dimwit. Jeb has a bit of a criminal record. He's been busted for shoplifting a couple times, and once, he got arrested for public indecency. He thought he was on a nude beach, but it wasn't. And so, when a crime occurred, he thought it would be best not to call attention to himself. So he took off, which was the perfect thing to do to call attention to himself. He's just over the border in Mexico, lying low until the heat blows over on this. Nuevo Laredo, I think."

Mom dug into her pie and moaned. "Oh my. This is amazing."

"My pastry chef trained in Paris," Harper said proudly.

"You have your own pastry chef?" I asked, astonished.

"It's one of the best things about being a billionaire," Harper told me. "Well, in the top hundred for sure."

Dad said, "Do you think Dmitri Kleskovich might have been involved in the theft of Minerva?"

"It's possible," Harper conceded. "Although I'd be surprised. The guy usually plays it safe, and it'd be really ballsy to steal something in America. But then, this *is* a *T. rex* skull. Those are rarer than Vibranium. So maybe he thought it'd be worth the risk. I still have no idea how he would have done it, though."

"There must be other shady dealers besides Kleskovich," Dad suggested. "Maybe it was one of them."

"Also possible," Harper agreed.

"Do you know who they might be?" I asked.

"That's not really my area of expertise, but hold on." Harper called out, "Computer, get me the contact information for Arin Singh."

"Yes, Commander," a computerized voice answered. "Sending it to your phone now."

A second later, Harper's phone pinged as the information arrived.

"Dr. Singh is one of the best paleontologists on the planet," Harper told me. "And one of the leads on combating fossil theft. He was the one who warned me about working with Kleskovich. I'll give you his number. Just call him up and mention my name. Maybe he even has an idea or two about who swiped Minerva. Only, don't call until tomorrow morning. He's on a dig in South Africa and it's the middle of the night there."

"Thanks so much," Mom said.

"My pleasure. You folks are super cool," Harper said. "Hey! I just got some new plans for a potential space hotel. But you need to use my virtual reality system to see them. Want to check it out? It feels like you're there."

"I'd love to!" Mom exclaimed, then grew slightly embarrassed. "Though maybe Teddy should go first."

"I can wait," I said.

"All right," Mom said, then looked to Harper expectantly. "How do we do this?"

"The rig's back in my bedroom," Harper said. "Which is also sort of my office. And my virtual reality lab. There's not too much space on this RV. Come on back and I'll hook you up."

Mom practically sprang from her seat to follow Harper.

Once they were out of earshot, Dad leaned over to me and whispered, "What do you think of Harper?"

"She's nice," I said. "But . . ."

"But what?"

I looked around the RV. Both the butlers had left to clean our dishes, but I wondered if there might be any listening devices around. If anyone had their RV wired like that, it was Harper Weems. So I lowered my voice and whispered, "She acted kind of weird when you asked about her arrangements with J.J. I don't think she's telling us everything."

"No," Dad agreed, casting a skeptical glance after Harper and Mom. "I don't think she is either."

THE LONG NIGHT

Mom and Dad suggested that we could all call
Dr. Singh in the morning. Both felt that handing the number over to Sheriff Esquivel or Officer Brewster would be the
same thing as throwing it away. Given the events of the day
before, the local police seemed to have their minds made up
that J.J. McCracken was behind the theft.

J.J. hadn't been arrested; his lawyers had prevented that
from happening. Dad suggested that Sheriff Esquivel had
probably never expected to make the arrest anyhow; he was
just making his accusation against J.J. as public as possible.
Whatever the case, it certainly hadn't worked out the way
Esquivel had hoped. The fracas in front of the FunJungle
administration building made the news all over the country, turning both our local police and the FunJungle security

team into a laughingstock. One clip had gone viral: Marge O'Malley had attempted to deck Officer Brewster, but missed and taken out Zelda Zebra instead.

More importantly, the secret of Minerva's existence was now out. The news of the stolen skull was the lead story on every news network. The Bonottos, Julie, Caitlyn, Madison, the Carvilles, and the Brocks all appeared on various TV reports, sadly discussing the dig and the fate of Minerva. Questions were raised about J.J. McCracken and Harper Weems, both of whom issued official press releases proclaiming their innocence and expressing their condolences.

I couldn't sleep that night. My mind was racing, thinking about all the possible suspects in the case.

The Weems family still seemed like the most obvious choice. Even though Harper Weems had gone out of her way to explain her innocence to us, Dad and I still had a nagging feeling that she wasn't being completely honest. (Mom didn't suspect her at all, however; she was crazy about Harper and she'd had so much fun touring the future space hotel on Harper's VR system that we'd had to forcibly drag her home.)

But even if Harper was innocent, that didn't mean Jeb was too. According to his own cousin, he had been arrested for theft before. And he was lying low in Mexico. So maybe he had tipped off some criminal fossil dealers in return for a cut of the profits.

Then again, any of the other people on the dig could have tipped off criminals too. Caitlyn had tried to make off with a rare tyrannosaur tooth. Mr. Brock had mysteriously hurt himself on the same night that a suspicious visitor to the dig site had run into a tree—and he had a son in the moving business. And then there were the Bonottos . . .

They were in financial trouble and, by Sage's own admission, hoping to sell the skull for a profit. They had been secretly taking offers from both J.J. McCracken and Harper Weems, looking to drive the price up. So maybe they had found a third party willing to buy the skull and then had merely *claimed* that it had been stolen.

Dr. Chen was another question mark. Where was she? Why hadn't anyone seen or heard from her? She certainly seemed to be distraught over the theft, but maybe that was an act—although I couldn't imagine why a renowned scientist would arrange for her own amazing find to be stolen. Unless maybe she was in some sort of financial trouble too.

I also couldn't completely rule out J.J. McCracken. Even though Summer was my girlfriend, I knew her father had been involved in some questionable business dealings. Maybe he simply wanted a *T. rex* skeleton for his living room, rather than one to display at FunJungle.

And then, there was the very good possibility that someone else entirely had been involved. Maybe Dmitri Kleskovich or another group of fossil thieves had found out about the skull. Jeb Weems had been posting about the dig on his website without permission. He hadn't given away the exact location, but a savvy thief who knew their way around the paleontology world could have probably figured things out.

Or perhaps word had leaked out another way. Maybe someone else from the dig had also violated the secrecy agreement and written an e-mail or text to the wrong friend. Or maybe J.J. or Harper had let word of Minerva slip to another billionaire who had the means to steal the skull.

None of which explained how the crime had even been committed in the first place. I found myself wondering about the two suspicious items my friends had found near the dig: the wooden plank with the hole in it and the neatly cut log. Had those been involved in the theft somehow, or were they merely random items? And if they were involved, how had they been used?

Was the pen from Weems Aerospace evidence against the Weems family? Or was someone trying to frame them with it? Or had Jeb simply dropped it by mistake?

And if all that wasn't enough to lose sleep over, I also had snakes on the brain.

After dinner I had received a message from Lynda in

J.J. McCracken's office. The snake control team had visited the Barksdale home and successfully located the escaped cobra, which they had found coiled in a pile of dirty laundry. Although FunJungle had a general policy of not taking people's pets, they had made an exception in this case, as the cobra in question had turned out to be a young Mandalay spitting cobra, which was rare and endangered. Given the scarring on it, the snake team determined that it had certainly been caught in the wild and smuggled into the United States.

Sadly, the team had not been able to take the baby alligator, as there was no room for another alligator at FunJungle, but they had given the boys a stern warning that maybe they should think twice about owning an animal that could grow to fifteen feet in length and would require a considerable amount of meat every month.

I wondered how many other people Rick had illegally sold reptiles to. There had been a decent number of animals in the back room at Snakes Alive, and yet he had claimed he was low on stock, indicating that he generally had a lot more to sell. Had most of those animals been captured from the wild and smuggled into the country? When was the next shipment coming in? And how long would it be before someone like the Barksdales got killed by something they had bought?

I finally gave up on sleep, got on my computer, and did some research into reptile trafficking. The numbers were much bigger than I had imagined. The popularity of reptiles had surged in the US in recent years; nearly five million homes were estimated to have one. And a significant portion of those were estimated to have been illegally captured in the wild. Even worse, for every reptile that made it into the country alive, an equal number were killed in the process, usually due to the horrible conditions they were often subjected to. To get them past customs, the poor animals were crammed into small containers with poor ventilation. They ended up crushed, frozen, overheated, suffocated, dehydrated, or starved to death.

As for the animals that did survive, some were certainly well-cared for and even loved by the people who bought them, but others were mistreated or dumped into the wild by people who discovered that owning them was far more difficult than they had expected. Often, the animals died in their new habitat, but sometimes, they thrived at the expense of local animals. For example, in Florida, Everglades National Park was under siege by Burmese pythons that had been illegally released there. The pythons could grow almost as large as anacondas, and without natural predators, their population had exploded. They were gobbling up everything, even the alligators, and some parts of the national park had been rendered almost completely devoid of life.

The whole thing was shocking and unsettling to me. Thanks to the illegal pet trade, ecosystems all over the planet were being destroyed, some by having species stolen from them, others by having invasive species introduced into them. And all so that someone could have a fancy pet, when it turned out that there were plenty of healthy, captive-bred animals available—not to mention all the animals they could adopt. A quick online search proved that in central Texas alone, there were hundreds of dogs, cats, and even more exotic animals like reptiles and amphibians in need of new homes.

While I was at it, I checked up on the members of the dinosaur dig. Jeb Weems had been uncharacteristically silent on his blog; he hadn't posted in days. I tracked down several social media accounts for Caitlyn, Madison, and Julie; now that the secret about Minerva was out, they had felt free to start posting their photos from the dig, which had all garnered hundreds of likes and comments by friends impressed that they had been involved in the discovery of a *T. rex* skeleton.

The Brocks and the Carvilles either hadn't posted anything, or I hadn't been able to find it. But I did find Robert Brock, whose website proclaimed that he owned an entire fleet of moving vehicles for every need, and over 1,200 secure storage units. Each unit was big enough to house the stolen skull.

Eventually, I returned to my bed, but still tossed and turned. When I finally did fall asleep, I was plagued by dreams of cobras, anacondas, and tyrannosaurs.

I awoke around seven, but felt as though I hadn't slept at

all. I headed into our tiny kitchen to find both my parents awake. Dad was scrambling eggs while Mom read the paper online. (My parents would have preferred a real newspaper every morning, but getting delivery to FunJungle employee housing had proven to be impossible.)

They both greeted me cheerfully, although I got the idea neither one of them had slept that well either.

"Any chance we can call Dr. Singh?" I asked. "It's well into the day in South Africa."

"Sure thing," Mom said. Then she brought up the number Harper Weems had given her and dialed it.

Dr. Singh answered on the third ring.

"Dr. Singh," Mom said, "my name is Charlene Fitzroy. I was given your number by—"

"Harper Weems?" Dr. Singh finished. "She told me to expect your call. I've been waiting to hear from you. Any friend of Harper's is a friend of mine."

Mom cupped her hand over the phone, beaming. "Harper thinks we're friends!" she said excitedly.

"Fangirl later," Dad told her. "Talk now."

"Right." Mom got back on the phone. "Did Harper explain what we would be calling about?"

"Yes. She said you would be interested in any illegal fossil dealers that might be operating in Texas. This is all about that stolen tyrannosaur that's on the news?"

"You've heard about it there?" I asked.

"That's my son, Teddy," Mom told Dr. Singh. "And my husband, Jack, is also listening."

"Ah yes," Dr. Singh said. "Harper thought I might be hearing from all of you. She had a very good time meeting you last night, by the way."

"Really?" Mom asked, getting excited again.

"I heard you got to see the virtual plans for her space hotel," Dr. Singh said. "That must have been amazing."

"It was incredible!" Mom exclaimed. She might have launched into a recount of the whole evening, but Dad put a calming hand on her shoulder and said, "Charlene, focus."

"So, yes, word of the stolen tyrannosaur has made it through to here," Dr. Singh said. "Although I'm not sure how much the press got right. They're saying the entire skull disappeared from an active dig site, even though it was over three miles from the closest road."

"That part is true," Dad said.

"Really? My goodness. That is quite unprecedented."

"Why's that?" I asked.

Dr. Singh said, "Usually, thieves hit sites that aren't being actively excavated. They either try to beat the paleontologists to the sites in the first place, or they rob the sites during the off-season. Due to weather and financial issues, most digs only operate for a few months a year. We generally can't remove all the fossils during that time, so many have to be left behind for subsequent excavations. That's why we go to such lengths to keep our sites secret. But perhaps, for a tyrannosaur skull, someone was willing to take a great risk. If this truly was a tyrannosaur in Texas, that would be a tremendous loss for science."

"That's exactly what Dr. Chen said," I told him.

"Ellen Chen from the University of Texas?" Dr. Singh asked.

"Yes," Mom said. "Do you know her?"

"Oh yes! We are very good friends. I was with her at a paleontology conference just last week."

"You were in Texas last week?" I asked.

"Texas? Goodness, no. This was in Berlin."

I shared a look of concern with my parents.

"Ellen Chen was in Berlin last week?" Dad asked.

"Yes, although she almost didn't make it. It's extremely hard to get to Germany from Mongolia."

"Mongolia?" Mom repeated.

"Where she's digging," Dr. Singh said. "Just like she has for the past ten years. Surely you must have known that if you've talked to her?"

My mind was suddenly racing, trying to make sense of how Dr. Chen could have been in Mongolia at the same time she had been in Texas, overseeing the dig at the Bonotto ranch. There was only one thing I could think of that made sense, and once that piece of the puzzle was solved, the other pieces quickly fell into place.

"We saw Dr. Chen *here*," Dad was telling Dr. Singh. "Only two days ago. She's the one who's in charge of the tyrannosaur dig."

"No, no, no," Dr. Singh replied. "That can't be. Ellen is in Mongolia excavating a new species of theropod. She was raving about it last week."

The picture of what had happened was becoming clearer and clearer to me. Everything that had been stumping me for the past few days now began to make sense.

My parents were putting things together as well. "I'm sorry, Dr. Singh," Mom said. "But we need to go."

"Don't you want my list of fossil thieves?" Dr. Singh asked.

"Not right now," Mom said. "I think we're okay. Thanks for your time." Then she hung up and looked to Dad and me. "Are you guys thinking what I'm thinking?" she asked.

"Our Dr. Chen is an impostor," Dad said.

"And she stole the skull," Mom added.

"Not quite," I told them. "I think I know where it is."

22

THE EVIL SCHEME

"The best way to commit a crime," I told the Bonottos, "is to commit one you have a perfect alibi for."

Back at my house, it had only taken a few minutes to confirm my theory about what had happened. Dad had already downloaded the hundreds of photos he had taken at the dig site to his computer. We had searched through all the photos to find the ones that mattered, and then sent the evidence to our phones.

Then we had called the Bonottos and told them we were on our way over. As ranchers, they were up early. In fact, Sage's father was already out, working the cattle on horseback.

We got to the ranch as fast as we could. Luckily, all the traffic at that time of day was heading toward FunJungle rather than away from it, so we made good time, although

Dad still had to exercise caution going up the Bonottos' driveway. Much of it had dried out in the summer heat since the storm, but many big patches of mud remained.

When we arrived at their house, Sage and his mother already had the ATVs prepped for us; Sage's father was going to meet us at the site. So now, I was explaining my theory of what had happened as we raced across the ranch, using the radios mounted in the helmets to talk to everyone, although I still had to yell to be heard over the ATV engines.

Since this was my third time heading to the dig site in as many days, I was starting to know the route. As we sped through the woods in the early morning, we startled grazing herds of deer and spooked flocks of birds into the air.

"How can you commit a crime when you have a perfect alibi?" Sage's mother asked me.

"You make everyone *think* the crime has been committed, when it hasn't," I said.

"Teddy, you're getting ahead of yourself," Mom told me. "Start at the beginning."

"Okay." I hit a muddy patch of ground on the ATV and slewed a bit, kicking up a spray of muck. "Mrs. Bonotto, how did you end up in touch with Dr. Chen in the first place?"

"We called the paleontology department at the University of Texas," Sage's mother said. "We told them what we had found, and then Dr. Chen called us. She came out to visit the site that day and got very excited and asked if we could start excavating right away. We agreed, and she had the dig going within two days."

"Did you ever ask her for any identification?"

There was a pause while Mrs. Bonotto thought about that. "Well . . . no. But we had looked her up online before we called the university. Her credentials were incredible—"

Sage interrupted. "Are you saying that the woman here wasn't really Dr. Chen?"

"Yes," I answered. "It was only a thief who *looked* like Dr. Chen. Although, to be honest, it's not like they're twins or anything. The photo of Dr. Chen on the university website isn't great. It's kind of grainy. And she's wearing a hat and sunglasses in it. But the woman who came here looked enough like her to pass. Because who would ever suspect an impostor to show up?"

"I . . . I can't believe this," Mrs. Bonotto stammered. "It never occurred to me to confirm she was who she said she was. I mean . . . we called the university and then she called us! Are you saying the University of Texas is corrupt?"

"No," I said. "Except for the receptionist who took your call. He never passed the message on to the real Dr. Chen, who's in Mongolia right now." I assumed it was the same receptionist who I had talked to the day before. The one who had told me that Dr. Chen was in the field. That was probably what he told everyone who called, unless it was someone who knew Dr. Chen personally.

"Mongolia?" Sage echoed. "That's on the other side of the planet!"

"Exactly." I drove over a portion of the path so rutted, it was like a washboard, and my voice vibrated as I spoke. "The real Dr. Chen is in one of the most remote places imaginable, and she's there for months. She's the perfect person to impersonate, because there's almost no chance that she's going to show up back here all of a sudden."

Mom said, "Our guess is, the fake Dr. Chen paid off the receptionist at the university to feed her tips, waiting for an opportunity like this to present itself."

We emerged from the woods into a clearing, where another herd of deer was grazing in the morning cool, six females and an equal number of fawns, with one big buck. They had heard us coming and were all on the alert, ears erect, noses twitching, eyes locked on us. Then the buck bolted and the rest followed, bounding away across the grass and melting into the forest.

"I can't believe this," Mrs. Bonotto repeated. "There's no way . . . We talked to our Dr. Chen at length. She knew *everything* about dinosaurs, and how to run a dig . . ."

"It's still her area of expertise," Dad explained. "The same as the real Dr. Chen. The fake one just does it illegally."

Sage asked, "So her whole team was in on it too?"

"No," I answered. "They were fooled like the rest of us. They had applied to be on another dig and were wait-listed. And Jeb Weems had recently called and asked if there were any digs he could be a part of. The receptionist at the university must have given the fake Dr. Chen their numbers. When she contacted them to help on the dig, they didn't think to question her either. They were just excited to be involved."

Dad said, "They all showed up where and when the fake Dr. Chen told them to and went to work. It probably looked like a perfectly normal dig to them. And even if it didn't, they were all first-time volunteers, so who would even know what a dig was supposed to be like?"

"They were all sworn to secrecy about the site," Mom added. "And they were camping out here, cut off from society. The person they *thought* was Dr. Chen was their authority figure. They were expecting her to tell them what to do. So they did what she asked and didn't question anything."

"I can't believe this," Mrs. Bonotto said again. She had been saying it over and over, like she was in shock. "How could we have been so stupid?"

"It *wasn't* stupid," Dad assured her. "You called the university and left a message for Dr. Chen. Someone claiming to be Dr. Chen called you back and sounded like the right person. *I* would never have thought she was a fake."

"No one would have," Mom said supportively.

"But how did she steal Minerva?" Sage asked. "Even if she was an impostor, it's not like she had superpowers."

"She *didn't* steal Minerva," I replied. "Not yet, at least."

Sage looked back over his shoulder at me, like he was trying to tell if I had gone crazy. "If she didn't steal the skull, then why is it missing?"

"I'll explain," I said, although I had to hold off on that for a few moments, as a large herd of cattle was blocking our path. Unlike the deer, they didn't feel threatened by us. Instead, they didn't even seem to care that we were there. Sage's mother had to shout to get them to move out of the way, and even then, we still had to find a meandering path through the stragglers.

I described what had happened while we slalomed through the cattle. "Obviously, there were a lot of difficulties with stealing the skull. Not only was it big and heavy and miles from the road, but the dig team was camping nearby every night, so it was impossible to move without being seen. But if Dr. Chen could make everyone *think* the skull had been stolen, then that changed things."

"How do you make someone think a skull has been stolen without stealing it?" Sage asked.

"The fake Dr. Chen waited for a night where a big storm was coming," I said. "Then she shut down camp and sent everyone off-site to a motel while she stayed behind, claiming to be preparing the site for the rain. Once everyone was gone, she moved the skull. Not very far, because she didn't have much time, but far enough to confuse everyone. That's what that cut log we found two nights ago was for, Sage. It was a roller. And if you had about ten more of them, then you could roll the skull along on top of them. Exactly like the ancient Egyptians moved the blocks for the pyramids."

Mrs. Bonotto said, "Still, Dr. Chen couldn't have done that by herself . . ."

"No," I admitted. "But she probably only needed two or three other people, and I'll bet she's had a whole team lying low around here for a while. The ones who helped that night were most likely waiting in the woods for the diggers to leave on the night of the storm. I'm sure they had already cut the logs for the rollers ahead of time. And when they were done with them, they chucked them into the river, figuring the evidence would sink or be carried way downstream."

"But even if they used rollers," Mrs. Bonotto said, "they still would have left a track."

"The wooden plank!" Sage exclaimed suddenly. "The one we found with the holes in it that the rope had gone through! They made that ahead of time too, then dragged it over the ground to smooth over their tracks!"

"Right," I agreed. "The ground wasn't muddy before the storm, so it wouldn't have been too hard to erase a short set of tracks in the dirt. And then the rains would have washed away any remaining evidence. They only spent about an hour there. Then the fake Dr. Chen went to the motel and spent the night with everyone at Ruby's, giving herself an alibi."

We finally made it through the cattle and were able to pick up speed again. We revved our engines and hauled through the forest, closing in on the dig site.

"I suppose all that makes sense," Sage's mother said, "but where could they have possibly moved the skull in only an hour? We were all over the area and didn't see any sign of it."

"That's not quite true," I told her. "We *did* see it. We just didn't realize what it was. Because most of it was hidden."

"The river!" Sage cried out. "They rolled it into the river!"

"Exactly," I said. "They only moved Minerva about thirty feet, if that. And it was all downhill. Then the rains came along and raised the water so high, it almost completely covered the skull. It simply looked like a rock, poking out of the water."

"Summer even stood right on top of it!" Sage exclaimed. "That's why fake Dr. Chen freaked out. She wasn't worried about Summer's safety! She was worried about Summer noticing what she was standing on!"

"Right," I agreed. "The plan was to make everyone *think* the skull had been stolen, but provide an alibi for the fake Dr. Chen. Then she could temporarily shut down the dig, claiming she was trying to figure out what to do, and come back later to remove Minerva—which is what she tried to do two nights ago. Only, she didn't expect to find you, me, and the guys camping out there. So she took off before we could see it was her."

"We thwarted her evil scheme!" Sage crowed triumphantly.

"For now," Dad cautioned. "But it's only a matter of time before she tries again. Which is why we thought we needed to get out here right away before—"

He didn't finish the thought, as we had just reached the dig site. The moment all of us saw it, we realized something was wrong.

Since it was nearly two days since the last big rain, the height of the river had crested and was dropping to its normal, significantly lower level. We could clearly see the boulders that Summer had been jumping on a few days before. They were the size of school desks, and half of each poked above the waterline.

There was no skull among them.

We all parked at the top of the small bluff, looking down at the river, and cut our engines.

The world instantly seemed incredibly quiet. The only sound was the soft burbling of the river, the chirp of birds, and the occasional distant moo.

Mom looked at Dad and me, concerned. "We would see the skull if it was there, wouldn't we?"

Dad whipped out his phone and pulled up the photos he

had taken of Summer on the rocks. "It was there the other day! Look! There are four boulders poking through the water in my photograph, but only three now."

All of us realized, to our horror, what that meant.

"They came back last night!" Mrs. Bonotto wailed. "No one was here to scare them off then!"

Sage jumped off his ATV, scrambled down the small bluff to the riverbank, and inspected the ground. "They left tracks this time! There are footprints here! Lots of them! And drag marks!" He pointed downriver, the way the people with the flashlights had fled two nights before. "Going that way!"

"They're heading toward the road," Mom said. "But if they're hauling a five-hundred-pound skull, they can't be moving that quickly."

"Then maybe we can still catch them," Dad said. He started his ATV again and looked to Sage's mother. "Lorena, lead the way."

Mrs. Bonotto's eyes steeled with determination. She wasn't about to let anyone get away with her dinosaur that easily. "Follow me," she announced, and then revved up her own ATV.

Sage clambered back up the bluff and leaped onto his ATV, and we all took off across the ranch. We raced down the river to a spot where it was quite broad and the water level had now dropped to only a few inches. The tracks of the thieves indicated they had waded across there. The wheels of our ATVs were big enough to take us across without any trouble. We even stayed relatively dry.

When we reached the other side, we gunned our engines and went as fast as possible. This time, we didn't talk, as we were focused on following the faint trail the thieves had left—and saving our breath. Even though we were on motorized vehicles, driving them was still a lot more work than using a car. We were constantly wrenching the handlebars one way or another, or standing high in the saddle to keep from being thrown off, and the constant bouncing and juddering battered us. After a while, I felt as though my brain was going to vibrate right out of my skull.

Fortunately, even though her ranch was enormous, Mrs. Bonotto knew the way to the road well, and we kept seeing evidence that the thieves had stuck to that route: fresh footprints in patches of mud, swaths of grass flattened by dragging the skull through, passages through the woods where small limbs had been recently snapped to make room for Minerva.

Along the way, Mom was trying to call the local police, but between her trying to drive the ATV and our remote location, the call kept dropping. Mrs. Bonotto had better luck reaching her husband. She let him know where we were heading, and eventually, he fell in beside us, riding his trusty horse as fast as it could go. Mr. Bonotto looked straight out of a movie western, with a creased cowboy hat pulled low over his eyes. The horse was breathing hard, its flanks heaving, after a long gallop to catch up to us.

I was the first one to see the truck. It was a white U-Haul, midsize, the kind you'd rent to move a few rooms of furniture. It gleamed in the sun, providing a distinct contrast to the miles of cedar trees, grass, and dirt we had just ridden through.

"They're still here!" I yelled, pointing ahead through the woods. We emerged from the trees and the entire scene came into view:

The truck was parked on the side of the road along with two other cars: a beat-up sedan and an even more beat-up minivan. The fake Dr. Chen and her team—eight big men in jeans and sweat-soaked T-shirts—had just finished loading the skull into the U-Haul after what had certainly been a long, hard slog across the ranch. They had heard us coming and were scrambling to escape before we could catch them, dropping the filthy tarp on which they had carried the skull and racing for their vehicles. Someone was already behind the wheel of the U-Haul, starting the engine. Dr. Chen yanked down the roll-up door at the rear of the U-Haul and ran for the passenger seat.

She limped as she ran. Apparently, she was the one who had been hurt while fleeing through the woods two nights before.

We all went after them as fast as we could. The last stretch to the roadside was open field, and we roared across it, Mr. Bonotto's horse galloping beside us.

As we got closer, I could see that instead of lifting the skull over the barbed wire, the thieves had simply cut the wires and flattened a section of the fence. We raced through the gap onto the shoulder of the road.

It was too loud and hectic for all of us on ATVs to coordinate our efforts. We all shouted our plans at once, with the effect that no one could hear what anyone else intended to do. Everyone went different ways, resulting in chaos. Sage and his mother crashed into each other and spun out in the dirt. Mom and Dad veered away to cut off the car and the van, while Sage's father and I went after the U-Haul.

The U-Haul's tires spun, kicking up a great spray of gravel that rained down on me, and then the truck lurched onto the road.

The fake Dr. Chen might have known a lot about theropods, but she didn't know much about U-Hauls. In her haste, she hadn't locked the roll-up door, and when the truck jounced onto the road, the jolt sent the door flying back up again, leaving the rear of the truck wide open. Inside, the giant skull, swaddled in plaster, was lashed down with cords of rope.

I swerved onto the road, right behind the U-Haul.

Mr. Bonotto used the last of his horse's strength to ride around to the front of the truck, trying to cut off the escape. The driver slammed on the brakes to avoid running him over, and the U-Haul skidded to a stop right in front of me.

It occurred to me that the truck was certainly much faster than an ATV, and that if it drove off again, we would never catch up to it.

In the cab of the U-Haul, I heard fake Dr. Chen yell, "Drive, you idiot! He'll move!"

In the moments before the driver could respond, I leaped from the ATV into the back of the truck.

Then the tires squealed and the U-Haul lunged forward. I nearly pitched right back out onto the road, but caught the rope that controlled the roll-up door at the last second and held on tight.

There was a frightened whinny and a clatter of hooves on asphalt as Sage's father and his horse abandoned their standoff before they got run over, and then the U-Haul was speeding down the road.

Behind me, my parents had managed to box in the sedan on their ATVs, preventing it from going anywhere, but the minivan got around them, swerving onto the road behind me.

Which meant I was now all by myself with the bad guys.

23

THE CHASE

My first instinct was to yank the roll-up door back down and lock it into place, but I decided against that: My plan was to stay with the U-Haul and let my parents know where it was going, and to do that, I had to see where I was. Out there in the boonies, I wasn't sure that I had enough cell service to load GPS and talk to my parents at the same time—and even if I did, I would need to see landmarks to help pinpoint my location. Since there were no windows in the back of the U-Haul, the only way I could see outside was through the open door. So, I cautiously made my way farther into the truck to ensure that I wouldn't tumble out into the road.

The U-Haul sped through the countryside with the minivan following closely behind.

The skull was so big that there was barely room for me to

get past it in the back of the truck. It had only been lashed down with two strands of rope so far. More was coiled on the floor, indicating that the thieves had probably intended to tie the skull down more securely, but we had scared them off before they could. The two strands were pulled taut over the skull and vibrating like plucked guitar strings.

My phone rang. I pulled it from my pocket and wasn't surprised to see it was my mother calling. I yanked off my helmet so that I could speak to her. "Hi, Mom."

"What on earth were you thinking, getting into that truck?" she demanded. She sounded angry, but I knew it was because she was worried for my safety.

"I figured if I was with the truck, then I could guide you to it," I said. "Otherwise, the bad guys would get away!"

"Your life isn't worth risking over a dinosaur skull!" Mom told me.

"Charlene," I heard Dad say, "this is not the time for this." Then he yelled, "We've commandeered the bad guy's car!"

"How?" I asked.

"There were only three of them, and Joe Bonotto's tougher than all of them put together," Dad replied. "We're trying the police again. Where are you?"

The U-Haul careened through a fork in the road, nearly throwing me off my feet.

The minivan stayed right behind us, running a stop sign.

"We just made a left turn," I reported, looking out the back of the truck for landmarks. "Although we'd been going straight until then. I can't see any road signs, but there's a big pond at the intersection with about forty cows around it."

"Keep us posted," Dad told me. "We're on our way."

"Will do." I edged closer to the cab of the U-Haul. I couldn't see into it, but through the wall, I could hear the driver and the fake Dr. Chen talking. They were raising their voices, sounding panicked and exasperated with each other.

"You said this wouldn't happen!" the driver yelled. He had a strong accent that I immediately recognized; he was the receptionist who had answered the phone at the paleontology lab.

"It wouldn't have happened if you idiots hadn't taken so many breaks!" That was the fake Dr. Chen. Her voice was a bit more shrill and nasally now, as though she had been acting all the times we had spoken to her before.

"It's not like we were carrying a bunch of throw pillows!" the receptionist said angrily. "That skull weighs a quarter of a ton!"

"I was carrying things too!" fake Dr. Chen snapped. "And you don't hear me whining about it."

I now noticed there were some other items tumbling around the back of the truck with me: two medium-size blobs wrapped in plaster. The longer one had HUMERUS written on it in Sharpie, while the bulkier one said ISCHIUM. Additional bones. That was probably what fake Dr. Chen had been carrying. As if making off with only the skull hadn't been enough, she had swiped a few extra pieces of Minerva from the dig.

I turned my attention to the skull itself. The plaster had eroded during its time in the river, but still remained mostly intact, save for a few small holes here and there through which I could see what might have been rock or bone. I assumed that meant Minerva was still in good shape.

We hooked through another turn, going so fast the bones and I were thrown against the inside wall of the U-Haul.

The minivan stayed right on our bumper, tires squealing on the road. The driver and the other four thieves inside the van were glaring at me menacingly.

"We just made a right," I informed my parents, looking out the back of the truck. "By a really big oak tree. Are the police on their way?" I asked.

"We haven't even talked to them yet," Mom said sourly. "We're still on hold."

My phone buzzed. It was Summer. "Can you guys hold on?" I asked my parents. "I've got another call."

"And you're taking it now?!" Mom asked.

I didn't bother arguing. I simply switched calls. "Hey—" I began, intending to tell Summer what was going on.

Only, she had news of her own she couldn't wait to

share with me. "I just heard from Rick. The shipment's coming in now!"

"Now?" I repeated. "Like right now?"

"Ten minutes from now. He actually called a little while ago, but I missed it because I was in the shower. Where are you? It sounds like you're in a tunnel or something."

"I'm in the back of a truck," I said. "With the dinosaur skull."

"You found it?!" Summer exclaimed.

"Yes. But we haven't quite recovered it yet. We're kind of in the midst of a high-speed chase."

"You always get to have all the fun," Summer said.

"This isn't fun!" I told her, then yelped as we took another turn and my feet went out from under me.

The giant skull pitched to the side. The ropes holding it groaned ominously under its weight.

"Uh-oh," I said.

"What now?" Summer asked.

Both ropes snapped with loud cracks, allowing the skull to roll free around the back of the U-Haul. To my chagrin, the first direction it rolled was toward me. I scrambled out of the way as it thudded into the wall of the truck, hitting so hard that it left a dent.

"What was that?" fake Dr. Chen exclaimed in alarm from the cab.

"I have to go!" I told Summer. "Get to Snakes Alive!"

"I'm already on my way!" she told me. "Daddy's driving me! And I called Tommy Lopez too. But he's an hour away."

I dodged to the left as the giant skull tumbled through the truck toward me again. I probably should have been focused on not getting crushed, but Summer's statement had alarmed me. "An hour away? He'll miss catching the guy making the delivery!"

"Maybe there's a way I can slow them down!" Summer told me. "You deal with your thing. I'll deal with this!" Then she hung up before I could ask *how* she intended to deal with it.

That concerned me, although I didn't have time to worry about it. We made another turn and the skull came tumbling back through the U-Haul again. I dodged, but not quite fast enough. The skull grazed my leg as it rolled by.

"I think something's loose back there," fake Dr. Chen said in the cab.

"Should we stop?" the receptionist asked.

"No way," fake Chen replied. "We can't let them catch us."

I returned to the phone call with my parents. "Mom, Dad, I'm back. But I'm in trouble. The skull is loose and rolling around in the truck with me."

"What?" Mom gasped, horrified.

"Hang in there, buddy," Dad said. "We're coming as fast as we can."

There was a slight shift in the ground below me. We had started to go up a hill. Unfortunately, the skull was now near the cab of the U-Haul while I was by the rear, meaning that as the truck tilted upward, the skull would come my way fast. Plus, the back of the truck was still wide open, meaning there was nothing to stop the skull—or me—from falling out into the road.

The skull started rolling toward me.

It would have been safest for me to simply jump out of the way and let the skull roll out of the truck, but I doubted it would survive tumbling down the hill—or smashing into the pursuing minivan. And if it was destroyed, then it would be lost to science in the same way as if it had been stolen.

So I dove for the rope that controlled the roll-down door.

At the same time, the hill suddenly got much steeper. My momentum picked up rapidly—as did that of the skull. It careened through the U-Haul like an enormous, prehistoric bowling ball.

In the minivan directly behind us, everyone's eyes went wide in terror as they saw the skull coming for them. The driver swerved off the road to avoid it.

I nearly went flying out the door ahead of the skull, but managed to snag the rope. My weight yanked on the door, which dropped down quickly.

Then I threw myself against the wall of the U-Haul to avoid being flattened.

The door didn't make it all the way down before the skull slammed into it. There was still a two-foot gap left. The door crumpled and part of it ripped off its track, but it held firm enough to keep Minerva from escaping.

The impact shook the U-Haul and made it veer wildly.

Out in the road behind us, I heard a screech of tires and a crash. I peered through the gap under the door and caught a glimpse of the minivan smashed into an oak tree on the side of the road.

The U-Haul evened out as we reached the hilltop, and then tilted steeply in the other direction as we started down the other side of the hill.

For a few seconds the skull remained wedged into the busted door at the back of the truck. And then gravity took over. The skull pulled free, skittered back through the U-Haul, and slammed into the wall behind the cab hard enough to put a two-foot dent in it.

I heard a cry of surprise from the receptionist and a groan of pain from fake Dr. Chen. The U-Haul skidded to a stop on the shoulder of the road. "Alice!" the receptionist yelled, sounding panicked. I figured that was fake Dr. Chen's real name. "Alice! Speak to me!"

There was no response from Alice.

"Dang it," the receptionist said, not sounding concerned so much as annoyed. "Stupid skull." I heard him turn off the engine, then open his door and jump down out of the cab.

I figured he was coming to see what the situation was with the skull. Which meant he was going to look into the back of the U-Haul and find me there.

I didn't know anything about the receptionist except that he was a thief, and thus probably a jerk, and I didn't want to be in the back of the truck when he got there. There was no exit besides the rear door, so if I stayed where I was, I'd be trapped.

The gap at the base of the broken door was just big enough for me to fit through. I slipped underneath and circled around the U-Haul on the passenger side, going the opposite way from the receptionist.

As I did, I glanced back at the minivan. Smoke billowed from under the smashed hood. The van was totaled. The thieves all seemed to be fine, however. They were all getting out, yelling at one another, angry about how everything was going wrong.

One of them spotted me, pointed my way, and yelled, "Stop that kid!"

On the other side of the U-Haul, I heard the receptionist pause and yell back, confused, "What kid?"

All the thieves started running my way.

I ran past the front of the U-Haul. Alice, the fake Dr. Chen, was slumped against the passenger door, unconscious.

The big dent the skull had put in the back of the cab was directly behind where her head would have been. It appeared that Alice had been knocked cold by Minerva.

The road ahead of the U-Haul sloped downward through a forest. Since I was at the crest of a hill, I could see far ahead; there wasn't another turn or junction for miles. It was one of those long, lonely Texas backcountry roads that almost no one ever drove on. Barbed-wire fences ran along both shoulders, indicating that I was between two ranches. My chances to outrun all the thieves on foot and get to safety weren't good.

There was only one secure place I could think of.

I scrambled around the cab of the truck. The driver's side door still hung open.

The receptionist was still by the rear of the U-Haul, trying to understand what was going on. He was a skinny guy with wiry hair and glasses who gaped in surprise when he saw me.

I climbed into the cab, slammed the door, and locked it.

Fake Dr. Chen moaned.

The receptionist ran back to the door and banged on it angrily. "Get out of there, you stupid kid!" he shouted.

In the side-view mirrors, I could see the other thieves running my way. They all looked angry too.

The keys to the U-Haul were still in the cab. The receptionist had left them there.

I now had a way to get away from all the bad guys and take the skull with me.

Of course, there was one big problem: I had never driven a truck. The only time I had ever driven at all was on Sage's ranch, and that was merely puttering along his driveway at ten miles an hour.

But I still knew the basics of driving. And driving seemed like a much better option than staying where I was. The thieves and the receptionist all looked like they would be perfectly happy to drag me from the truck and cause me some serious bodily harm.

So I started the truck.

"No!" the receptionist yelled. "Do not do this! If you start driving, I will kill you!"

I inspected the steering wheel and the gear shift of the U-Haul. They looked similar enough to the ones on Sage's old car.

I put the truck into drive. It instantly started creeping forward, due to gravity.

The receptionist ran alongside it, banging on the door. "Pull this truck over right now!" he demanded.

I didn't. Instead, I veered back onto the road. The truck was more sluggish than Sage's car had been, but I was already getting the hang of things. I placed my foot lightly on the gas pedal. The speedometer moved up slightly, to ten miles an hour, and the receptionist dropped away, screaming curses at me.

In the side-view mirrors, the looks on the thieves' faces went from anger to surprise and concern.

I sped up to twenty miles an hour, which seemed good enough, and drove on for a minute, leaving the thieves and the receptionist behind.

Then I stopped the truck on the shoulder of the road and got back on my phone. "Mom? Dad? Are you still there?"

"We are!" Mom exclaimed, thrilled to hear from me again. "Where are you now?"

"I've taken the truck from them," I replied.

There was a pause. "Did you say you've taken the truck?" Dad asked.

"Yeah." I looked in the side-view mirrors again. The thieves and the receptionist were all running after me. I was a few hundred yards away from them, but I realized I would still be safer if I kept moving. I looked down the long road ahead; in the distance, I could see a single billboard. It was too far to read, but I could make out the image on it: the head of a cobra. Suddenly, an idea came to me. "Have you guys been in touch with the police yet?"

"Yes!" Mom said. "They're trying to find you! Just like we are!"

"I'll make it easier for everyone," I said. "Call them back and tell them to go to Snakes Alive."

24

TOTAL CHAOS

Right after I told my parents where to go, the call dropped. As I had feared, the cell phone service was extremely weak out on that desolate road. That provided me with one advantage: Maybe the thieves couldn't make calls either, which would mean they would be stranded out there until I could send the police for them.

However, no cell phone service meant I couldn't use the GPS on my phone. But then, I didn't need my GPS to find Snakes Alive. I simply had to follow the billboards.

The way I figured it, the police wanted to recover the dinosaur skull, and if I could lure them to Snakes Alive with it, then maybe they could bust the reptile smuggler too.

I started up the U-Haul again. The thieves were still coming down the road after me. In the side-view mirrors,

I watched their faces fill with dismay as I drove off, leaving them in the dust once again.

I headed down the road at thirty miles an hour, which seemed like the maximum speed I should attempt, given that I'd never had any driving lessons.

At that speed, it took me two minutes to get to the billboard with the cobra on it. It sat at the junction of two roads and announced that Snakes Alive was only seven miles away. I turned and headed for it.

Driving the U-Haul turned out to be easier than I had expected—at least on long country roads with few turns and even fewer cars—and I was getting the hang of it quickly. Meanwhile, I wasn't sure how long the smuggler would be at Snakes Alive. So I stepped on the gas and increased my speed.

The skull seemed to have wedged itself into the wall of the cab, so it wasn't rolling around anymore. Fake Dr. Chen remained blissfully unconscious, although she did startle me at one point by sleepily murmuring, "I swim, but the potatoes come."

The only real challenge arose when I reached the highway. Thankfully, I only needed to drive on the access road, which moved much slower, but I was still encountering traffic for the first time. My first merge onto a road with other drivers resulted in a chorus of angry honks and shouts and one middle finger aimed in my direction—although I knew from watching drivers in the FunJungle parking lot that this was extremely common. I continued onward, white-knuckling the wheel, and managed to get within sight of Snakes Alive without enraging too many more drivers.

The sound of sirens echoed along the road. In the side-view mirrors, I saw three police cars far behind me, bubble lights flashing. For a moment, I feared they were coming to bust me, then realized they were heading to Snakes Alive, as I had requested. So I kept on driving that way, hoping to get there at the same time.

It was still relatively early in the day. Snakes Alive wasn't open yet, so the parking lot was empty—except for two vehicles.

One was a beat-up old pickup that I realized, with concern, belonged to Vance Jessup. (Vance was technically only two grades above me, but he had been held back a grade several times, which made him old enough to drive.)

The second vehicle was a midsize cargo truck almost the exact same size and shape as the U-Haul I was driving. It was parked so that the rear faced a side door of Snakes Alive. The smuggler's truck, I guessed.

I didn't see any of the McCrackens' cars. Apparently, I had beaten Summer there.

Rick and the smuggler were moving back and forth between the truck and Snakes Alive. The smuggler was a young guy with long, stringy hair and heavily tattooed arms. They were carrying large plastic tubs like the kind Rick had kept reptiles in. I assumed that each one had a smuggled reptile in it.

Tim and Jim Barksdale were following them.

Everyone looked up, surprised, at the sound of the police sirens.

The police cars had almost caught up to me. I started to pull off the road to let them pass.

Then fake Dr. Chen woke up.

Her eyes snapped open, then widened even farther when she saw I was at the wheel. "You!" she exclaimed, then desperately tried to make sense of things, although she was still dazed and groggy. "What are you . . . ? How did we . . . ? Where are . . . ?" She trailed off, hearing the sirens. "Cops! We need to get out of here!"

"Sorry," I said. "I'm stopping."

"No!" Fake Dr. Chen was either scared stiff or not thinking straight after her accident. Possibly both. She seized the wheel of the U-Haul and tried to steer me back onto the road, sliding over and slamming her own foot down on the gas pedal.

Meanwhile, the tattooed smuggler was also frightened by the approaching police. He dropped the plastic tub he was carrying, leaped into the cab of his truck, and started to drive away, not even bothering to lower his own roll-down rear door first.

I stomped on the brake at the same time fake Dr. Chen was trying to speed us up. The U-Haul swerved into the parking lot while the police cars came flying around us. The smuggler, who was trying to speed away, did his best to avoid us, but we sideswiped his truck, making him veer wildly. He smashed into the fence of the Snakes Alive petting zoo, tearing it from the ground.

All the fainting goats immediately passed out.

The smuggler's truck then clipped the corner of the hyena paddock. A smart person would have realized the game was up and hit the brakes, but the smuggler was desperate and made a last-ditch effort to try to speed across the parking lot of Jerk-ee's. The police cars cut him off and he lost control of his truck once more, crashing right through the grand entrance of the giant convenience store.

Despite the early hour, there were already plenty of customers at Jerk-ee's. They fled for cover as the truck smashed through the front windows.

My own U-Haul stopped with far less fanfare, spinning out right by the petting zoo, where two dozen regular, non-fainting goats, and the single, ornery llama, had just discovered their freedom and were scattering into the parking lot.

Before fake Dr. Chen could try to speed off again, I turned the truck off, took the keys, and leaped out.

Fake Dr. Chen took one look at the police, then fled.

Rick did the same thing. He tore past me in the parking lot.

Tim and Jim Barksdale followed him, oblivious of the police. "You owe us for that cobra!" Tim yelled. "FunJungle wouldn't have taken it if you hadn't given us a lousy carrying case!"

"No refunds!" Rick yelled back at them. "Under any circumstances!"

The police were all climbing out of their cars, trying to make sense of what was going on. I spotted Officer Brewster, who looked bewildered, and Sheriff Esquivel, who seemed to realize that the situation was rapidly about to become a serious headache for him.

Rick and fake Dr. Chen ran away from the police and into Jerk-ee's.

The goats and the llama followed them, probably recognizing Rick as the person who fed them.

Tim and Jim went after Rick, still wanting their money, and the police followed them, figuring they ought to go after the criminals. It looked like the strangest parade of all time.

Vance Jessup exited Snakes Alive, zipping up his jeans, having missed everything while he was in the bathroom.

Then he spotted me and grew enraged. "You!" he yelled.

So I ran too. I figured the safest thing to do would be to follow the police, who were all running toward Jerk-ee's.

With a screech of metal, a section of the damaged fence around the hyena enclosure collapsed.

"Oh boy," I sighed.

The three hyenas bounded through the hole.

The fossil thieves' remaining getaway car pulled into the parking lot. My father was driving, with Mom and the Bonottos all crammed into it.

J.J. McCracken's pickup truck was right behind them. J.J. was driving, with Summer in the passenger seat.

All of them jumped out at once. I didn't have time to explain to anyone what was going on. Pursued by Vance, I ran through the brand-new hole in the front entrance of Jerk-ee's.

The sight that greeted us was enough to make even Vance stop and gawk in surprise.

The superstore was two football fields in length. In the distance, I could see aisle after aisle of every snack food imaginable—there was an entire section simply devoted to "gummy objects"—while the walls were lined with the glass doors of refrigerated cases displaying several hundred varieties of chilled drinks. However, the front of the store was devoted to Jerk-ee's merchandise, almost all of which featured the company mascot, a sentient piece of beef jerky named, obviously enough, Jerk-ee. As mascots went, he wasn't very cute; personally, the first time I had seen him, I thought it was supposed to be a piece of poop with eyes. But for some reason, people adored him, and his likeness was slapped on everything from T-shirts to beer mugs to dish towels. The smuggler's truck had crashed into an enormous bin full of Jerk-ee plush toys, sending them flying. They now lay like tiny disaster victims all through the store.

The driver's side door of the truck hung open, but the smuggler was gone.

The back of the truck was still open, and dozens of tubs with rare reptiles in them had tumbled over. Thanks to the wreck, many tubs had come open, freeing their captives. Some of those reptiles had stayed put, but many had fled for their freedom, dispersing into the store, causing a great panic among the customers.

To my relief, none of the escapees appeared to be venomous snakes. However, nearly a dozen were monitor lizards, which weren't dangerous but could be quite scary: They looked like wingless dragons, were up to two feet long, and moved really fast. Terrified customers ran screaming down the aisles as the monitors scampered after them.

A few small children seemed excited about the presence of the goats from the petting zoo—until the hyenas bounded into the superstore. I didn't think the hyenas would be a threat to the humans, as they were well fed and probably didn't even know how to hunt, given that Rick hand-delivered chicken to them every day. But the customers were understandably frightened. Parents grabbed their children and clambered atop the many racks of snack foods while the hyenas gamboled past. The goats fled too, bleating in fear.

However, the thing I was *really* concerned about was the Komodo dragon.

The Komodo is the biggest lizard in the world, a type of monitor that can grow as large as an alligator. They are extremely endangered, only living on one small island in Indonesia. Somehow, the smuggler had managed to get ahold of one. I spotted it lumbering past a Doritos promotion, looking like something that had shown up straight out of the Jurassic age. It wasn't full grown, but it was big enough to be dangerous. I knew that Komodos could move surprisingly fast, and although goats weren't their natural prey, they *did* eat them. At Komodo National Park, the rangers lured the lizards into view of visitors by catapulting goat carcasses to them. The giant lizard in the store had smelled the fugitive goats from the petting zoo and was on the hunt.

The store's public address system, which usually said things like, "Today's Jerk-ee's special is two MegaDogs for three dollars," was now saying, "All customers, be advised that we have a minor invasion of wild animals. Please take cover in our clean and spacious restrooms while our staff attends to this issue."

Despite the announcement, the staff didn't appear to be taking care of anything. Most of the Jerk-ee's employees I saw were running in fear from the animals, often shoving elderly women and small children out of their way. Although one cashier was trying to shoo a water monitor out of the aerosol cheese aisle with a mop.

Meanwhile, Sheriff Esquivel and his police officers weren't handling things much better. Given that the main job of this force was doling out speeding tickets, the presence of multiple crises at once appeared to be overwhelming them. No one seemed to know what to deal with first.

I started toward Officer Brewster, hoping to enlist her help wrangling the Komodo, when I was suddenly tackled from behind. Vance Jessup had blindsided me. We smashed into a rack full of Jerk-ee's T-shirts and crashed to the floor.

I scrambled to get away, but Vance pinioned me and cocked a fist back. "I've been waiting a long time for this," he said.

"Touch him and you're dead," a voice behind him warned.

Vance looked back to see Summer standing over him. She was holding a green tree python in her hands. Green tree pythons aren't big or venomous, so they're not dangerous to humans, but Summer had already witnessed Vance's serious fear of snakes. "This is a Vietnamese poison viper," she said. "It's ten times deadlier than that snake you saw the other day. One bite from it will kill you instantly."

Vance rolled off of me and raised his hands. "I'm only joking around with him," he lied.

Summer held the snake out toward Vance and said, "Sic him."

Vance screamed like a kindergartner and ran for his life. He tore back through the store and was out the door so fast, he would have left gold-medal-winning sprinters in his dust.

"Thanks," I told Summer, getting back to my feet.

"Help!" fake Dr. Chen shrieked from nearby. "Someone please help me!"

"There's never a dull moment with you, is there?" Summer asked me.

We ran past a few aisles of cheap Jerk-ee's souvenirs to find fake Dr. Chen surrounded by hyenas in the beef jerky department.

There was a thirty-foot-long glass case of the type in which other markets would have displayed fresh meat and poultry, but this store's case was full of jerky. Any animal that you could farm-raise had been filleted, dried, and seasoned: cattle, turkeys, deer, elk, pigs, boars, ostriches, impala, springbok, and dozens of others. Fake Dr. Chen was perched atop the case right above the bohemian garlic turkey jerky, while the three hyenas stood on their hind legs with their front paws against the glass, drooling hungrily. Pools of slobber had formed on the floor.

I was certain the hyenas were interested in the jerky, but fake Dr. Chen believed they were drooling over *her*. "Help!" she yelled to us. "They're trying to eat me!"

"Stay right there!" I warned her as we rushed past. "We'll go get help! It shouldn't be more than a half hour!"

"A half hour?!" fake Dr. Chen wailed. "What am I supposed to do for a half hour?"

"Don't make any sudden movements!" Summer warned. "Or they'll rip your guts out!"

Fake Dr. Chen whimpered in fear and did her best to remain still.

Summer and I ran on, leaving the beef jerky area and entering the hunting supply section. Here you could get shooting targets, duck blinds, decoys, and almost every possible article of clothing in camouflage, from jackets to pants to onesies, in case you wanted to take your newborn baby hunting. And while there were no guns, Jerk-ee's had a large array of hunting knives and archery equipment.

As Summer and I passed, someone armed with a machete lunged out from behind the knife counter.

Summer and I screamed and leaped several feet backward, only to discover that it was Tim Barksdale. He had swiped a whole bunch of camo gear and was dressed for battle. "Sorry!" he said sheepishly. "I thought you were one of them big old freaky lizards!"

"We're quite obviously humans!" I yelled.

Jim emerged from behind the counter as well, where he had been lying in wait with a bowie knife. He was also dressed in stolen camouflage and had painted his face as well. This might have made sense if he had been trying to hide in the forest, but inside the store, he stuck out like a sore thumb. "We're just being on guard, is all. This place is crawling with wild animals."

"The most dangerous thing in this store right now is both of you," Summer told them. "And why are you even wearing camouflage? You're indoors!"

Jim thought that over, then said, "We're camouflaged as houseplants."

Tim spotted a large tree monitor running past the beer coolers. "Lizard at twelve o'clock!" he cried, and whipped the machete at it. He missed the monitor by a mile. The machete shattered one of the refrigerator doors and mortally wounded a case of Budweiser.

"It's getting away!" Jim yelled. He and Tim grabbed more weapons and raced after it.

"Leave it alone!" I yelled. "These animals are harmless!"

The Barksdales were too wrapped up in the thrill of the chase to listen to me, though. They probably wouldn't have listened to anyone . . .

Except for the one person who began speaking over the public address system.

"Everyone who is holding a weapon, this is J.J. McCracken, and I have a message for you." His voice was instantly recognizable, and it boomed throughout the store. The Barksdales paused to listen. "The animals in this store might look scary, but they are not a threat. So please put down your weapons and leave them alone."

The Barksdales looked at each other, still wary about doing this.

"Fine," J.J. said. "I'll pay you a hundred bucks not to hurt anything."

That worked. The Barksdales immediately dropped their weapons.

"All right!" Tim exclaimed. "We're rich!"

There was still one more major problem to deal with.

The police had cornered Rick and the smuggler in the center of the store, next to an array of fourteen separate ICEE machines.

The police all had their guns out, but Rick had taken a hostage.

It was a cobra. Rick was holding it directly behind the head so it couldn't bite him, with the casual style of someone who did this all the time. The cobra wasn't happy. It was hissing and writhing, whipping its tail about angrily.

Rick held a hunting knife by the cobra's neck. "This is an endangered cobra!" Rick announced to the crowd. "But I will kill it if you don't let me go!"

"*Us,*" the smuggler corrected. He was staring at the police, goggle-eyed, as though trying to fathom how any of this could have happened. "You'll kill it if they don't let *us* go."

"Right," Rick said. "I want you all to lower your guns and kick them over to me. Then Bill and I are gonna walk out of here nice and easy and drive away."

The police looked to Sheriff Esquivel, unsure whether they should even care about the snake. Esquivel didn't seem to think so. "You're not going anywhere," he told Rick and the smuggler.

"Don't test me!" Rick warned, pressing the knife against the snake's skin. "I'll kill it!"

"So what?" Esquivel asked. "It's one less snake in the world."

"Wait!" Mom yelled, running up with Dad and the Bonottos. "That cobra really is endangered!"

"Don't care," Esquivel said coldly.

There was a frightened bleat behind us. A goat came

racing up the pretzel aisle, pursued by the Komodo dragon. We all leaped out of the way, but Rick didn't move fast enough. As the Komodo scuttled past, it knocked Rick's legs out from under him with a sweep of its powerful tail. Rick landed flat on his back, letting go of the angry cobra, which promptly bit him in the hand.

Rick screamed, more out of fear than pain.

"That's bad," Dad observed. "I'll be right back." He raced off toward the hunting supplies.

Mom quickly dialed 911 for an ambulance.

The cobra slithered away. The police fired after it, though it made it to the safety of a bin of Cheetos without being wounded.

The smuggler saw his chance to escape, and ran.

He was coming toward Summer and me. There was an ICEE machine close by. I considered throwing a cup of frozen slush into the criminal's eyes and blinding him the way that Xavier had done with the Smoothie of Justice a few days before.

But then I realized it would be much easier to just trip him.

So I stuck out my leg.

Summer had the exact same idea. We caught him in both legs at almost the same time. The smuggler went down hard, whacked his head on the floor, and passed out with a groan.

Officer Brewster handcuffed him anyhow.

Sheriff Esquivel and the other police weren't so quick to cuff Rick, as Rick's life was in severe danger, but then Dad came running back with a snake bite kit he'd found in the emergency hunting supplies.

Dad had handled snake bites before, and he dealt with Rick's quickly and professionally, although Rick still needed to go to the hospital just to be safe.

"By the way," Sage told Sheriff Esquivel, once we were sure Rick would survive, "the stolen dinosaur skull is in a truck out in the parking lot. Teddy here recovered it. And the woman who stole it is over in the beef jerky aisle, surrounded by hyenas. So any time you'd like to apologize to my parents for being a jerk and suggesting they were making the whole thing up, I'm sure they'd love to hear it."

"Also," I added, "all the other thieves are stranded on a country road about eight miles from here. If they haven't found a ride, they might still be out there. I can give you directions."

"That'd be nice," Sheriff Esquivel said, chastened. He took the directions from me, but he didn't apologize to the Bonottos.

My parents, Sage and his family, Summer, and I headed toward the front of the store. By now, several Snakes Alive employees had arrived on the scene and were dealing with the escaped animals. One team was wrangling the hyenas so that fake Dr. Chen could be apprehended by the police. Another team had captured the Komodo dragon, which they insisted was a legitimate delivery for Snakes Alive, although the same couldn't be said for the other animals. Lamar, the guy who had shown off the albino python to Summer and me the day before, was helping round up the monitors and venomous snakes, but warned that it might take days to find them all. The goats and the llama had been left alone for the moment, as they didn't pose much danger to anyone. The goats were happily gorging themselves on gummy objects.

At the front of the store, the police had stretched yellow plastic crime tape across the entrance, which was bad news for anyone who wanted to buy hunting supplies or desperately needed a clean restroom. (Snakes Alive was insisting that people had to pay full admission to use theirs.) A crowd had gathered in the parking lot. With everything else that was going on, no one was paying any attention to the banged-up U-Haul.

Tommy Lopez slipped under the crime tape with his fellow Fish and Wildlife agents. "I hear you've already done our job for us," he said to me, then looked over the remains of Jerk-ee's. "In your usual, subtle way."

"This wouldn't have happened if you'd been on time," I teased.

"Thanks. We'll handle things from here." Tommy headed into the store.

"Watch out for the hyenas," Summer warned.

Tommy laughed, thinking she was joking. "Sure thing," he said.

Sage was looking at the U-Haul. "Since our paleontologist is a fake," he asked, "does anyone know what we're supposed to do with Minerva?"

"Leave that to me," J.J. McCracken said confidently, emerging from the wreckage of Jerk-ee's. "I know exactly where she should go."

Epilogue

THE BASEMENT OF BONES

A week later, I found myself standing in a laboratory next to the femur of an *Argentinosaurus*. The lab belonged to the University of Texas's paleontology department, which was housed in an unassuming brick building at the rear of the J. J. Pickle Research Campus. The lab was where fossils were cleaned, inspected, and prepared after being brought in from the field. The *Argentinosaurus* was one of the largest animals that had ever lived, as long as three school buses and weighing seventy-seven tons. Its femur was as tall as I was. It stood on end by the laboratory entrance, held in a metal brace, the way a piece of sculpture might have been mounted in a normal office. Everyone who worked in the lab seemed to have forgotten it was even there.

The lab workers were all far more interested in the skull

of Minerva, which now sat smack in the middle of the room. Everyone was carefully removing the remaining plaster from the skull under the watchful eye of the real Dr. Ellen Chen, who had flown back from Mongolia to oversee the project. Even though she had been excited about the theropod she was excavating in Asia, it paled in comparison to finding a tyrannosaur in her own state.

Dr. Chen had invited Summer, Sage, and me to see what was being done with Minerva, and our parents had eagerly tagged along. Before we had come to the lab, she had given us a tour of the facility, which was primarily used to store ancient bones. According to Dr. Chen, only about 1 percent of any natural history museum's bone collection was on display; the rest was inevitably stockpiled away. The storage area was surprisingly low-tech: the smaller bones were housed in cabinets, while the bigger ones were merely on shelves in the basement. There were a startling number of artifacts: The building was almost as big as Jerk-ee's, and it was chock-full. Dr. Chen had shown us mastodon tusks, the plates from a stegosaur's back, the club from the tip of an ankylosaur's tail, and even the only known bones from a *Quetzalcoatlus*, the largest animal that had ever flown. It was bigger than a Cessna airplane.

To my surprise, many of the bones were still wrapped in their original plaster casts, and some had been there for decades. "It's easier to excavate the bones and wrap them up than it is to unwrap them again and determine what they are," Dr. Chen had explained. "And it's easier to get volunteers to help with the digging, since it's a lot more exciting. Sadly, we don't have the funds or the manpower to handle the backlog. To examine all these bones properly would take years."

Eventually, we had made our way to the fossil lab, which seemed more like a workshop; it had a cement floor, lots of tools, and white walls that were bare save for a few dinosaur movie posters. Bones in the process of being extracted from their plaster casts were laid on white tables around the edges of the room, although they had all been forgotten in the excitement over Minerva. Now all five lab employees were working on different parts of the skull at once, using fine tools like scalpels and dental picks to carefully remove the plaster.

"Generally, removing the bones from the cast is painstaking work," Dr. Chen said. "When the bones are wrapped in the field, they come with a lot of debris as well, which we call matrix, and we want to analyze that carefully, as it can contain all sorts of important microfossils. Plus, we want to make sure that we don't damage the fossil itself. Unfortunately, Minerva got bounced around a lot, so any matrix inside the skull has probably been compromised, and the skull was banged up a bit too."

"Sorry," I said.

"Oh!" Dr. Chen exclaimed. "I wasn't upset with *you*, Teddy. If it wasn't for you, we wouldn't even have Minerva. You did what you had to do to save her." She gave me a reassuring smile. Her appearance was somewhat similar to the fake Dr. Chen, which made sense, as they had turned out to be second cousins.

The fake Dr. Chen, whose real name was Alice Soon, had plotted for years to use their family resemblance to her own advantage. As I had suspected, she had paid off the receptionist at the lab, waiting for exactly the right circumstances to present themselves—although even Alice had never dreamed that would lead her to a tyrannosaur. She had been expecting a much less glamorous set of fossils, like a set of dinosaur tracks, which were relatively common in central Texas. But when the discovery of a lifetime had presented itself, she had jumped at the chance.

The receptionist, Darnell Scroggs, had been arrested on the day of the Jerk-ee's chaos. Following my instructions, Sheriff Esquivel and his officers had found Darnell and the five thieves from the minivan still stranded on the lonely road where I had abandoned them. As I had hoped, due to the lack of cellular service, they had been unable to call anyone to pick them up. Mom, Dad, and the Bonottos had left the remaining three thieves hog-tied back by the ranch. Darnell and the thieves had all proclaimed their innocence until Alice Soon implicated them in an attempt to reduce her own jail sentence. They were all going to do time.

Meanwhile, Tommy Lopez and his team had arrested Rick from Snakes Alive and Bill the reptile smuggler, although Tommy still wasn't satisfied. "These were the lowest guys on the totem pole," he had told me a few days afterward. "They're just pawns in the game. Same goes with the guys who steal these animals in the wild, or the poor schlubs who try to smuggle animals into the country. They take all the risks and get paid a pittance. The *real* guys we're after are the kingpins who control it all." Unfortunately, he suspected that many of those kingpins were based in other countries, where he had no jurisdiction. The best he could hope for was to put a case together and bring a foreign law enforcement agency in on it, although he didn't seem very hopeful that would happen.

Still, the pipeline of illegal animals to our area had been shut off. Without Rick, fewer people like the Barksdales would be able to get their hands on exotic reptiles and would hopefully get normal pets instead. J.J. had made good on paying the Barksdales a hundred dollars each for putting down their weapons at Jerk-ee's, and they had promised to spend it on adopting a cat to replace Griselda for their mother.

Vance Jessup was being sent to a juvenile detention camp for the rest of the summer; repeatedly threatening me with bodily harm had violated the terms of his release. I was pleased to hear it was located several hours away from me, in an area known to have an abundance of wild snakes.

Snakes Alive was under investigation for being complicit in the trade of illegally obtained animals, seeing as Rick had conducted his sales there. However, the owners claimed that Rick had lied to them about the nature of his business— and that they had acquired all their display animals legally. Tommy was sure the owners were lying about Rick, but he doubted he could prove it. Chances were, Snakes Alive would be able to continue operating.

There was better news where the zebra spankers were concerned. The fad already seemed to have peaked, partly due to increased zoo security (at FunJungle, Marge O'Malley had tackled two potential camel whackers) and partly due to a rash of zebra-spanking copycats getting seriously wounded in the process (four people had been bitten, three had received concussions from kicks to the head, and one had broken a leg simply by falling into an exhibit). But the real change in popularity was due to Summer. She had over three million followers on social media, and she had started a campaign to declare animal harassment at zoos uncool. It had quickly caught on as more famous people spoke out, and soon, anyone who harassed a zoo animal stood to be chastised online, rather than praised. Videos of the morons who still attempted stunts started to get only a few hundred hits, rather than millions. "Sometimes there's an upside to being famous," Summer had told me.

In the lab, one of the assistants cautiously removed a large section of the cast, revealing one of Minerva's eye sockets. Suddenly, the skull looked less like a rock that had been encased in plaster and more like a part of a living being. We all gasped in delight, although no one looked more pleased than Dr. Chen.

"I've already noted some distinct differences between this skull and the ones that have been found in Montana," she told us. "They're subtle, but important."

"What does that mean?" Sage asked.

"That this is another subspecies of tyrannosaur," Dr. Chen replied excitedly. "One that is entirely new to science."

J.J. McCracken was the only one who didn't seem excited by this. "So, when we put Minerva here on display, we can't call her a *Tyrannosaurus rex*?"

It turned out that even before the theft, J.J. McCracken, Harper Weems, and the Bonotto parents had been working on a top-secret deal for Minerva. That was what Harper had been hiding from us. The ultimate plan was that J.J. and Harper would collectively pay seven million dollars in a preemptive bid to take Minerva off the market. But instead of splitting the bones, they would donate them to the University of Texas, which would get to display the originals at the Texas Memorial Museum on campus. In return for their investment, J.J. and Harper would each get copies of the skeleton. Harper was donating a revolutionary supersize 3-D printer to the paleontology department to make the bones. It would be years before the excavation and scanning were complete, but eventually J.J. would have one dinosaur replica for FunJungle and Harper Weems would have another for herself. The university could sell skeletons to other museums, but J.J. and Harper would be the only private owners. Harper hadn't announced what she would do with her skeleton, but she was leaning toward keeping it in her rocket factory. She was so excited about the deal, she was thinking of naming her new rocket lines after dinosaur species: *T. rex*, *Carnotaur*, *Raptor*, and so on.

The deal would also allow the Bonottos to keep their ranch going, which was a great relief to the entire family. The fake Dr. Chen had known about the deal, and had played along, though she was plotting to steal Minerva the whole time. Now the real Dr. Chen was thrilled to have not only a new tyrannosaur, but also a deal to finance its presentation in place.

"You'll still be able to call it a tyrannosaur," she informed

J.J. "It just won't be a 'rex.' As a brand-new species, it will have a different name."

"Who gets to name it?" Mr. Bonotto asked.

Dr. Chen said, "Normally, it would be the person who describes the dinosaur for science."

"Which would be you," Mom observed.

"Officially," Dr. Chen replied. "But that's not a hard and fast rule. There is a lot of precedent for other people naming new species. Sometimes the rights are auctioned off at charity. Sometimes a friend simply comes up with a great name. To be honest, there's no absolutely correct way to do it, as long as it sounds remotely scientific."

"So it could be called *Tyrannosaurus funjungleus?*" J.J. asked.

"Er . . . yes," Dr. Chen replied, looking a bit queasy at the thought.

"Or *Tyrannosaurus bonotto?*" Sage suggested.

"Or . . . ," I began, fully intending to suggest *Tyrannosaurus mccracken*. Only Summer slapped a hand over my mouth before I could.

"*Tyrannosaurus theodorus,*" she suggested. "Because no one would even know this species existed if it wasn't for Teddy."

Everyone smiled at the thought of that, even Dr. Chen.

"Tyrant Lizard Theodore," Dad translated, looking at me. "Seems fitting."

Summer whispered in my ear, "You've already named a rhino and a nature preserve after me. It's your turn to be famous for once."

"You're all okay with that?" I asked the room.

My parents and the Bonottos and the McCrackens and Dr. Chen and the lab staff all nodded agreement. I found myself feeling overwhelmed by their support and respect.

I looked into the vacant eyes of the dinosaur skull. Part of the upper jaw was exposed, and in a weird way, it looked like Minerva was giving me a 65-million-year-old smile. I smiled back. "*Tyrannosaurus theodorus*," I said proudly. "Sounds good to me."

The Reptiles in This Book Are Not the Only Ones in Danger!

Animal trafficking is an enormous problem. By many estimates, it is the second-biggest criminal enterprise on Earth after the drug trade.

So what can you do to stop it? Plenty.

The first thing is, be very cautious about purchasing exotic pets—especially reptiles—to make sure that they were captive-bred and not caught in the wild. I had expected that the people I interviewed at the World Wildlife Fund and various zoos would recommend that people not buy reptiles as pets at all—but to my surprise, most of them were okay with this, as long as buyers do their research first. First of all, don't take the purchase of an exotic animal lightly. Know what the care of this animal will involve. Know how big it will grow and what it will need to eat. Know which animals do well in captivity and which don't. And no matter how cool a venomous snake might seem, it's probably in your best interests not to own one.

Then, learn which animals are guaranteed to be captive bred or sustainably harvested. (Examples include leopard geckos, ball pythons, and bearded dragons.) Third, look for legitimate merchants. Petco and PetSmart both have reptile sales systems that have been vetted by the WWF. Be extremely cautious about reptiles purchased at reptile shows. As I pointed out in this book, if an animal has wounds or parasites or doesn't look like it has been pampered, there's a decent chance it was stolen from the wild and smuggled, or bred in an illegal facility. An animal that looks like it has been well taken care of its whole life was probably born and raised in captivity.

Here's something that really surprised me: Many experts suggested that you purchase a designer reptile—one that has been captive-bred for its looks. At first, this sounded bizarre to me, but then I realized that this is what dog owners have been doing for centuries. We all know that a labradoodle or a mutt from the pound isn't a wolf that has been stolen from the wild. The same thing applies to designer snakes. If a snake has a pattern that doesn't exist in nature, then it wasn't stolen from the wild. (And to be honest, some of the patterns on these designer snakes are amazingly beautiful.)

Of course, it's not only reptiles that are victims of the illegal wildlife trade, so what I've said here certainly applies to exotic birds, fish, and mammals as well. Getting a pet isn't something to be taken lightly. Do your research—and remember, while an exotic pet might seem really cool and unusual, there are probably hundreds, if not thousands, of dogs and cats in your community in need of adoption. They might not be unusual—but they'll be loving and devoted. So it couldn't hurt to drop by your local animal shelter, right?

Acknowledgments

One of the most amazing things about writing this series is the amazing people I have been able to meet—and the amazing places I have been able to visit—while doing research.

For example: Alan Zdinak, preparator of vertebrate paleontology at the Natural History Museum of Los Angeles County, was kind enough to spend hours showing me—and my son—around the labs and answering all our questions. Deborah Wagner, the paleontology laboratory manager at the John A. and Katherine G. Jackson School of Geosciences at the University of Texas at Austin, was also incredibly helpful, and even took the time to give me a spur-of-the-moment tour of the university's amazing collections. (For the record, the lab really is located on the J. J. Pickle Research Campus. I didn't make up that name.)

Giavanna Grein and her cohorts at the animal crimes division of the World Wildlife Fund first tipped me off to how serious the issue of trafficking illegal animals is. Robin Sawyer and Julia Criscuolo at the WWF discussed the details of reptile laundering with me. At the Los Angeles Zoo, Candace Sclimenti; Mike Maxcy, curator of birds; and Ian Recchio, curator of reptiles, gave me more of the scoop on trafficking and how zoos can be overwhelmed with requests to take exotic pets. (Plus, Candace really did once bust a passenger for smuggling a monkey on a passenger plane.) At the Maryland Zoo, Lori Finklestein, VP of education, interpretation, and volunteer programs, and Sharon Bower, education manager, gave me a tour of their facilities and discussed how important it is for everyone to understand the difference between zoos that are AZA certified (like your municipal zoo, most likely) and ones that aren't (like Snakes Alive). Also, thanks are due to Jeanne Brodsky, the office manager of Strictly Reptiles in Florida, and Jay Brewer, owner of Reptile Zoo in Fountain Valley, California, who gave me a tour of his facilities and his designer anaconda breeding operation.

My amazing intern, Kelly Heinzerling, located all these fascinating people and took incredible notes. And my dear friend Lennlee Keep joined me on an investigative expedition along Interstate 35 in Texas, where we visited a certain place (that will remain unnamed) that served as the inspiration for Snakes Alive.

I should also point out that Bonotto Ranch in the book is closely based on my experiences on the ranch of my childhood friend Paul Dague, whom I reconnected with when his kids ended up reading my books. So thanks to Paul and his family for all the great fun I had on their ranch when I was a kid. (For the record, Paul really did have a car he used to go up and down the driveway.)

As usual, I need to thank my entire team at Simon & Schuster: Liz Kossnar, Justin Chanda, Anne Zafian, Lucy Cummins, Milena Giunco, Audrey Gibbons, Lisa Moraleda, Jenica Nasworthy, Chrissy Noh, Anna Jarzab, Nicole Benevento, Devin MacDonald, Christina Pecorale, Victor Iannone, Emily Hutton, Caitlin Nalven, and Theresa Pang. And as usual, I must give massive props to my incredible agent, Jennifer Joel, for making all this possible.

Plus, huge thanks to my ever-supportive community of writers: James Ponti, Sarah Mlynowski, Christina Soon-tornvat, Julie Buxbaum, Leslie Margolis, Karina Yan Glaser, Elizabeth Eulberg, Ally Carter, Varian Johnson, Julia Devil-lers, Adele Griffin, Michael Buckley, Chris Grabenstein, AJ Jacobs, Rose Brock, and Maggie Stiefvater (who first taught me about fainting goats and told me "this is going to change your life" before showing me videos of them). Thanks to all the school librarians and parent associations who have arranged for me to visit, all the bookstore owners and employees who have shilled my books, and all the amazingly tireless festival organizers and volunteers who have invited me to participate. On the home front, thanks to the Sterns, the Reismans, the Heisens, the Rotkos, the Delmans, the Berloffiluses, the Kuklinskis, the Bosnaks, the Steinbergs, the Johnsons, the Middlemans, the Lyons, and the Heys.

Finally, thanks to my team who helps get me through every day—and makes sure I can still travel around to do research, visit schools, and meet excited readers at festivals: Ronald and Jane Gibbs; Darragh, Suz, and Ciara Howard; Barry, Carole, and Alan Patmore and Sarah Cradeur; Andrea Lee Gomez; and Georgia Simon.

Last but certainly not least, thanks to my children, the real Dashiell and Violet, who are now old enough to come with me on the occasional research trip (and to ask better questions than I do) and to help edit my books with me. I love you both to the moon and back.

A Reading Group Guide to
Tyrannosaurus Wrecks
by Stuart Gibbs

About the Book

In the latest novel in *New York Times* bestselling author Stuart Gibbs's FunJungle series, Teddy Fitzroy returns as FunJungle's resident sleuth to solve his most improbable mystery yet—with a victim that's 65 million years old.

Discussion Questions

The following questions may be utilized throughout the study of *Tyrannosaurus Wrecks* as reflective writing prompts, or, alternatively, they can be used as targeted questions for class discussion and reflection.

1. Teddy tells readers, "All the trouble with the tyrannosaur started the same day Xavier Gonzalez and I helped apprehend the Zebra Spanker." What do you think makes that statement unusual? Given what you know about Teddy's past experiences, predict what's in store for Teddy and his friends.

2. Consider the Zebra Spanker's behavior. In your opinion, why can getting attention online and on social media cause people to behave poorly? What kind of effect can this have on their lives and those of the people around them? Explain your answers.

3. When Sage asks Teddy for help, Teddy asks if Sage's family is getting assistance from the local authorities. Xavier tells Teddy, "'You're way better than the police.'" In what ways might Teddy benefit from having his friends' support and confidence in his abilities? Can you think of ways that this can also become problematic for Teddy?

4. After seeing tourists in Snakes Alive T-shirts, Xavier tells them, "'You shouldn't support Snakes Alive. It's not accredited by the Association of Zoos and Aquariums. Zoos in the AZA are required to maintain high levels of animal care.'" Why is an organization like the Association of Zoos and Aquariums important to the overall well-being of animals? In what ways can unaffiliated attractions and small zoos like Snakes Alive be detrimental? How might you go about educating the public about this distinction?

5. Were you surprised to learn that Sage was in second grade when he started driving on his family's property? Would you like to have a similar opportunity? Why do you think there is a driving age requirement? Explain your answers.

6. Upon visiting the dig site and hearing Mrs. Bonotto's praise for successful investigations, Summer tells everyone, "'We know how to handle a crime scene. This isn't our first.'" Do you think Summer is right to be so confident? Why is Teddy less assured?

7. Consider how law enforcement treats Teddy's and Summer's presence at the crime scene. Why might the police and other law enforcement officials be bothered by their role in the investigation?

8. Throughout *Tyrannosaurus Wrecks*, readers learn a great deal about dinosaurs as well as snakes, lizards, and other animals that are often part of the illegal animal trade. Which animal facts most interested or surprised you? Which animals would you like to explore further?

9. After discovering that only the dinosaur's skull has been stolen, the sheriff is told, "'But as far as we're concerned, the skull pretty much *was* the dinosaur.'" Why is that the case? Think about what you've learned; what makes finding a *T. rex* skull so incredibly rare and valuable? What information can it tell you? Did you have any idea of its importance?

10. Historically, Teddy's and Summer's investigations have been incredibly successful; however, their parents have continued to resist allowing their children to participate in solving mysteries. Why do you think that is? Did you find their behavior to be any different in this book? Can you think of any reasons for changes in attitude?

11. When Jim Barksdale reaches out to Teddy for help, he tells Teddy, "'Tim and I just got this new pet snake, and it sort of ate our cat.'" What does learning that Jim hopes their cat is still alive reveal?

12. Based on what you know about them, what makes learning the Barksdale twins acquired an anaconda as a pet so problematic?

13. What do you think would be the best part of getting to participate in a dig such as this one? Can you think of any drawbacks or challenges to this kind of experience?

14. Sage tells Teddy, "'Minerva's the only thing that can save us. . . . If that skull was really worth millions, it'd be enough to save our ranch. It was like stumbling across a treasure chest.'" Do you think knowing Sage and his family are in a financial crisis affects Teddy's willingness to help solve this mystery? What other motivations might he have? Explain your answers.

15. After getting no answers as to where the Barksdales acquired the anaconda, Summer takes matters into her own hands by being flirtatious to get more information. Did you expect her plan to be effective? Why are the Barksdales hesitant to provide information about their snake source? Explain your answers.

16. Consider Teddy's reaction to news that Summer's father is the number one suspect in the case of the missing dinosaur skull. How did it make you feel? How do you think Summer would feel? How might you have reacted if you were in Teddy's shoes?

17. Tommy shares Summer's and Teddy's frustration toward Rick's illegal animal trading ring. Though he also wants justice to be served, he tells them, "'The wheels of justice don't move that fast.'" Do you agree with this statement? Explain your answer. How does this knowledge affect Summer and Teddy? In what ways does it motivate them to accelerate the process?

18. After learning that the Zebra Spanker inspired copycats who also want attention, Teddy tells Summer, "'And every time we watch the videos, we feed the beast.'" Summer defensively counters by retorting, "'Hey, it's not our fault this is happening.'" Do you agree more with Teddy or Summer? Explain your position, and what you feel their role should be.

19. As *Tyrannosaurus Wrecks* closes, Teddy and Summer have once again solved another important mystery. Predict what new mystery will come their way in the next FunJungle installment.

Extension Activities

1. Paleontologists are at the center of this mystery surrounding a missing artifact. Readers are introduced to the work done by these specialists at universities and site locations around the world. Using library resources and the Internet, have students research to learn more about paleontology. What specialized training does one need to do this work?

Be sure to learn the following:

• What kind of education is a paleontologist expected to have?

• Which major universities have specialized programs?

- What types of jobs do paleontologists typically hold?

- What are some of the ways people interested in the science of paleontology can become involved in discovery and excavation?

After gathering this information, have students create a visual presentation that illustrates their findings.

2. Readers learn that dinosaur excavation first gained great attention around 1880. Given that historical time line, use research resources to investigate the process of dinosaur excavation to learn more about how it has changed over time. Consider choosing a dig from the early 20th century and a dig from the last twenty-five years to lead your examination of the following:

- What tools are used during excavations?

- Where have other dinosaur bones been located?

- How is ownership assigned?

- How are these excavations generally funded?

- What are the benefits to an organization or institution?

After students finish their research, have them prepare presentations to share with others.

3. Readers also learn about the illegal international pet trade that involves animal trafficking. Using the World Wildlife Fund as a resource, investigate animal trafficking to learn more about the following:

- What types of animals are typically trafficked?

- What countries have the highest incidences of animal trafficking?

- What problems does the United States face with this issue? Can you find any data?

- What are the most trafficked or sought-after animals?

- What can be done to reduce the number of incidences of illegal animal trafficking?

- What are the general legal consequences for animal traffickers and illegal traders?

Have students take what they've learned and work in small groups to discuss possible solutions and ways they can actively help raise awareness for this issue.

4. The Barksdale twins' idea to keep a pet anaconda turns out to be far more complicated than they bargained for. Using library resources, learn more about these magnificent reptiles; alternatively, students can research other common types of wild snakes, such as a Mangshan pit viper or an emerald tree boa. Be sure to focus on the following:

• What are some of the reptile's general characteristics?

• Where are they typically found in the wild?

• What makes them such dangerous creatures?

• Why are they not ideal pets?

• Are there special sanctuaries available for their protection?

• Are there any national or global conservation efforts to protect them?

• What other snakes are often sold illegally as pets?

After students collate information, have them create posters to share what they've learned with their classmates.

5. As Dash and his friends camp out around the dig site, they hear a distant sound that Ethan suspects could be a chupacabra. Research to find out more about this mythical creature, being sure to focus on the following:

• What is a chupacabra believed to be?

• How is it described?

• Are there specific geographic areas that have reported sightings?

• What are other examples of cryptids around the world?

Have students write short essays sharing why they think these sightings and stories remain popular.

6. Readers learn that the illegal pet trade has destroyed ecosystems all over the planet. Have students discover more about how the illegal pet trade has had such a negative impact. Begin by reading this article from *Time* magazine at https://time.com/longform/florida-python-hunters/. Working in small groups, ask students to discuss this topic using other research resources to inform and support their thoughts on the impact. Have them think about the following:

- What are some additional examples of ecosystem destruction?

- Are there any plans in place to combat this?

- Who leads or funds these endeavors?

Using their new knowledge, ask students to create a visual that can be showcased and shared with others to spread awareness.

Lexile ® 830L

The Lexile reading level has been certified by the Lexile developer, MetaMetrics.

Guide written by Dr. Rose Brock, an assistant professor at Sam Houston State University. Dr. Brock holds a Ph.D. in Library Science, specializing in children's and young adult literature.

This guide has been provided by Simon & Schuster for library and reading group use. It may be reproduced in its entirety or excerpted for these purposes.

Turn the page for a
sneak peek at
Bear Bottom.

THE SELFIE OF DOOM

My family was delayed on our return to the bison ranch because we were trying to prevent a tourist from getting mauled by an elk.

We were leaving Yellowstone National Park, having spent the day exploring, on our first vacation in two years. My parents had been working overtime at FunJungle Adventure Park, the world-famous theme park/zoo, since before it had even opened. Mom was the head primatologist and Dad was the official photographer, and their jobs kept them extremely busy.

I had always thought that FunJungle attracted an unusual number of dumb tourists. But at Yellowstone, I discovered that there were dumb tourists *everywhere*.

It was the week after the Fourth of July, and thus the

height of tourist season; Yellowstone was flooded with visitors from all over the planet. That day we had witnessed dozens of people doing incredibly boneheaded things, often directly in front of signs warning them not to do so: attempting to pet wild animals, climbing over the safety railings at scenic viewpoints, swimming in rivers with life-threatening rapids—and positioning their young children dangerously close to bison for photographs. Two rangers had to arrest a college student who had attempted to use Monarch Geyser as a hot tub; apparently, he hadn't realized that the 204-degree water would have boiled him alive.

I had also overheard tourists ask the park rangers startlingly uniformed questions, such as: "What time do you turn off the Old Faithful Geyser every night?" "Why do we have to stay on the hiking paths when the deer don't?" And "Where can we see the presidents carved into the mountain?" (The answers were: "It's a geological feature, not a fountain"; "The deer are wild animals"; and "You're thinking of Mount Rushmore, which is five hundred miles away in South Dakota.") I also heard one person angrily claim that a raccoon had stolen his bag of Cheetos and demand that the park service refund his money. Tourists did things like this so often that the park rangers had a name for them: tourons.

Despite all of that, it had been a good day. Yellowstone featured some of the most beautiful scenery I had ever seen, and we had also been lucky enough to spot three bald eagles, a moose, and a pair of wolves. Plus, my girlfriend, Summer, was with us. Summer was fourteen, a little bit less than a year older than me. She was smart and fun and liked seeing wildlife and hiking as much as I did. Her father, J.J. McCracken, was the owner of FunJungle, and he had invited us to join him—along with a few other FunJungle employees—at his friend's ranch in West Yellowstone for a week. While my parents were big fans of Summer and her mother, Kandace, they were a bit wary of J.J., whose actions often concealed ulterior motives. However, the offer had been too good to pass up: a free place to stay, a flight on J.J.'s private jet, *and* a visit to one of Dad's favorite places on Earth. (Mom and I had never been to Yellowstone, and Dad had always wanted to take us there.) We had eagerly accepted the offer.

Our group had arrived the evening before, too late to visit Yellowstone, so my parents and I had been raring to go this morning. J.J. had some business to deal with, while Kandace hadn't arrived yet; she was flying in from a fashion shoot in New York City that afternoon. So Summer came with my family to see the park. Sidney Krautheimer, the owner of the ranch, happily lent us a car.

We were leaving the park in the late afternoon, on the road to West Yellowstone, when we saw the biggest touron of the day.

The road was a picturesque, winding route along the bank of the Madison River. It was relatively free of traffic, which was unusual in Yellowstone, as the roads in the park were prone to traffic jams. Usually, these were due to wildlife sightings; a bear, a moose, or even a common white-tailed deer could cause backups several miles long. But there were also plenty of car wrecks, often caused by tourons who had rented massive recreational vehicles that they couldn't control. So a wide-open road through the gorgeous landscape was a pleasant surprise.

The first thing that tipped us off that we were dealing with an unusually dumb tourist—even by Yellowstone standards—was the fact that he had abandoned his car in the middle of the road. Rather than taking a few seconds to pull over onto the shoulder, he had simply stopped, put on his hazard lights, and leaped out. He hadn't even bothered to shut his door. We nearly plowed right into the car as we came around a bend.

For a moment, we feared we had stumbled upon an emergency situation, but then we saw what had caused the man to abandon his car in such a hurry: a small herd of elk, grazing by the river. The touron was trying to get a photograph of them.

I understood why he wanted the photo; it was a spectacular scene. There were five females, six fawns, and a large bull watching over them. The fawns were adorable, certainly only a few weeks old, while the bull had an impressive ten-point rack of antlers. And amazingly, there were no other tourists around. Still, the man was making a very big mistake—in addition to having left his car in the road.

Instead of keeping a respectful distance, he was trying to get as close as possible to the elk, tramping directly across the meadow toward them. This had put all the elk on the alert. The bull looked particularly agitated, but I knew that a mother elk who felt her young were threatened could be very dangerous as well.

Dad parked our car on the shoulder. "I'm gonna see if I can talk some sense into this guy before he gets himself killed," he said, and hopped out.

Mom climbed out too, so Summer and I did the same. After all, it was a beautiful spot and there was no point in sitting in the car.

It was only then that we discovered the man's family was still in his car. His wife was in the passenger seat, while his two teenage children sat in the back. All three were making it obvious that they were irritated with the father. None seemed remotely aware that their car was a serious driving hazard.

"Dad!" the daughter yelled out the window. "We've seen, like, ten million elk already today and you've taken pictures of every one of them! We don't need any more!"

"These are *better* elk!" the father yelled back. "This photo's gonna be amazing!"

"Yeah right," the son said sarcastically. He wasn't even looking at the scenery; instead he was riveted to his phone. "It's just a stupid deer."

"Morton!" the wife called. "Enough is enough! I'm hungry!"

"I'm sorry to bother you," Mom said as pleasantly as possible, "but do you think that maybe you could move your car? It's blocking the road."

The woman sighed with annoyance, as though my mother had asked her to do something unreasonable. "I can't move it. That darn fool took the keys." She pointed toward her husband.

Her daughter noticed Summer and gaped with astonishment.

Summer was famous. Although she didn't want to be. Since her father was a famous businessman and her mother was a fashion model, she'd never had any choice in the matter. She usually did her best to keep a low profile; today she was wearing sunglasses and had her blond hair tucked up under a baseball cap, which had worked well. We had made it through the entire day without anyone recognizing her—until now.

So Summer resorted to her usual trick in such circumstances: She pretended to be someone else.

"You're Summer McCracken, aren't you?" the girl asked. She was staring at Summer in the same way that a bird watcher would have regarded a bald eagle.

"Sorry, no," Summer said, speaking with a fake western twang. "I get that all the time, though."

The daughter narrowed her eyes suspiciously. "Are you *sure* you're not her?"

"Oh, I'm positive," Summer said.

The daughter started to press the issue, but her brother cut her off. "It's obviously not her. Do you really think Summer McCracken would be driving around Yellowstone in that car?" He pointed toward our run-down loaner. "Summer wouldn't come here. She goes places like Paris. Or Dubai."

The daughter looked from Summer to our car and back to Summer again. "I guess you're right," she said.

Meanwhile, their father, Morton, was now attempting to sneak up on the family of elk, even though they were all staring directly at him. He had uprooted a small shrub from the ground—killing it in the process—and was holding it front of him while he waddled across the meadow in a low crouch, apparently hoping that the elk would think we was just a walking bush.

The elk did not appear to be fooled by this at all. Instead, they were growing increasingly agitated as Morton approached. Due to the bend in the river, they had water on three sides of them, and Morton was coming from the only land direction; they were boxed in.

"Hey!" Dad shouted at Morton. "You're getting much too close to those elk! You need to come back to the road!"

"Shhhh!" Morton hissed. "You're going to scare them away! I'm trying to sneak up on them!"

"Well, you're not doing a very good job of it!" Summer shouted. "They're looking right at you! And if you get much closer, they're going to attack!"

"I saw people getting way closer than this to plenty of animals today!" Morton told her.

"That doesn't mean it's right!" I yelled.

Morton ignored us and continued toward the elk, which were visibly nervous now. The fawns edged closer to their mothers, while the bull moved forward and gave an angry snort.

That was certainly meant as a warning to get Morton to back off, although Morton completely failed to comprehend this. Instead, he doubled down on his idiocy. Rather than retreating to his car, he turned his back on the herd of elk—and tried to take a selfie.

"Of course," Dad said, exasperated.

As a professional wildlife photographer, Dad was extremely annoyed by the proliferation of phone cameras. He had spent his entire life trying to take photos in ways that impacted his subjects as little as possible, like using telephoto lenses, which allowed him to work from so far away that the animals rarely even knew he was there. But now even the best camera phones only worked from relatively close by, which often compelled inexperienced amateur photographers like Morton to get much too close to the animals.

However, it was the ability to take selfies that had caused the most problems. Since a selfie required photographers to turn their back on their subject, it led to even more disruptive—and often hazardous—behavior. At FunJungle, there was at least one incident each day of a tourist falling backward into an exhibit while attempting to take a selfie. In the national parks, there was even more potential for disaster; a ranger had told me that selfie takers at Yellowstone were regularly falling off scenic viewpoints, riverbanks, canyon edges, and cliffs. Or, like Morton, they were getting dangerously close to wild animals and then not paying attention to them.

Mom, Summer, and I all started shouting at once, trying to get Morton to listen to reason—or scare the elk off. I figured we had a much better chance of scaring the elk. Even Morton's family now grew concerned. They started shouting at him too. They even got out of the car to do it.

Morton ignored us all. Even worse, he ignored the bull elk behind him, which was growing more and more perturbed.

Since elk look somewhat similar to deer, many people don't realize exactly how powerful and threatening they can be. A bull elk can grow to over eight feet long and weigh 750 pounds, which is far bigger than a black bear. With their sharp hooves and multipronged antlers, they can fend off full-grown mountain lions—or do serious damage to dumb tourists.

The bull behind Morton was a large specimen. It now pawed the ground and lowered its head, pointing its rack of antlers toward Morton's backside.

"Morton, you idiot!" his wife screamed at the top of her lungs. "Look behind you!"

"Why?" Morton asked. "Is there something better to get a photo of?" He finally turned around—just in time to see the bull charge him.

Morton yelped in fear and fled across the meadow as fast as he could—which wasn't very fast at all. He had the build of a man who hadn't done much exercise in the past decade, and the bull quickly closed in on him.

I actually felt bad for the guy—until, in the midst of his flight, he actually tried to take a selfie. While he should have been completely focused on his own well-being, he stiff-armed the camera in front of him and clicked away.

Meanwhile, his own children were also recording the event. Both had their phones trained on the chase and were laughing as they watched their father run for his life, as though the entire event were taking place on TV.

There was nothing my parents, Summer, or I could do to help Morton. He was too far away from us.

While Morton focused on his selfies rather than fleeing, the bull elk lowered its head—and rammed its antlers into Morton's ample bottom. Then, with a heave of its powerful neck, it scooped him up and flung him aside. Morton tumbled across the meadow while his phone sailed through the air and plunked into a beaver pond.

I was worried that the bull might now trample Morton, but thankfully it stopped, gave one last snort, and then trotted back to join its herd.

"Morton!" his wife shrieked. She ran across the meadow toward her husband. My parents, Summer, and I joined her, although Morton's children remained on the shoulder of the road, trying to upload their videos to YouTube.

Morton was howling, which made me fear he was badly hurt, but as we got closer, it became clear what was really upsetting him. "My phone!" he wailed. "That stupid deer made me lose my phone!"

I kept a wary eye on the bull as we approached. "Do you think he might attack again?" I asked my parents.

"No," Dad replied confidently. "I think he knows he got his point across. Literally." He pointed to the bull, which still had a shred of Morton's boxer shorts impaled on the tip of its antler.

Tires screeched on the road behind us, which was followed by a loud crash. We turned around to see that a large recreational vehicle had plowed into the rear of Morton's car. (As we would learn later, the driver had been so focused on watching the elk gore Morton, she had taken her eyes off the road until it was too late.) The car slid off the side of the road and smashed into a tree, while the front end of the RV crumpled. A geyser of steam erupted from its radiator, like a miniature Old Faithful.

"My car!" Morton wailed. "And my phone!" He rolled over and shook his fist at the bull elk. "You stupid deer! I'm gonna sue this park for everything they've got!"

The bull ignored him and resumed grazing by the river.

We finally arrived at Morton's side. Given what I'd seen the elk do to him, the injury wasn't nearly as bad as I'd expected. Morton had a small gouge in the right cheek of his rear end but was otherwise all right. Physically, at least. Mentally, he was enraged over the loss of his car and his phone.

"You saw what that crazy deer did to me, right?" he asked us. "It just attacked me out of nowhere!"

"Actually, you provoked it," Mom told him, without an

ounce of sympathy. "After we repeatedly warned you not to."

"How was I supposed to know it was dangerous?" Morton demanded. "There's no warning signs!"

He was completely wrong. There had been plenty of signs throughout Yellowstone warning visitors that the wildlife was dangerous.

By the roadside, the driver of the RV was now arguing with Morton's children, most likely about who was at fault in the accident. Just as the daughter leaned in to let the driver have it, the family car burst into flames.

Morton screamed again. So did his wife. She seemed to forget that her husband was wounded and raced toward the flaming car. "Our clothes!" she shouted to her children. "Get our clothes!"

Mom sighed heavily. "I think we're going to have to take this guy to the hospital."

I wasn't happy about that. And I could see that Dad and Summer were disappointed too. But we couldn't leave Morton wounded in the middle of the wilderness.

"Darn right I need to go to the hospital," Morton said. "Lousy, no-good deer! This is the last time I ever go on vacation in a national park!"

"I'm sure the park service will be happy to hear that," Summer informed him.

Morton ignored her and kept on ranting. "We should have gone on a cruise. They don't have any homicidal deer on cruise ships."

Dad looked to me and rolled his eyes. "Welcome to Yellowstone," he said.

I laughed, figuring this was the strangest thing that would happen to me that day.

It wasn't even close.

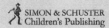

LIVING ON A MOON BASE SHOULD BE EXCITING—BUT NOT *THIS* EXCITING.